BIRTHRIGHT: BOOK THE THIRD

IN THE AGE OF LOVE AND CHOCOLATE

GABRIELLE ZEVIN

MACMILLAN

First published in the US 2013 by Farrar Straus Giroux
First published in the UK 2013 by Macmillan Children's Books

This edition published 2014 by Macmillan Children's Books
a division of Macmillan Publishers Limited
20 New Wharf Road, London N1 9RR
Basingstoke and Oxford
Associated companies throughout the world
www.panmacmillan.com

ISBN 978-0-330-53791-9

1 3 5 7 9 8 6 4 2

A CIP catalogue record for this book is available from
the British Library.

Printed and bound by CPI Group (UK) Ltd, Croydon CR0 4YY

To the ones with the porcupine hearts, who believe in love but can't stop wanting other things, too.

Often a sweetness comes

as if on loan, stays just long enough

to make sense of what it means to be alive,

   then returns to its dark

source. As for me, I don't care

where it's been, or what bitter road

   it's traveled

to come so far, to taste so good.

       – Stephen Dunn, "Sweetness"

CONTENTS

THE AGE OF CHOCOLATE

THE AGE OF LOVE

THE AGE OF CHOCOLATE

I

I BECOME A RELUCTANT GODMOTHER;
ON THE BITTERNESS OF CACAO

I HADN'T WANTED TO BE GODMOTHER, but my best friend insisted. I tried to demur: 'I'm flattered, but godparents are supposed to be Catholics in good standing.' In school, we had been taught that a godparent was responsible for the religious education of a child, and I hadn't been to Mass since Easter or to confession in over a year.

Scarlet looked at me with an aggrieved expression that she had acquired in the month since she had given birth to her son. The baby was beginning to stir, so Scarlet picked him up. 'Oh, sure,' she drawled in a sarcastic baby-talk voice, 'Felix and I would positively adore a fine, upstanding Catholic as a godparent, but *malheureusement*, the person we are stuck with is Anya, who everyone knows to be a bad, bad Catholic.' The baby cooed. 'Felix, what could your poor, unwed, teenage mother have been thinking? She must have been so exhausted and overwhelmed that her brain stopped working. Because no one in the entire world has ever been worse than Anya Balanchine. Just ask her.' Scarlet held the baby toward me. The baby smiled – it was a happy, apple-cheeked, blue-eyed, blond-haired creature – and wisely said nothing. I smiled back, though truth be told, I was not entirely comfortable around babies. 'Oh, that's right. You can't talk yet, little baby. But someday, when you're older, ask your godmother to tell you the story of what a bad Catholic – no, scratch that – bad person she was. She cut off someone's hand! She went into business with a terrible man and she chose that same business over the nicest boy in the world. She went to jail. To protect her brother and her sister, but still – who, when presented with other options, wants a juvenile delinquent for a godparent? She poured a steaming tray of lasagne over your daddy's head, and some people even thought she tried to poison him. And if she'd succeeded, you wouldn't even be here –'

'Scarlet, you shouldn't talk like that in front of the baby.'

She ignored me and continued chattering to Felix. 'Can you imagine, Felix? Your life will probably be ruined because your mother was so thick as to choose Anya Balanchine to be your godmother.' She turned to me. 'Do you see what I'm doing here? I'm acting like it's a done thing that you're going to be the godmother, because it *totally* is.' She turned back to Felix. 'With a godmother like her, it's probably straight to a life of crime for you, my little man.' She kissed him on his fat cheeks, and then she nibbled him a bit. 'Do you want to taste this?'

I shook my head.

'Suit yourself, but you're missing out on something delicious,' she said.

'You've gotten so sarcastic since you became a mother, you know that?'

'Have I? It's probably best if you do what I say without argument then.'

'I'm not sure I'm even Catholic anymore,' I said.

'OMG, are we still talking about this? *You are the godmother*. My mother is making me have a baptism, so you're the godmother.'

'Scarlet, I really have done things.'

'I know that, and now Felix does, too. It's good that we go into this with our eyes open. I've done things myself. *Obviously*.' She patted the baby on the head, then gestured around the tiny nursery that had been set up in Gable's parents' apartment. The nursery had once been a pantry, and it was a tight squeeze, containing the three of us and the many items that make up a baby's life. Still, Scarlet had done her best with the miniature room, painting the walls with clouds and a pale blue sky. 'What difference does any of that make? You're my best friend. Who else would be godmother?'

'Are you honestly saying you won't do it?' The pitch of Scarlet's voice had shifted up to an unpleasant register, and the baby was still fussing. 'Because I don't care when the last time you went to Mass was.' Scarlet's pretty brow was furrowing and she looked like she might cry. 'If it's not you, there's no one else. So please don't get neurotic about this. Just stand next to me in church and when the priest or my mother or anyone else asks you if you're a good Catholic, lie.'

On the hottest day of summer, in the second week of July, I stood next to Scarlet in St Patrick's Cathedral. She held Felix in her arms, and the three of us were sweating enough to solve the water crisis. Gable, the baby's father, was on the other side of Scarlet, and Gable's older brother, Maddox, the godfather, stood beside Gable. Maddox was a thicker-necked, smaller-eyed, better-mannered version of Gable. The priest, perhaps aware of the fact that we were about to pass out from the heat, kept his remarks brief and banter-free. It was so hot he did not even feel the need to mention that the baby's parents were unwed teenagers. This was truly the boilerplate, no-frills baptism. The priest asked Maddox and me, 'Are you prepared to help these parents in their duties as Christian parents?'

We said we were.

And then the questions were directed to the four of us: 'Do you reject Satan?'

We said we did.

'Is it your will that Felix be baptized in the faith of the Catholic Church?'

'It is,' we said, though at that point we would have agreed to anything to get this ceremony over with.

And then he poured holy water on Felix's head, which made the baby giggle. I can only imagine that the water must have felt refreshing. I would not have minded some holy water myself.

After the service, we went back to Gable's parents' apartment for a baptismal party. Scarlet had invited a couple of the kids we had gone to high school with, among them my recently crowned ex-boyfriend, Win, who I had not seen in about four weeks.

The party felt like a funeral. Scarlet was the first one of us to have a baby, and no one seemed to know quite how to behave at such an affair. Gable played a drinking game with his brother in the kitchen. The other kids from Holy Trinity chatted in polite, hushed tones among themselves. In the corner were Scarlet's and Gable's parents, our solemn chaperones. Win kept company with Scarlet and the baby. I could have gone over to them, but I wanted Win to have to cross the room to me.

'How's the club coming along, Anya?' Chai Pinter asked me. Chai was a terrible gossip, but she was basically harmless.

'We're opening at the end of September. If you're in town, you should come.'

'Definitely. By the way, you look exhausted,' Chai said. 'You've got dark circles under your eyes. Are you, like, not sleeping because you're worried you'll fail?'

I laughed. If you couldn't ignore Chai, it was best to laugh at her. 'Mainly I'm not sleeping because it's a lot of work.'

'My dad says that ninety-eight per cent of nightclubs in New York fail.'

'That's quite a statistic,' I said.

'It might have been ninety-nine per cent. But Anya, what will you do if you fail? Will you go back to school?'

'Maybe.'

'Did you even graduate high school?'

'I got my GED last spring.' Need I mention she was starting to annoy me?

She lowered her voice and cast her eyes across the room toward Win. 'Is it true that the reason Win broke up with you is because you went into business with his father?'

'I'd rather not talk about that.'

'So it *is* true?'

'It's complicated,' I said. That was true enough.

She looked at Win, and then she made sad eyes at me. 'I could never give up *that* for any business,' she said. 'If that boy loved me, I'd be, *What business?* You're a way stronger person than me. I mean it, Anya. I totally admire you.'

'Thanks,' I said. Chai Pinter's *admiration* had managed to make me feel horrible about every decision I'd made for the past two months. I pushed out my chin with resolve and pulled back my shoulders. 'You know, I think I'm going to step on to the balcony for some fresh air.'

'It's like one hundred degrees,' Chai called after me.

'I like the heat,' I said.

I opened the sliding door and went outside into the sweltering early evening. I sat down in a dusty lounge chair with a cushion that was bleeding foam. My day had not begun in the afternoon with Felix's baptism, but hours before at the club. I'd been up since five that morning and even the meagre comforts of that old chair were enough to lure me to sleep.

Though I have never been much of a dreamer, I had the oddest dream in which I was Scarlet's baby. Scarlet held me in her arms, and the feeling overwhelmed me. All at once, I remembered what it was to have a mother, to be safe, and to be loved by someone more than anything else in the world. And in the dream, Scarlet somehow transformed into my mother. I

8

could not always picture my mother's face, but in this dream, I could see her so clearly – her intelligent grey eyes and her wavy reddish-brown hair and the hard pink line of her mouth and the delicate freckles sprinkled across her nose. I had forgotten about the freckles, and that made me even sadder. She had been beautiful, but she didn't look like she took guff from anyone. I knew why my father had wanted her even though he should have married anyone *but* her, anyone but a cop. *Annie*, my mother whispered, *you are loved. Let yourself be loved.* In the dream, I couldn't stop crying. And maybe that is why babies cry so much – the weight of all that love is simply too much to bear.

'Hey,' Win said. I sat up and tried to pretend I hadn't been sleeping. *(Aside: Why do people do that? What is so embarrassing about being asleep?)* 'I'm leaving now. I wanted to talk to you before I went.'

'You haven't changed your mind, I suppose.' I did not look him in the eye. I kept my voice cool and even.

He shook his head. 'You haven't either. My dad talks about the club sometimes. Business continues, I know.'

'So what do you want, then?'

'I wondered if I could stop by your place to get a few things I left there. I'm going to my mother's farm in Albany and then I'll only be back in the city for a bit before I leave for college.'

My tired brain tried to make sense of this statement. 'Leave?'

'Yes, I decided to go to Boston College. I don't have a reason to stay in New York anymore.'

9

This was news to me. 'Well, good luck, Win. Have a *fantastic* time in Boston.'

'Was I supposed to consult you?' he asked. 'You certainly never consulted me about anything.'

'You're exaggerating.'

'Be honest, Anya.'

'What would you have said if I had told you I was going to ask your father to work for me?' I asked.

'You'll never know,' he said.

'I do! You would have told me not to do it.'

'Of course I would have. I would have told Gable Arsley not to work with my father, and I don't even like him.'

I can't say why, but I grabbed his hand. 'What things of yours do I have?'

'You have some of my clothes and my winter coat and I think your sister might have one of my hats, but Natty can keep that. I left my copy of *To Kill a Mockingbird* in your room, and I might like to read it again someday. But mainly I need my slate back for college. It's under your bed, I think.'

'There's no need for you to stop by. I can put the stuff in a box. I'll bring it to work, and your dad can take it to you.'

'If that's what you want.'

'I think it would be easier. I'm not Scarlet. I don't crave pointless, dramatic scenes.'

'As you like, Anya.'

'You're always so polite. It's irritating.'

'And you always keep everything inside. We're a terrible match, really.'

I crossed my arms and turned away from him. I was angry.

I wasn't certain why I was angry, but I was. If I hadn't been so tired, I feel quite sure I would have been better able to keep my emotions in check.

'Why did you even come to the launch party for the club if you weren't going to at least *try* to forgive me?'

'I *was* trying, Anya. I wanted to see if I could get past it.'

'So?'

'It turns out I can't.'

'You can.' I didn't think anyone could see us, but I wouldn't have cared anyway. I threw my arms around him. I pushed him into the side of the balcony and pressed my lips against his. It only took me a couple of seconds to notice that he was not, in fact, kissing me back.

'I can't,' he repeated.

'So that's it. You don't love me anymore?'

For a moment, he didn't reply. He shook his head. 'Not enough to get past this, I guess. I don't love you that much.'

To restate: *He had loved me, just not enough.*

I couldn't argue with that, but I tried to anyway. 'You're going to regret this,' I said. 'The club is going to be a huge success, and you're going to regret that you didn't stand by me. Because if you love someone, you love them all the way. You love them even when they make mistakes. That's what I think.'

'I'm meant to love you, no matter how you act, no matter what you do? I couldn't respect myself if I felt that way.'

He was probably right.

I was tired of defending myself and of trying to convince him to see things from my point of view. I looked at Win's

11

shoulder, which was less than six inches from my face. It would be so easy to let my neck drop and ease my head into that cosy space between his shoulder and his chin, which seemed designed specifically for me. It would be easy to tell him the club and the business with his father were terrible mistakes and to beg him to take me back. For a second I closed my eyes and tried to imagine what my future would look like if Win were in it. I see a house somewhere outside the city – Win has a collection of antique records, and maybe I learn to cook a dish besides macaroni and frozen peas. I see our wedding – it's on a beach and he's wearing a blue seersucker suit and our rings are white gold. I see a dark-haired baby – I call him Leonyd after my father, if it's a boy, and Alexa, after Win's sister, if it's a girl. I see everything and it is so very lovely.

It would be so easy, but I would hate myself. I had a chance to build something, and in the process, to do what my father had never been able to do. I couldn't let that go, even for this boy. He, alone, was not enough.

So I held my tired neck erect and kept my eyes fixed forward. He was going, and I would let him.

From the balcony, I heard the baby start to cry. My former schoolmates took Felix's tears as a sign that the party was over. Through the glass door, I watched them as they filed out. I don't know why, but I tried to make a joke. 'Looks like the worst prom ever,' I said. 'Maybe the second worst if you count junior year.' I lightly touched Win's thigh where my cousin had shot him at the worst prom ever. For a second he looked like he might laugh, but then he repositioned his leg so that my hand was no longer on it.

12

Win pulled me to his chest. 'Goodbye,' he whispered in a gentler tone than I'd heard from him in a while. 'I hope life gives you everything you want.'

I knew it was over. In contrast with the other times we'd quarrelled, he did not sound angry. He sounded resigned. He sounded as if he were already somewhere faraway.

A second later, he released me and then he really did leave.

I turned my back and watched the city as the sun went down. Though I had made my choices, I could not bear to know what he looked like when he was walking away.

I waited about fifteen minutes before I went back into the apartment. By that time, the only people left were Scarlet and Felix. 'I love parties,' Scarlet said, 'but this was miserable. Don't say it wasn't, Annie. You can lie to the priest, but it's too late for you to start lying to me.'

'I'll help you clean up,' I said. 'Where's Gable?'

'Out with his brother,' she said. 'Then he has to go to work.' Gable had a truly wretched-sounding job as a hospital orderly, which involved changing bedpans and cleaning floors. It was the only work he could find, and I suppose it was noble of him to have taken it. 'Do you think it was a mistake to invite the kids from Trinity?'

'I think it was fine,' I said.

'I saw you talking to Win.'

'Nothing has changed.'

'I'm sad to hear that,' she said. We cleaned up the apartment in silence. Scarlet started to vacuum, which is why I didn't notice right away that she had begun to cry.

13

I walked over to the vacuum and turned it off. 'What is it?'

'I wonder what chance any of the rest of us have if you and Win can't make it work.'

'Scarlet, it was a high-school romance. They aren't meant to last forever.'

'Unless you're stupid and get yourself knocked up,' Scarlet said.

'That's not what I meant.'

'I know.' Scarlet sighed. 'And I know why you're opening the club, but you're certain Charles Delacroix is worth the trouble?'

'I am. I've explained this to you before.' I turned the vacuum cleaner back on and vacuumed. I was pushing the vacuum in long, mad strokes across the rug: angry-vacuuming. I turned the vacuum off again. 'You know, it's not easy to do what I'm doing. I don't have any help. No one is supporting me. Not Mr Kipling. Not my parents or my nana, because they're dead. Not Natty, because she is a child. Not Leo, because he is in jail. Not the Balanchine family, because they think I'm threatening their business. Certainly not Win. No one. I am alone, Scarlet. I am more alone than I have ever been in my entire life. And I know I chose this. But it hurts my feelings when you take Win's side over mine. I'm using Mr Delacroix because he is the connection I have to the city. I need him, Scarlet. He has been part of my plan from the beginning. There is no one else who could replace him. Win is asking me for the one thing I can't give him. Don't you think I wish I could?'

'I'm sorry,' she said.

'And I can't be with Win Delacroix just so my best friend doesn't give up on romance.'

Scarlet's eyes were tear-filled. 'Let's not argue. I'm an idiot. Ignore me.'

'I hate when you call yourself an idiot. No one thinks that of you.'

'I think it of myself,' Scarlet said. 'Look at me. What am I going to do?'

'Well for one, we're going to finish cleaning this apartment.'

'After that, I meant.'

'Then we're going to take Felix and go to my club. Lucy, the mixologist, is working late and she has a bunch of cacao drinks for us to sample.'

'And then?'

'I don't know. You'll come up with something. But it's the only way I know how to move forward. You make a list and then you go and do the things on it.'

'Still bitter,' I said to my recently hired mixologist as I handed her the last in a series of shot glasses. Lucy had white-blonde hair cropped short, light blue eyes, pale skin, a big bow of a mouth, and a long, athletic body. When she was in her chef's coat and hat, I thought she looked like a bar of Balanchine White. I always knew when she was working in the kitchen because even from my office down the hall, I could hear her muttering and cursing. The dirty words seemed to be part of her creative process. I liked her very much, by the way. If she hadn't been my employee, maybe she would have been my friend.

'Do you think it needs more sugar?' Lucy said.

'I think it needs . . . something. It's even more bitter than the last one.'

'That's what cacao tastes like, Anya. I'm starting to think you don't like the taste of cacao. Scarlet, what do you think?'

Scarlet sipped. 'It's not obviously sweet, but I definitely detect sweetness,' she said.

'Thank you,' Lucy said.

'That's Scarlet,' I said. 'You're always looking for the sweet.'

'And maybe you're always looking for the bitter,' Scarlet joked.

'Pretty, smart, and optimistic. I wish you were my boss,' Lucy said.

'She isn't as sunny as she seems,' I told Lucy. 'An hour ago, I found her crying and vacuuming.'

'Everyone cries when they vacuum,' Lucy said.

'I know, right?' Scarlet agreed. 'Those vibrations make you emotional.'

'I'm serious, though,' I said. 'In Mexico, the drinks weren't this dark.'

'Maybe you should hire your friend from Mexico to come make them, then?' My mixologist had trained at the Culinary Institute of America and at Le Cordon Bleu, and she could be touchy when it came to criticism.

'Oh, Lucy, you know I respect you enormously. But the drinks need to be perfect.'

'Let's ask the heartbreaker,' Lucy said. 'With your permission, Scarlet.'

'I don't see why not,' Scarlet said. She dipped her pinky into the pot and then held it out for Felix to lick. He tasted tentatively. At first he smiled. Lucy began to look intolerably smug.

'He smiles at everything,' I said.

Suddenly, his mouth crumpled into the shape of a dried-out rose.

'Oh, I'm sorry, baby!' Scarlet said. 'I'm a terrible mother.'

'See?' I said.

'I suppose cacao is too sophisticated a flavour for a baby's palate,' Lucy said. She sighed and dumped the contents of the pot into the sink. 'Tomorrow,' she said, 'we try again. We fail again. We do better.'

I OFFICIALLY BECOME AN ADULT; HAVE A SERIES OF UNKIND THOUGHTS ABOUT MY FRIENDS AND FAMILY; AM COMPARED UNFAVOURABLY TO THE ELEMENT ARGON

'THERE ARE A MILLION perfectly good reasons a venture fails, Anya,' Charles Delacroix lectured. He had proven himself to be a decent enough business partner, but he did like to hear himself talk. 'The failure is the only part people remember. For instance, no one remembers that the man who was to be the district attorney of New York City was taken down by a seventeen-year-old.'

'Is that what happened?' I asked. 'As I recall, the man who *did not become* district attorney had an unwise obsession with his son's love life, and his opponents preyed on it.'

Mr Delacroix shook his head.

'Like a lion felled by a tiny burr,' I said. 'Also, I'm not seventeen anymore.'

'I was waiting for you to object to that.' He held his fingers to his mouth and whistled like he was hailing a cab. The sound echoed across the club, which still didn't have much furniture in it. Several members of my newly hired staff came out with a birthday cake. HAPPY BIRTHDAY, ANYA was spelled in pink icing.

'You remembered,' I said.

'August 12, 2066. As if I could forget your eighteenth. No more trips to Liberty Children's.'

The staff sang and clapped for me. We didn't know one another very well yet, but I was the boss so it wasn't like they had a choice. I was glad when the compulsory merriment was over and everyone returned to work. I did not relish being the centre of attention, and there was so much to do before we opened in a month. I had already hired (and fired) contractors, waitstaff, designers, chefs, publicists, doctors, security, and event planners. There was a never-ending series of permits to get from the city, though most of that was Mr Delacroix's responsibility. I had tried (unsuccessfully) to broker a peace with my cousin Fats and the Family, and had (successfully) negotiated a great deal on cacao from my friend Theo Marquez at Granja Mañana. There were tiles, linens, and paint colours to be selected; ovens to be leased; menus and press releases to be written. There were glamorous jobs like arranging for garbage pickup and choosing toilet paper for the bathrooms.

'Vanilla,' I noted, looking at the sliced cake. 'Not chocolate.'

'We can't have you brought down by minor indiscretions,' he said. 'You're an adult now. The next time you're in trouble, it's off to Rikers. I'm headed home. Jane and I have plans. Promise me you'll settle on a name before tomorrow. We have to start getting the word out.'

Naming the club had proven difficult. I couldn't use *my*

19

name because that would have associated the business with organized crime. *Cacao* or *chocolate* couldn't be in it, though it was necessary for people to know that they could get chocolate here. The name needed to sound fun and exciting, but not illegal in any way. I still clung to the probably foolish idea that it should evoke good health.

'Honestly, I'm not even close,' I said.

'That won't do.' He looked at his watch. 'I still have a little time before Jane will murder me.' He sat back down. 'Let's have your top five then.'

'Number one, Theobroma's.'

'No. Hard to pronounce. Hard to spell. Ridiculous.'

'Number two, Prohibition.'

He shook his head. 'Nobody wants a history lesson. Plus, it seems political. We don't want to seem explicitly political.'

'Three, the Medicinal Cacao Company.'

'These are getting worse. I've already told you, you cannot have *medicinal* in the name of a nightclub. Sounds like sick people and hospitals and bacterial outbreaks.' He shuddered.

'If you're going to shoot down everything, I don't know why I should go on.'

'Because you have to. Something has to be painted on the sign, Anya.'

'Fine. Four, Hearts of Darkness.'

'Is that a reference? It's a bit pretentious. But I like "dark" – "dark" is better.'

'Five, Nibs.'

'Nibs. Are you kidding?'

'That's what they process the cacao into,' I explained.

'It sounds dirty and weird. Trust me. No one will ever go to a club called Nibs.'

'That's what I've got, Mr Delacroix.'

'Anya, I think we can go by our given names now.'

'I'm used to Mr Delacroix,' I said. 'Frankly, I think it's rather presumptuous of you to call me Anya.'

'You want I should call you Ms Balanchine?'

'Or ma'am. Either one. I'm your boss, aren't I?' After what he had put me through in 2083 (prison, poison), I felt entitled to josh.

'Partner, I'd say. Or legal counsel to *unnamed* Manhattan club.' He paused. 'Mrs Cobrawick was a formidable woman. When you were at Liberty didn't she teach you anything about respecting your elders?'

'No.'

'That institution is a waste of the land it sits on. Returning to the discussion at hand. How about the Dark Room?'

I considered it. 'Could be worse.'

'There's the unavoidable photography reference of course. But it's a little bit evil. It references what we're selling. And, at this point, we have to choose a name. Don't you know how publicity works, Anya? You repeat the same message over and over again in as loud a voice as possible. To do this, though, we need to have something to say.'

'The Dark Room,' I said. 'Let's do it.'

'Good. I'm off for the night, then. Happy Birthday, *ma'am*. Big plans for later?'

'I'm going to a play with my best friend, Scarlet, and

21

Noriko.' Noriko was my brother's wife and she was also working as my assistant.

'What are you seeing?'

'Scarlet bought the tickets. A comedy, I hope. I hate crying in public.'

'It's a good policy. I try never to do it myself,' he said.

'Unless it served your interests somehow, I imagine. How's your son?' I asked casually. We never talked about Win. It was a tiny present to myself to even ask the question.

'Yes, him. Change of plans. The boy has decided to go to college in Boston,' Mr Delacroix reported.

'He mentioned that.' I'd boxed up his possessions, but I still hadn't managed to bring them to work.

'He'll be back for holidays and summers, I imagine,' Mr Delacroix said. 'Jane and I will miss him, of course, but Boston isn't very far.'

'Well, give him my regards, will you?'

'You could always come give them yourself. His father won't object.'

'I think that's done, Mr Delacroix,' I said. 'He doesn't understand about the business.'

Mr Delacroix nodded. 'No, I can't imagine that he would. He's prideful and he's been too sheltered.'

I wanted to know if Win ever asked about me, but the question was too humiliating. 'Relationships aren't always meant to last forever,' I said, trying to sound wise. If I said this enough times, maybe I would start to believe it. 'Isn't that what you've always told me?'

'Life is not easy for the ambitious, Anya.'

22

'I'm not ambitious,' I said.

'Sure you are.' His mouth was amused, but his eyes were annoyingly certain. 'I should know.'

'Thanks for the cake,' I said.

He held out his hand for me to shake. 'Happy birthday.'

Not long after Mr Delacroix departed, I took a bus back to my apartment.

The truth was, I did not miss that boy.

Maybe I missed the idea of that boy.

(NB: No, it wasn't just the idea. It was him. *I missed that stupid boy, but what was the point of that? I had no right to miss him. I'd made my choice. Forgive me the honeyed lies I told myself – I was still so young. And when we are young, we don't even know completely what we are giving up.)*

(NB: What I mean to say is that you can make a choice, be reasonably satisfied with it, and still regret that which you did not choose. Maybe it's like ordering dessert. You have it narrowed down to either a warm peanut-butter torte or strawberries jubilee. You choose the torte, and it's delicious. But you still wonder about those strawberries . . .)

(NB: So yes, from time to time, I thought about the strawberries.)

Noriko and I had been waiting outside the theatre for a half-hour. 'Should we go inside without her?' Noriko's English had improved a remarkable amount since she'd arrived in America four and a half months ago.

'I'll go call her from the payphone,' I said. I hadn't had time to procure my, as of today, perfectly legal cell phone.

Scarlet picked up on the fifth ring. 'Where are you?' I asked.

'Gable was supposed to watch Felix, but he never showed up. I can't make it. You guys should go to the play without me. I'm really sorry, Annie,' Scarlet said.

'Don't worry about it,' I said.

'I am worried about it. It's your birthday, and I wanted to see the play. Can I come meet you later? We'll dance or have drinks.'

'Honestly, I've been working since six in the morning. I'll probably go home and go to bed.'

'Happy birthday, my love,' Scarlet said.

The play Scarlet had chosen was about an old man and a young woman who switch bodies with each other at a wedding. The young woman's husband has to learn to love the young woman, even though she's in the old man's body. And in the end, everyone learns a lot of lessons about love and acceptance and how it doesn't matter what body you're in. It was romantic, and I was not in the mood for a romance, which you'd think Scarlet could have guessed.

When the actors took their bows, they were given a standing ovation, but I stayed in my seat. Romance was a lie. It was so much of a lie that it made me angry. Romance was hormones and fiction. 'Boo,' I whispered. 'Boo to this whole stupid play.' No one heard me. There was too much applause. I could boo all I wanted and I found this liberating.

And the worst part was I didn't even like the theatre.

24

Scarlet liked the theatre and she hadn't bothered to show up. And it wasn't the first time she'd missed an appointment with me either. I honestly didn't know why I bothered making plans with her anymore. 'Boo to Scarlet. Boo to the theatre.'

Noriko was weeping and clapping like a crazy person. 'I miss Leo,' she said. 'I miss Leo so much.'

Maybe Noriko did miss Leo, but in that moment, I was sceptical. They barely spoke the same language. They had known each other a little over a month when they decided to marry. And we were talking about my brother. He was a nice person, but . . . I'd been working with Noriko the whole summer. She was smart and, not to be mean, Leo was not.

I defrosted some peas and was about to close the chapter on my unmemorable eighteenth birthday when the phone rang.

'Anya, this is Miss Bellevoir.' Kathleen Bellevoir was Natty's math teacher at Holy Trinity, but in the summer she worked at genius camp. 'There's some trouble with Natty up here, and I wanted to let you know that she's going to be home tomorrow.'

I put my hand over my heart. 'What's wrong? Is she sick?'

'Oh no, nothing like that. But there has been an incident. Several incidents, I should say. Everyone on staff has decided that it's best if she comes home early. The purpose of my call is to ensure you'll be there when she arrives.'

'What kind of incidents?' I asked.

All the Things Natty Had Done
1. Failed to participate in science and math labs

25

    2. Generally disrespected staff and other campers
    3. Was caught with chocolate on the campus
    4. Was caught in a boy's room after hours
    5. Snuck out of camp, stole the camp's van, and
       drove it into a ditch

The last and latest incident had marked the official end of genius camp's patience.

'Is she hurt?' I asked.

'Bumps and bruises. The van made out less well. I love your sister, and she had such a success here last summer that everyone, myself included, tried to ignore it when she started having trouble. I probably should have called you sooner.'

I wanted to yell at Miss Bellevoir for not watching Natty closely enough, but I knew this wasn't rational. I bit my lip, which was chapped and began to bleed.

Natty arrived at the apartment at six the next night, which was a Sunday. My sister was pretty banged up. She had bruises on her cheek and forehead and a deep cut on her chin. 'Oh, Natty,' I said.

She opened her arms as if to hug me, but then her face morphed into a snarl. 'For God's sake, Annie, don't look at me that way. You're not my mother.' She stalked to her bedroom and slammed the door.

I gave her ten minutes before I knocked.

'Go away!'

I turned the knob, which was locked. 'Natty, we need to talk about what happened.'

'Since when do you want to talk? Aren't you Miss Stiff Upper Lip? Miss Keep Everything Inside?'

I picked the lock on Natty's door with the nail we kept over Leo's (now Noriko's) room.

'Go away! Can't you please leave me alone?'

'I can't,' I said.

She pulled the blanket over her head.

'What happened this summer?'

She didn't answer.

I had not gone into her room for a while. It was like two people lived there: a child and a young woman. There were bras and dolls, perfume and crayons. One of Win's hats, a grey fedora, hung from a hook on the wall. She had always liked his hats. Next to the mirror was a periodic table, and I noticed that she had circled some of the elements.

'What do the circles mean?' I asked.

'They're my favourite ones.'

'How do you choose?'

She emerged from under the covers. 'Hydrogen and oxygen are pretty obvious. They make water, which is the source of life, if you care about that kind of thing. I like Na, sodium, and Ba, barium, because those are my initials.' She pointed to Ar, which wasn't circled. 'Argon is totally inert. Nothing affects it, and it has a hard time forming chemical compounds, i.e., having relationships. It's a loner. It doesn't ask for anything from anybody. It reminds me of you.'

'Natty, that isn't true. Things affect me. I'm upset right now.'

'Are you? It's hard to tell, Argon,' Natty said.

'Maybe the point is, it doesn't matter what happened to you at camp. Summer is summer. Summer is never real life anyway.'

'It isn't?'

I shook my head. 'You had a bad summer. That's all. School starts in a couple of weeks. It's your junior year, and I think it's going to be a great one for you.'

'OK,' she said after a while.

'I've got to go to the club, but I'll be back later,' I said.

'Can I come?'

'Some other time,' I said. 'I think you should rest up tonight. You look terrible, by the way.'

'I think I look tough.'

'Troubled maybe.'

'Criminal. A real Balanchine.'

I kissed Natty on the forehead. I had never been good with words. On the path from my heart to my brain to my mouth, phrases became twisted and hopelessly convoluted. The intent – what I meant to say – never quite made it out. My heart thought, *I love you*. My brain warned, *How embarrassing. How foolish. How dangerous*. My mouth said, *Please go away*, or worse, it made some senseless joke. I knew I needed to do better for Natty in this moment. 'No, you're nothing like that,' I said. 'You're the smartest, best girl in the world.'

Instead of taking the bus, I walked to the club. It was after dark and a bit late to be walking alone, but even Argon the Seemingly Unaffected sometimes needed to clear her head. I was halfway there, almost to Columbus Circle, when it began to rain. My hair frizzed, but I didn't care. I loved New York City in the rain. The rotten smells faded, and the sidewalks looked almost clean. Colourful umbrellas sprouted like upside-down tulips, and the windows of the empty skyscrapers shone, if only for the night. In the rain, it did not seem possible that we might run out of water, or that anyone you loved could truly be gone forever. I believed in the rain.

As I walked, I thought of Natty and whether I had said and done the right things this evening. I had been miserable at that age. My parents were dead, and Nana's condition had been getting worse every day. At school, my only friend was Scarlet. I had been obsessed with the idea that everyone was insulting me, and maybe some of them were. I got in and picked fights constantly. (In retrospect, it is amazing I was not tossed out of Holy Trinity years earlier.) At fourteen, I was not at the height of physical attractiveness either – I was a big head of hair and a too-round face and breasts that were still in the process of figuring out how to be breasts. By the time I was fifteen, I had improved looks-wise, and that was the year I started dating Gable Arsley, who had been my first real boyfriend and the first boy to say I was pretty. See, the rain was so clever it could even trick me into having a nice memory about Gable.

I was walking up the steps that led to the club when a man emerged from the darkness and grabbed my hand. 'Anya, where is Sophia?' He pulled me roughly behind one of the headless-lion statues that guarded the entrance.

It was Mickey Balanchine, my cousin and Sophia Bitter's husband. He had lost weight and even in the dark his skin seemed jaundiced. I hadn't seen him since he and Sophia had abruptly left the city months ago. 'I don't know what you're talking about.' I tried to wrest my hand from his, but he pulled me closer. I could smell his breath, which was sickly sweet and strangely repellent. It reminded me of wet leather.

'We were in Switzerland opening a new Bitter factory,' he said. 'We were staying in a hotel, and one morning she went down to breakfast with her bodyguard, but she didn't come back. I know you think she tried to kill you—'

I interrupted. 'She did, didn't she?'

'But she's still my wife and I need to find her.'

'Listen, Mickey, you're not making any sense. I haven't seen you or her in months, and I have no idea where she is.'

'I think you kidnapped her in retaliation.'

'Kidnapped her? I wouldn't kidnap her. I'm opening a business. I don't have time to kidnap anyone. Believe it or not, I haven't thought about her in months. I'm sure a woman like that has enemies other than me.'

Mickey pulled out a gun and poked it into my ribs near my heart. 'You have every reason to wish Sophia ill, but the only way we can help each other is if you tell me where she is.'

'Mickey, please. I honestly have no idea. I honestly –' I started reaching for the machete that I kept in my backpack during the summer months. Without a coat, I couldn't strap the weapon to my belt – too obvious. I had never gotten around to acquiring a sheath.

Another voice said, 'Mickey Balanchine, welcome home. There's a gun pointed at the back of your head so I suggest you drop your weapon.' Mr Delacroix was pushing an object into Mickey's skull, but even in the darkness, it didn't look like

30

a gun to me. It was a bottle of something. Wine? 'Unless there's somebody else with you, I suggest you drop the gun. You're one against two, and I know Ms Balanchine is probably itching to pull out that machete she thinks no one knows about.'

'I'm alone,' Mickey said as he slowly lowered his weapon.

'Good man,' Mr Delacroix said.

'I don't want to hurt her,' Mickey said. He coughed and the sound was deep and rattling. 'I only want information.' Mickey set the gun on the ground, and I picked it up. Despite how this scene may appear, I was not particularly happy to have Mr Delacroix's intervention at that moment. I did not believe my cousin would shoot me, nor did I want Mr Delacroix involved with the Family in any way. Frankly, his hero act annoyed me. I saw through it. As I had known when I asked him to work for me, Mr Delacroix was self-interested above all else, and it felt false for him to pretend otherwise. Besides, I did not require heroism – I had been the hero of my life for some time.

'If that's true, come inside and discuss the matter like a civilized person,' Mr Delacroix said to my cousin. 'We're all getting soaked, and you look as if you might get pneumonia if we stay out here much longer.'

'OK,' he said.

Once the three of us were inside, I went to the guard's station to tell Jones, who ran security for the club, that I needed him to stay with Mickey.

Our party now expanded by one, we went up the stairs and past the club space to my office. I unlocked the door and told

31

Jones and Mickey to wait inside. I then went back out to the hallway to dismiss Mr Delacroix for the evening. He handed me a thin towel that must have come from the club's kitchen.

'You need personal security,' he said. 'I'm not going to be around to rescue you—'

I interrupted him. 'I'm glad you bring that up, Mr Delacroix. I wanted to remind you that you were not hired for heroics.'

'Heroics?' he asked. '*Hired?*'

'Hired,' I said. 'You are my employee.'

'Your partner. I assume I understand the contracts *I* vetted.'

'My share in this business is far greater than yours and I don't need your permission to do anything.'

He looked at me with an even expression. 'Fine, Anya. What does madame require?'

'Legal counsel,' I said. 'Nothing more.'

'So I understand my responsibilities . . . If I see you at night – let's say it's dark and stormy – and you are being attacked by a man I recognize as the *mafiya* cousin who may or may not have tried to murder you and your family, protocol dictates that I should' – he shrugged – 'look the other way and let you die?'

'Yes, but—'

Now *he* interrupted me. 'Good. I'm glad that's cleared up.'

'I wouldn't have died. I haven't died yet. I even survived being poisoned, if you can believe that.'

'Be that as it may, as your legal adviser and *only in that capacity* – I wouldn't want to overstep here – I think it

32

would be useful for you to have security.'

'You're taking this the wrong way. I'm saying we need boundaries. Our roles need to be defined. I appreciate your need to know everything, but didn't we both agree that it was better for the club and for you if there were some matters, and particularly ones involving the Family, that I kept from you?'

He considered my question for a moment. 'As you wish. What happened to that giant woman who used to follow you around?'

'I let Daisy go.'

'Why would you do that?'

'Since I'm trying to do everything legally, I didn't think it made the best impression to have a bodyguard with me. And I still believe this. I won't walk around the city with a bodyguard like a two-bit gangster. You know perfectly well that appearances matter.'

'You seem to have made up your mind,' he said. 'I don't agree, but I understand the rationale.'

'Goodnight, Mr Delacroix.'

I went into my office. Mickey and Jones were crammed together on my love seat. I dried my hair with the towel Mr Delacroix had given me, and then I handed the towel to Mickey so that he could use it, too.

'Is he your boyfriend?' Mickey nodded toward the hallway.

'Boyfriend? Are you kidding me? That's Charles Delacroix. You must remember him from when he ran for district attorney back in '83.'

'Right, him.'

'He lost and now he's legal counsel for my club.'

'Fancy,' Mickey said.

'Boyfriend!' I was unnerved by the notion that anyone could think Charles Delacroix was my boyfriend. 'That's disgusting, Mickey. He's probably twice my age, maybe more. He's old enough to be my father. He's Win's father. Remember my ex-boyfriend Win?'

'Hey, I don't judge how people live their lives.' His eyes were glazed and unfocused. I felt like he was on the verge of passing out, and I needed to get information before he did.

'Did you know about the plot to kill Natty, Leo, and me?' I asked.

'No, I was in the dark as much as you. By the time I found out Sophia was involved, it had already happened. She convinced me that we had to run or the Family would kill me. She said that you were the most famous and the most beloved Balanchine and that the Family would surely take your side and happily tie up the loose end that I represented. She insisted that everyone would think *I* had orchestrated the plot because I had the most to gain from getting rid of Leonyd Balanchine's children. So I went with her. Maybe it was dumb, but I didn't have time to think and she is still my wife. But less than a month later, an old friend told me that you had let Fats Medovukha take over the Family, and then I knew that Sophia must have lied.'

'Who else was involved?'

'Yuji Ono, obviously.' Mickey coughed so hard I worried he might choke. I thought I saw drops of blood on the towel I had given him. 'They were in love, you know.'

There had been rumours, but all I knew for certain was

that Yuji and Sophia had been schoolmates. 'Anyone else?'

'No. Not that I know of. No one important.'

'Simon Green?'

'The lawyer?'

My father's bastard, I wanted to say.

'So many lawyers,' Mickey said. 'Simon's not the worst.'
He coughed yet again and it sounded like his lungs were filled
with marbles.

'What's wrong with you?' I asked.

'I think I caught something when I was overseas.'

'Something contagious?' Jones asked. My head of security
rarely felt the need to add commentary.

'I don't know,' Mickey said.

Jones scooted as far away from Mickey as the love seat
would allow.

'Why are you looking for Sophia? If someone kidnapped
her, you should leave well enough alone. Let her be gone,'
I said.

'I have unfinished business with her. I need to see her.'

'Care to say what that business is?'

'If she hasn't been kidnapped, I think she set me up. She
got me out of New York City so that Fats could take over.
Maybe she thought you would take over, I don't know. I don't
understand any of it.' Despite the fact that rain had cooled the
late-summer night, Mickey was covered in sweat. 'She –' He
coughed again, but this time he expectorated an enormous clot
of bloody sputum that bounced across my desk like a rubber
ball.

'Mickey, you're not well,' I said, though that was more

35

than evident. 'Would you like a drink of water?'

Mickey did not, or I should say *could not*, reply. His eyes rolled toward the back of his head, and his body convulsed.

Jones looked at me without emotion. 'Take him to the hospital, Ms Balanchine?'

'I don't see what choice we have.' I had no particular love for my cousin, but I did not want him to die in my office either.

Three days later, Mickey Balanchine was dead. He had outlived his father by less than a year. The official cause of death was an incredibly rare strain of malaria, but official causes of death are wrong all the time.

(NB: For many reasons, I suspect poison.)

I ENLIST THE HELP OF AN OLD FRIEND;
INDULGE IN A MOMENT OF DOUBT;
GRAPPLE WITH THE CONCEPT OF DANCING;
KISS A HANDSOME STRANGER

'THE DOCTORS' CREDO IS DO NO HARM,' Dr Param said. 'Well, a bit of chocolate never hurt a soul, and I'll sign my name to that on as many prescriptions as you want.' He was sixty-two years old and losing his eyesight, which left him unable to perform surgery and thus willing to accept a position at the Dark Room. The seven other doctors I had hired had their reasons for working at my club, too – the most important reason and the one that they collectively shared was that they needed the money. Cacao could be used to treat everything from fatigue to headaches, from anxiety to dull skin. However, the unofficial policy of our club was to give prescriptions to everyone who was over eighteen and wanted one. For this service, we paid our doctors well and expected them not to scruple very much. I told Dr Param he was hired. 'This is a baffling world we live in, Miss Balanchine.' He shook his head. 'I remember when chocolate became illegal –'

'I'm sorry, Dr Param. I'd be superinterested in discussing this with you some other time.' The club was opening tomorrow and I had so much to do before then. I stood and shook his hand. 'Please give your uniform size to Noriko.'

I went down to the newly constructed bar and then passed through it to the immaculate kitchen. I had never seen such a resplendent kitchen anywhere in Manhattan. It was like a place out of an early twenty-first-century advertisement. Lucy, the mixologist, and Brita, the Parisian chocolatier I had hired, were frowning over a bubbling pot. 'Anya, taste this,' Lucy said.

I licked her spoon. 'Still too bitter,' I said.

Lucy swore and emptied the contents of the pot into the double sink. They were working on our signature drink. We had mostly finished the menu, but I felt we should have a house beverage. I hoped it would be as distinctive as the drinks I'd had in Mexico. 'Keep trying. You're getting closer, I think.'

Behind them, I could see into the pantry where the shelves were stocked with weeks' worth of supply from Granja Mañana, the cacao farm where I had spent the previous winter. In retrospect, I probably should have had the *abuelas* or at least Theo come out to teach my chefs how this was done.

I went back to the bar, where Mr Delacroix waited for me. 'Would you like to read the interview in the *Daily Interrogator*?' he asked.

'Not particularly.' Mr Delacroix had insisted that we hire a publicist and a media strategist. I had given endless interviews over the past two weeks, and in that time I'd learned that

Argon the Unaffected was not suited to talking about herself. 'Is it bad?'

'Listen, it takes a while to be good at giving interviews.'

'You should have done all of them,' I said. He had given his share, but he had insisted that I be the face of the business. 'I feel dumb talking about myself.'

'You can't think of it that way. You aren't talking about yourself. You're letting people know that you're involved with this great project.'

'But they dredge up parts of my life that I'm not comfortable discussing.' The difficulty was this: they felt that nothing was off limits while I, who was reserved by nature, felt that everything was. I did not wish to speak of my past – this included my mother's murder, my father's murder, my relatives in general, the time I'd spent at Liberty, the reason I'd been thrown out of school, the fact that my brother was in prison, the fact that my ex-boyfriend had been poisoned, and the fact that my other ex-boyfriend had been shot. 'Mr Delacroix, they want to unearth ancient history that has nothing to do with the club.'

'Ignore the questions. Discuss what you *do* want to discuss. That's the secret, Anya.'

'Do you think the club's going to flop because I'm awful at interviews?'

'No. It's too good to flop. People are going to come. I believe in this enterprise. I do.'

I wanted to run my fingers through my hair but then remembered that I had no hair. The media strategist had thought it would be a good idea if I got a new look before the launch of the club. Gone were my curls, which I was told made me look like an unkempt pre-teen and not like the owner of – her words – 'the hottest new nightclub in New York City!' Instead, I had a sleek, choppy bob, chemically relaxed and flat-ironed within an inch of its life. I did not mean to sigh, but I did.

'You miss your hair, poor thing.'

'You are mocking me, Mr Delacroix,' I said. 'Anyway I've worn it short before. It's only hair.' It *was* only hair, but I had cried after it was cut. The hairdresser had spun around the chair for the big reveal. I regarded an alien in the mirror, who looked as if it might have trouble surviving life on the hostile planet where its spaceship had crashed. I looked vulnerable, which was my least favourite way to look. *Who was that girl?* She certainly couldn't be Anya Balanchine. She certainly couldn't be me. In a display that I considered so unlike myself as to be disturbing, I had buried my shorn head in my hands and wept. How embarrassing. One wept at funerals; one did not weep over hair.

'You hate it,' the poor hairdresser had said.

'No.' I took a shuddery breath and tried to come up with an excuse for my behaviour. 'It's . . . Well, my neck is awfully cold.'

Luckily, only the stylist had been privy to my moment of weakness.

'I forget. Girls are sensitive about their hair. When my daughter was in the hospital –' Mr Delacroix cut himself off with an ironic nod. 'And this is not a story I want to tell right now.' He studied me. 'I like the new hair. I liked the old hair, too, but the new hair is not bad.'

'What an endorsement,' I said. *'Not bad.'*

'Now I have a silly but potentially awkward matter to run by you.' He paused. 'In her infinite wisdom, the media strategist thinks it would be good for the club if you brought a date to tomorrow's opening.'

'Other than my sister, I suppose?'

'I believe they are willing to arrange someone suitable for you if you don't have anyone lined up.'

'I suppose Win's away at college,' I joked.

'He left last week.'

'And also he hates me.'

'Yes, that,' he said. 'I didn't become New York City's district attorney, but I did manage to squelch that little high-school romance.'

'Well done, you.'

I honestly didn't have anyone to take me. I'd been working, not dating. And I was not on good terms with my exes. 'I don't want an arranged date,' I said finally. 'I was planning to take my sister and I think I'm going to stick with that.'

'OK, Anya. I will inform the team. I told them you would say that, by the way.' Mr Delacroix started walking to the door.

'You always did think you knew my moves.'

He came back to me. 'No. I did not predict this.' He gestured around the space, which had, in the last several weeks, begun to look like a club. The floors were buffed and polished. The painted-cloud ceiling had been restored. Silvery velvet curtains covered the windows, running from the ceiling to the

41

floor, and the walls were painted a deep chocolate brown. A mahogany bar the length of one side of the room had been added, and a bandstand, too. A red carpet would be laid out that afternoon. The only feature we lacked? Paying customers. '*This* is rather enormous,' he said. 'Now don't stay too late, and get a good night's sleep if you can.'

Despite Mr Delacroix's instructions, that night I lay in my bed not sleeping. As was my custom, I tortured myself by listing everything that might go wrong. It was almost a relief when my cell phone rang and Jones came on the line.

'Sorry to wake you, Ms. Balanchine. There's been some vandalism. Someone poured acid – we think it's acid at least – over the cacao supply.'

When I arrived, Jones led me to the pantry. The entire batch of cacao had been doused in a chemical that looked like either bleach or acid. Holes were burned into the sacks, and I could see dark mud-like clumps of damp cacao.

'You shouldn't spend too long in there,' Jones said. 'There's not much ventilation.'

My eyes were already watering. I had to think. It was not going to be an easy matter, finding two hundred and fifty pounds of raw cacao for tonight's opening.

I was about to leave the room when I noticed a Balanchine Special Dark wrapper sitting on a shelf. Not very subtle, I thought. Of course, subtlety hadn't been the point.

I hadn't heard much from Fats, who was now the head of the Balanchine family. At the prelaunch party in June, he had threatened me that there would be consequences for opening

42

the club. I guess this was what he had meant. I knew I would have to deal with him later. In the meantime, triage. I took out my phone to call my cacao supplier in Mexico.

'Anya, this hour is insanity. It is too early for me to be speaking English,' Theo said when he picked up.

'Theo, I'm in trouble.'

'I am serious as the grave when I say that I will kill for you. I am small but tough.'

'No, you ridiculous boy. I don't need you to kill for me.' I explained what had happened. 'I wanted to know if anywhere locally might have, say, two hundred and fifty pounds of cacao for tonight?'

Theo didn't speak for several seconds. 'This is a disaster. My next delivery is not supposed to arrive to you until *miércoles*. Nowhere in your country can you obtain such a large quantity of cacao, and even if you were able to, you could not be sure of the quality.' He yelled to his sister, '*Luna, despiértate! Necesitamos un avión!*'

'*Un avión?*' My Spanish had atrophied in the months since I had left Casa Marquez. 'Wait, isn't that *a plane*?'

'Yes, Anya, I am coming to you. I cannot let you start your business with subpar cacao. In Chiapas, it is now five a.m. Luna thinks I can get to New York City by afternoon. You will arrange a truck to come meet me?'

'Of course. But Theo, a cargo plane is very expensive. I can't let you and your family absorb such a cost.'

'I have money. I am a rich chocolate baron of Mexico. I will do this for you in exchange for' – he paused to come up with a figure – 'fifty per cent of your first week's profits.'

'Fifty per cent is kind of high, Theo. Besides, shouldn't you have negotiated this up front? You've already told Luna to get the plane, no?'

'You speak the truth, Anya. How about fifteen per cent of your profits until I'm paid back for the cost of the plane and the fuel and the cacao?'

'Theo, now you're asking for too little. My business could flop, and then you'll get nothing.'

'I believe in you. I taught you everything you know, did I not? Plus, it gives me a good chance to see New York and I can help you, if you like. I would not mind to see you. Is your hair grown out?'

I told him that he'd have to see when he got here. 'Theo, *buen viaje*.'

'Very good, Anya. You have not forgotten completely your Spanish.'

I did not return to the apartment, as I knew I wouldn't be able to sleep anyway. I sat in my office, in my father's chair, the same one in which he'd been murdered, and I brooded. What if the plane crashed? What if I failed and everyone laughed at me? I was thinking of Sophia Bitter, Yuji Ono, Simon Green, and, obviously, Fats. What if they were right to laugh? What if my idea had been stupid and what if I was a stupid girl for believing I could build something new? What if Mr Kipling had been right, too? What did I know about running a business? What if the cacao arrived, we made the drinks, and still no one came? What if people did come, but they hated the cacao and refused to accept it as chocolate? What if I had to

44

fire the people I had just hired? What would they do for work? For that matter, what would I do for a job? I had a high-school equivalency diploma, no college prospects, and a criminal record. What if I ended up broke? Who would pay for Natty's college? What if I lost the apartment? What if, at eighteen years old, I had ruined my entire life? Where would I go from here? I was totally alone and ugly with silly, short hair.

What if I had told the boy I loved to leave and it ended up being for nothing?

I didn't talk about Win that much, even or especially with Scarlet, but I still missed him. Of course I did. At times like this, I felt the loss of him especially intensely.

It had been three and a half months since we broke up for good, and this was how I had come to understand what had happened.

I was not innocent. I knew what I had done. I knew why I was wrong (and why he was wrong, too). We had met in high school so the chance of us ending up together in the long run had probably been pretty slim, even if we hadn't been star-crossed from the start.

Yes, I had made my choices. And choosing this club meant not choosing Win. I had sacrificed him to a cause I believed to be greater. But, dear God, if you have the idea that letting Win leave had cost me nothing, you are mistaken. I know I am an infuriating character, that I have a tendency to sound stoic and dry. More than most people, it is my nature to conceal what is most sacred in my heart. But though my feelings may be concealed, it does not mean they aren't felt.

I missed Win's smell (pine, citrus), his hands (soft palms,

long fingers), his mouth (velvet, clean), and even his hats. I wanted to talk to him, to run ideas by him, to tease him, and to kiss him. I missed having someone love me, not because they were related to me, but because they thought I was irresistible, unique, and definitely worth the trouble.

And so, I could not sleep.

The cacao arrived around two o'clock, and Theo with it.

'Your hair is so ugly!'

'I thought you'd like it.'

'I despise it.' He circled me. 'Why must girls torture their hair so?'

'It was a business decision,' I told him. 'And if you go on about it much longer, you're in danger of hurting my feelings.'

'Anya, have we been apart so long that you have forgotten what a fool I am? I should be ignored. Eh, maybe the hair, maybe it is not so bad. Maybe it is growing on me. I hope it is growing on you.' He kissed me on my cheeks. 'The place looks handsome at least. Let us see the kitchen.'

When Theo and I brought in the sacks of raw cacao, the staff cheered and Lucy even kissed Theo. He was very kissable, that boy. She made him the signature drink, which was still a work in progress. Theo tasted it, swallowed slowly, smiled politely at Lucy, and set the glass on the counter. Then he pulled me aside and whispered in my ear, 'Anya, this is no good. You can't serve this.'

I explained to Theo that no American mixologist had experience making drinks with cacao on account of cacao

46

being banned. We were doing the best we could under the circumstances.

'I am serious. This tastes like dirt. Cacao requires more finesse than this. She needs to be teased, to be provoked. I am here. Let me help you.' He rolled up his sleeves and put on an apron.

He looked at Lucy. 'Listen, I mean you no disrespect, but we have different ways of dealing with the cacao in Mexico. Would you mind if I showed you?'

'I've been working on this drink for months,' Lucy protested. 'Not to mention, I have a special diploma in Beverages and Pastries from the Culinary Institute of America. I highly doubt you'll come up with a better recipe in an afternoon.'

'I only want to help my friend by showing you some techniques. I've been working with cacao my entire life so, humbly I tell you, I know a few things.'

Lucy stepped aside though she didn't exactly look happy about letting Theo take over her kitchen.

'OK, good. *Gracias.* I appreciate very much you letting me use your kitchen. I need orange zest, cinnamon, brown sugar, rose hips, coconut milk . . .' He reeled off a long list of ingredients and the sous-chefs scrambled to get them.

Twenty minutes later, Theo had finished mixing his attempt at the club's signature drink. 'The Theobroma,' he said. 'You must get orchids to put in the glasses.'

I sipped. The flavour was chocolatey, but not heavily so. The cacao was rich but almost in the background. Instead, what I tasted was the coconut and the citrus. It was fresh and had exactly the flavours I had craved.

'You know, Theo, orchids aren't exactly easy to come by here,' I said.

Theo was staring at me. 'But what do you think of the drink?'

'It's good. It's really good,' I said.

Lucy drank tentatively, but when she was done, she took off her chef's hat to Theo. She nodded toward me. I raised my glass and said, 'To the Theobroma! The signature drink of the Dark Room!'

'We have to leave in twenty minutes or we'll be late,' I called as I ran into the apartment. I had come home to change and pick Natty up. I dropped my keys in the foyer, and then I went into the living room, where my sister sat on the couch with an older-looking boy. They must not have heard me come in and they separated as soon as they saw me, which made them seem guilty – I didn't think they were even doing anything. Still, the sight of my little sister entertaining a gentleman companion was scandalous to say the least. 'Natty, who's your friend?'

The boy stood up and manfully introduced himself. 'I'm Pierce. I was a year behind you at Trinity actually. Natty and I have science together.'

I narrowed my eyes at him. 'Nice to see you, Pierce.' The boy was familiar and seemed friendly enough. However ... though he was only one grade ahead of Natty, Pierce was much too old to be my sister's boyfriend. I turned to Natty. 'We have to leave in twenty minutes. Would you mind asking Pierce to go so that we can get ready?'

Pierce was barely out the door when Natty turned on me. 'What was that? Why were you so rude to him?'

'Why do you think? He's eighteen at least.'

'Nineteen. He spent a semester working on the wells.'

'You are fourteen. He is much too old for you, Natty.'

'You're being completely unfair. I'm a junior. He's a senior.'

'But you're supposed to be a freshman.' She had skipped two grades.

'I can't help it if I'm young for my grade. And five years is nothing.'

'Is he your boyfriend?' I asked.

'No!' She sighed. 'Yes.'

'Natty, I forbid it. You cannot date a nineteen-year-old. He is a man, and you are still a child. And men have expectations.'

'You forbid it?' she screamed. 'You aren't ever around. You don't have a right to forbid me to do anything.'

'I do, Natty. The state of New York says that I am your legal guardian, and I do actually get to forbid you to do anything I want. If you don't break this off, I will call Pierce's parents, and I will let them know that if he tries anything with you, I will press charges. Do you know what statutory rape is?'

'You wouldn't!'

'I would, Natty. Don't test me.' I felt absurd even as I was saying this.

Natty had started to cry. 'Why have you become so horrible?'

'I don't want to be,' I said. 'I'm trying to protect you.'

'Protect me from what? Protect me from having friends? Protect me from having a life? I have no friends at school, do you know that? I'm, like, a freak. Pierce is seriously my only friend there, Annie.'

I looked at my sister and realized I had no idea what was going on with her. 'Natty, listen. We have to get ready for tonight. We can talk about this later. I'm sorry I haven't been here more. I really do want to know what's happening in your life.'

Natty nodded. She went to her room, and I went to mine. I no longer had time to shower.

For the opening, the branding people had chosen for me a pure white dress, skintight, made from a stretchy silk-wool blend. The dress had a very low back with multiple straps running horizontally across it. The neckline was an extreme V that ended in the southernmost region of my cleavage. The dress left nothing to the imagination. I was told that the colour of the dress was meant to convey innocence, but that the cut said the Dark Room was the most exciting place in New York. What the dress said to me was nudity.

I flat-ironed my hair, put on red lipstick and dark eyeliner, threw on black bondage-style heels that Scarlet had picked out, and went down the hall to Natty's room.

Natty was lying in bed with her head under the covers. 'Annie,' she said, 'I don't feel well.'

'You have to get ready. The car is going to be here in two minutes, and you're supposed to be my date.'

She poked her head out. 'Oh, you look pretty.'

'Thank you, but seriously, Natty, you have to hurry up. I can't be late.'

Natty didn't move.

'If you're doing this because you're mad at me, I think it's incredibly childish.'

'I'm a child. Isn't that what you said before?' I started to pull the blanket off her, and she pulled back even harder.

'Please, Natty. Come on.'

'I don't want to go.'

'I want you there.'

'You didn't want me there before. So, what? Am I supposed to show up now? Your obedient little sister? I had nothing to do with the club so I'd like to continue to have nothing to do with it.'

I did not have time for this. 'Fine. Don't come,' I said, and then I left.

At the club, the steps were already scattered with people. I could see photographers and journalists lining the red carpet, preparing for the VIP arrivals. The media blitz had worked. Now we'd have to see if actual people came. One of the journalists called me over. 'Anya Balanchine! Have a minute for an interview with the *New York Daily Interrogator*?'

I was in a terrible mood after my discussion with Natty, and I did not like giving interviews in the first place. But I was a grown-up and that meant doing things I didn't want to do. I shook off my bad mood, smiled, and went over to the reporter.

'This is fantastic!' the reporter enthused. 'The buzz is deafening! How does it feel to be the girl who is single-handedly giving chocolate back to New York City?'

'Well, it's not chocolate per se. It's cacao. Cacao is the—'

The reporter cut me off. 'In two short years, you've gone from being the most infamous teenager in New York City to a club impresario with the most audacious idea this city has seen in a decade. How did it happen?'

'Back to your other question. I wouldn't say single-handedly – I've had a lot of help in making this come together. Theo Marquez and Charles Delacroix, for instance, have both been instrumental.' Theo was inside, but I could see Mr Delacroix down the steps from where I stood. He was talking to a different group of reporters. He was much more skilled than I.

Although the alliance had cost me my relationship with Win, Mr Delacroix had absolutely been the right choice for my business partner. He knew everyone in the city and he knew how government worked. As I had hoped, people had believed him when he said our venture was legal.

'Interesting,' the reporter said. 'Delacroix was once your greatest enemy and now he seems to have become your greatest ally.'

I took Mr Delacroix's advice and steered the conversation back to what *I* wanted to talk about. 'Once you taste Theo Marquez's cacao drinks, you might think *he's* my greatest ally,' I said. I answered a few more questions, and then I thanked the reporter for her time.

When I went inside, I did a quick walk-through. The doctors were in their carrels. The chandeliers were lit. The big band was warming up. The ceiling fans kept the rooms cool and carried the soft, melancholy scent of chocolate – I mean, *cacao* – from room to room. For once in my life, all seemed right with the world.

I went into my office. I hadn't slept in close to twenty-four hours, and I was contemplating a short nap when Mr Delacroix came into the room.

He studied me for a second. 'You look very sleepy. Awaken, Anya Balanchine. Our doors open in ten minutes and there is still much for us to do and to see.'

'Like what?'

He offered me his hand to help me out of my chair, and I followed him to a window with a view of the eastern exterior stairs of the club.

He parted a red velvet curtain. 'Look,' he said.

Every space on the steps was filled with a body. The line to get inside extended down the sidewalk. I could not see where it ended.

'They haven't even tasted it yet,' I whispered.

'It doesn't matter,' he said.

He was smiling and that was a rare occurrence. When he smiled, I could see a bit of his son in him and I couldn't help wishing that Win were here.

He went on. 'You're giving them something they wanted, something they missed. In this small way, you're making people whole again. I wanted to do such things myself, once upon a time.' He paused. 'It's probably not my place to say, but I'm sure your parents would be proud of you.'

'How are you sure? Based on what evidence exactly do you conclude that my parents would have been proud?'

He laughed at me. 'Oh, you can never have a nice moment, can you? You can never let anything go. It must be exhausting in that head of yours.'

'Please. I'd like to know. You don't say anything without having considered your angle, so give me your rationale for my parents' theoretical pride. Or was it only a load of politician crap? Were you offering up a few benedictory words, like a low-level government official at a ribbon-cutting ceremony?' I was cranky from lack of sleep and this might have come out more harshly than I had intended it.

'I think I should be insulted.' He furrowed his brow. 'OK, proof of dead parents' pride. I can come up with that. Your mother was a cop, wasn't she?'

I nodded.

'Is it a stretch to suggest that she would have been proud of you for figuring out how to turn your father's business legal?'

'Maybe it would have irritated her that I was bending the law.'

He continued. 'And your father. At the end of his life, he was trying to push Balanchine Chocolate into the modern era, was he not? The Russians killed him for it. You're barely out of high school and you've already managed to do what your father could not. And without any bloodshed.'

'Any bloodshed *so far*.'

'You're in a cheery mood. In any case, I think I've presented ample evidence that both your parents would have been absolutely delighted with you, my colleague.' He offered me his hand, and I shook it.

Glasses were broken. Drinks were spilled. The occasional punch was thrown. Girls cried in the bathroom. Men and women left with people different from those they had arrived with. We ran out of cacao – we were going to need to increase our supply – and only half of the people who wanted to come in were able to get through the door. It was dirty and noisy and I loved it more than I had ever dared hope.

A small miracle: I, who always worried, stopped worrying. Maybe it was toward the end of the night when Lucy beckoned me to the dance floor, where a group of women who worked at the club were dancing together. I liked these women, though they were my employees, not my friends. (Indeed, I had barely seen my best friend that night – she'd left early, kissing me on the cheek and whispering a rushed apology about Felix's babysitter.)

'I don't dance,' I yelled to Lucy.

'You're wearing a dress that was made for dancing,' she yelled back. 'You can't wear a dress like that and not dance. That would be criminal. Come on, Anya.'

Elizabeth, who worked in the press office, waved her arms at me and said, 'If you don't dance with us, we'll think you're a snob and we'll probably talk about you behind your back.'

Noriko was with them, too. 'Anya! Silly to start dancing club and not dance.'

These were valid points, and so I made my way to the dance floor. Noriko put her arms around me and kissed me.

Years ago, Scarlet, who loved to dance, and I had been at Little Egypt, uptown. I had said to her, 'The more I think about dancing, the more I don't get it.'

'Stop thinking,' she had said. 'That's the key.'

At the Dark Room that night, I finally understood what she meant. Dancing was a kind of surrender to feeling, to sound, to the present.

I had been dancing for a while when a pillow-lipped, bedroom-eyed man in his twenties pushed his way into my circle.

'You dance well,' he said.

'No one has ever told me that before,' I said honestly.

'I find that hard to believe. Is it OK if I dance with you?'

'Free country,' I said.

'Interesting place, right?'

'Yeah.' I could tell he had no idea that I was the owner, and that was fine with me.

'Girl, that dress is stupid-sexy,' he said.

I blushed. I was about to tell him how it wasn't really my taste and how someone else had picked it out for me, but then I changed my mind. As far as he knew, I was exactly what I appeared to be. I was a sexy girl in a sexy dress, who'd gone out to a club to have a good time with her friends. I put my hand on his neck, and I kissed him. He had these big dark lips that looked as if they needed to be kissed.

'Wow,' he said. 'So do I get your name?'

'You seem nice, and you're incredibly cute, but I'm not dating right now.'

'Pour la liberté!' Brita said, pumping her fist.

'Freedom! Freedom!' Lucy echoed. I hadn't even known they'd been paying attention to me.

'Sure,' he said. 'I get that.'

We danced for a few more songs and then he left.

How strange it was for me to kiss a man and know he meant nothing to me, to know with certainty that I would never see him again, that what I was feeling at that precise moment I would only feel once. How different it was from kissing Win – those kisses had seemed consequential, ponderous even. But when I kissed that man, my only obligation was to the present. I had always tried to be a good girl, and until that night, it had never occurred to me that some people you kissed wouldn't become your boyfriend and that this was, in fact, perfectly fine. Maybe even desirable.

I was still on the dance floor when a hand grabbed mine. It was Natty. 'I couldn't miss your big night,' she said. 'I'm sorry I didn't tell you about Pierce.'

I kissed her on the cheek. 'We'll talk about it later. I'm glad you came. Come dance with me, OK?'

She smiled, and we danced for what felt like hours. I forgot that I had a body that was capable of being tired. I wouldn't even notice the blisters until the next day.

The sun had started to come up by the time Natty and I finally went home. She asked if we might stop at our church, as it only sent us slightly in the wrong direction.

At sixteen, I had still been convinced that piety could protect me and mine from the realities of living in this world and from the fact that all that lives must die. At eighteen, after everything that had happened to me, I did not much believe in anything anymore.

Still, I did not mind if my sister believed. In fact, I found the idea comforting.

At St Patrick's, we lit candles for our mother, our father, Nana, and Imogen. 'They're watching us,' Natty said.

'Do you really believe that?' I asked.

'I don't know, but I want to. And even if they aren't, I don't think it can hurt.'

I woke in the afternoon. My business ran on vampire hours, and in that first year of running the Dark Room, my whole life, perhaps appropriately, would pass in a series of dark rooms. I ambled out to the living room, where I found Theo, impossibly bright-eyed, sitting on my couch. I had told him he could use Nana's old room for as long as he stayed in New York.

'Anya, I have been waiting hours and hours for you.' He probably had been; Theo's work on the farm required him to rise at dawn, and it must have been difficult for him to break the habit. 'Listen, we have business to discuss.'

'I know,' I said, pulling my bathrobe around myself. 'But maybe some breakfast first?'

'It is past lunchtime,' Theo said. 'Your kitchen is the saddest place I have ever seen.' He produced an orange from his pocket and held it out to me. 'Here, eat this. I brought it from home.'

I took the orange and began to peel it.

'I have already arranged for the next month's cacao shipments,' Theo said. 'Looking through your books and seeing how last night went, I believe you underestimate demand by half.'

'I'll up my order. Thanks for doing that, Theo.' I arranged

the orange peels into a tidy stack.

'I am not being nice, Anya! I want to work for your club. No, I lie. I want to work *with* you. I see how successful the club could be and, if you want to keep it that way, you are going to need someone to supply your cacao. And in the kitchen you need an overseer with a deep understanding of cacao, too. I can be both someones.'

'What are you saying, Theo?'

'I am saying that I want to be your partner. I want to stay here in New York and become the director of operations for the Dark Room.'

'Theo, won't they miss you on the farm?'

'We are not talking about that. Pretend you know nothing about me. Pretend we are strangers. But no, they do not miss me. I will make a bucket of money supplying our cacao to you, and Luna takes care of much on the farm since I was sick last year.' He looked at me. 'Listen, Anya, you need me. And not because I am the most handsome boy you know. But I look around last night. Delacroix, he raises money for you. He talks to the press. He takes care of the law. But you do some of that and everything else, too. I am not criticizing you, but you are a young business and you need someone else to help you with the kitchen and supply aspects. I make sure everything we serve is delicious, safe, and of highest quality. It would have been certain disaster last night if not for me—'

'You're always so modest.'

'I want to organize your club so that you never again experience a supply shortfall. No matter what happens – *la*

59

plaga, el apocalipsis, la guerra – the Dark Room will keep serving drinks.'

'What do you get out of it?'

'I supply you with cacao and offer my services in exchange for ten per cent of the business. Also, I want to be a part of this. I want to build something with my own two hands. It is exciting here. My heart beats like a madman's!' He grabbed my citrus-coated hand and held it over his heart. 'Feel, Anya. Feel how it beats. Last night, I am so tired but I cannot even sleep. I have waited to be a part of something like this my whole life.'

His proposal did not seem unreasonable. Cacao was one of our larger expenses, and Theo had been indispensable since his arrival yesterday. (Had it only been yesterday?) If I had a hesitation, it was probably that I considered very few people to truly be my friends, and Theo was one of them. 'I don't want this to spoil our friendship if the business doesn't work out,' I said.

'Anya, we are the same. No matter what happens, I know the risk I take and I will not blame you. Besides, we will always be friends. I could just as soon hate you as I could my sister. My sister Luna, I mean. Not Isabelle. Isabelle, I could hate. You know how she gets.'

He held out his rough farmer's hand, and I shook it. 'I'll have Mr Delacroix draw up the papers,' I said.

It was only right. Theo Marquez had taught me everything I knew about cacao, and without him, there probably wouldn't have been a Dark Room.

I GO FROM INFAMOUS TO FAMOUS;
CONSEQUENTLY, ENEMIES
BECOME FRIENDS

THE NIGHT BEFORE MY BIRTHDAY, I had been sternly warned by Mr Kipling not to expect the club to be a success right away – or ever. 'Bars are tricky,' Mr Kipling had said. 'Nightclubs are worse. In this economy, do you know what the rate of failure for nightclubs is?'

Hadn't Chai Pinter said it was ninety-nine per cent? But that figure seemed high. 'I'm not sure,' I said.

'And that's precisely what worries me, Annie,' Mr Kipling had said. 'You have no idea what you're getting into. The rate of failure is eighty-seven per cent, by the way. And most people aren't foolish enough to open a nightclub in the first place.'

However, Mr Kipling had been wrong about the Dark Room. For whatever reason, the idea had instantly caught fire. From the first night we opened, every table was filled, and the lines got longer every night. People I hadn't heard from in years contacted me trying to get tables. Mrs Cobrawick, formerly of Liberty, was turning fifty and wanted to spend her birthday at the Dark Room. She was an awful woman, but she had once done me a good turn. I gave her a table by the window and even sent her a round of Theobromas on the house. District Attorney Bertha Sinclair wanted to bring her mistress but needed to arrange to come in through the back door to avoid the press, who were always posted out front. Bertha Sinclair was not my favourite person either, but it was good to have powerful friends. I hooked her up with our most secluded table. I heard from kids I'd gone to school with, teachers (a few of whom had voted to expel me), friends of my father's, and even the cops who had investigated me for poisoning Gable Arsley in 2082. I said yes to everyone. My father used to say, *Generosity, Anya. It's always a good investment.*

I had been written about my whole life because of who my father was, but now for the first time, I became the story. Instead of being identified as a '*mafiya* princess,' they called me a 'nightclub darling,' a 'raven-haired impresario,' and even a 'cacao wunderkind.' People wanted to know what I was wearing, who cut my hair, who I was dating. (I wasn't dating anyone, by the way.) When I walked down the street, people sometimes recognized me, waving to me and calling my name.

During this period, the Family remained silent. I had braced myself for more disturbances like the destruction of the cacao supply, but none came.

At the end of October, Fats contacted me. He asked if he might come to the club for a sit-down, and I agreed.

Fats arrived at our meeting with only one other person in

tow, and that person was Mouse, the girl who had been my bunk mate at Liberty. 'Mouse,' I said. 'How are you?'

'Very well,' she said. 'Thanks for recommending me to Fats.'

'She's become indispensable,' Fats said. 'I trust Mouse here with everything. Best hire I ever made, if you want to know the truth. You got good instincts, Annie.'

They sat on the love seat in my office, and Noriko brought in drinks. I asked what I could do for them.

'Well,' Fats said, 'I've had a change of heart, and I don't want there to be bad blood between us anymore. You've obviously made a real success of it here, and I'm the kind of person who can admit when he was wrong.'

I sat back in my father's chair. I did not feel the need to address the ruined cacao supply. I knew it had been him, and he knew I knew. Best to move on. 'Thank you,' I said.

'From this point in time forward, you got my hundred-per-cent backing. But there's something you need to know.'

'What's that?'

'The Balanchiadze, the Balanchines in Russia, are furious with you.'

'Why?'

'Because they see your business as a threat. If people go to your club to get cacao, maybe they lose their taste for black-market chocolate. That you, the daughter of Leonyd Balanchine, are the face of this new way of business threatens them even more.

'They keep pressuring me to sabotage you, but I won't. I did it once, but you probably know that.'

I nodded.

'Since then, I've done everything in my power to keep the heat off you. Me and Mouse both. And I'll keep on this way until I'm dead or someone else becomes the head of this Family. Also, I wanted to say that I'm proud of you, kid. I'm sorry I was slow to see the light. I hope this won't sound presumptuous but maybe you learned a little from me about how to run a club. You and your friends used to spend so much time in my speakeasy.'

'Maybe so,' I said. I clasped my hands and set them on the table. 'What do you need from me?'

'Nothing, Anya. I only wanted you to know what was happening and that you didn't have anything more to fear from me.'

He stood, and then he kissed me on both sides of my face. 'You done good, kid.'

I PREVENT HISTORY FROM REPEATING;
EXPERIMENT WITH OLDER FORMS
OF TECHNOLOGY

IT IS A TRUTH universally acknowledged that when something goes well in one part of your life, something else will just as certainly fall apart.

I was in a meeting with Lucy and Theo when my cell phone whistled. I hadn't had one for very long – you weren't allowed to have one until you turned eighteen – and I was always forgetting to turn the ringer off. I glanced at the caller identification: HT School. For a moment, I wondered what I had done wrong. I turned to the group. 'Apologies. This is so rude, but my sister's school is calling.'

I walked over to the window to take the call. 'We need you to come get Natty. She's being suspended,' Mr Rose, the secretary from Holy Trinity, said.

I excused myself, dashed out to the street, and then took a cab down to Holy Trinity. As I walked the familiar path to

Headmaster's office, I paused in the doorway of the lobby to consider my sister. Natty was still wearing her fencing whites, though a single drop of blood on her sleeve spoiled their pristine look. She was not sitting in a particularly ladylike position either. Her legs were spread aggressively and wide, as if to create a boundary between her and everyone else. She was hunched over – that chip on her shoulder was palpable and probably weighed her down. A scratch was slashed jauntily across her cheek. Her eyes were proud and murderous. I think you can guess who she reminded me of.

Another girl was exiting the office with a red nose and dried blood around her nostrils. Her mother had her arm around her shoulders.

'Your sister is an animal,' the mother said to me.

I didn't know what had happened, but I wasn't about to let that woman insult Natty. 'That's not called for,' I said. 'It looks like they both got hurt.'

'Everyone knows what type of people you come from,' the mother said.

She was leaving. I should have let her leave, but at the last minute I called out, 'Oh yeah, what type of people?'

'Scum,' she said.

I began to ball my hand into a fist, and then I reminded myself I was a prominent business owner and an adult and above such violent shenanigans. I let my fist unfurl. While I was busy taking the high road, Natty charged at the woman. I was barely able to hold Natty back.

'Just go,' I said to the woman. 'Go.'

'Before you even say anything,' Natty said, 'that girl came at me first.'

'What happened?'

'So I'm in Mr Beery's class, and we're studying Prohibition.'

God, I could already see where this was going.

'And then he says, "The best criminals are the ones that decide to use the law to their advantage. Take Natty's sister . . ." And then I'm screaming in Mr Beery's face about how you're the opposite of a criminal. And he sends me to Headmaster's office.'

Why hadn't the school fired this man? 'Natty,' I said, 'you can't fight with everyone who decides to call me a name.'

She rolled her dark green eyes at me. '*I know*, Anya.'

'I don't understand. How did the other girl get involved?'

'I have lunch after Beery, and then Beginners' Fencing. And all through Fencing, the girl is making cracks about how I'm too much of a baby to control myself and how Pierce must like babies. She's his ex, so she has it in for me. And then we're sparring with each other, and she keeps talking crap, and I pull her mask off and punch her in the face. And she pulls mine off, and that's how I got scratched.'

The secretary poked his head out of his office. 'Balanchines. Headmaster will see you now.'

The scene with Headmaster was one I'd starred in many times before. Natty was suspended for a week. If her grades hadn't been so stellar, her punishment probably would have been worse.

I dropped Natty off at home. 'I have to go back to work.

We'll talk about this later. I don't want you to go anywhere. Understood?'

'Whatever.'

'I'm on your side, Natty, and more than that, I can relate. Remember the first day of my junior year?'

'You dumped an entire tray of lasagne over Gable Arsley's head.' She laughed a little. 'He deserved it, too.'

'He did, but I still shouldn't have done it. I should have gone to him or his parents or Nana or Mr Kipling with my grievance. Please, Natty, look at me. Nothing in my life or anyone else's has ever been improved by violence or fighting.'

'I need a speech from you right now like I need a hole in my head.' Natty sighed. 'Why are we like this? Why are we so out of control?'

'Because terrible things happened to us when we were young. But it gets easier, Natty, I swear to God. And it will get even easier for you because you're so much smarter than me. Not to mention, your hair is naturally straight.'

'What does that have to do with anything?'

'Do you have any idea how much work it is to get my hair straight? I'm in a constant battle with frizz. It's a wonder I haven't murdered someone.' I kissed her on the cheek. 'Everything's going to be fine, you'll see.'

'I'm tired, Annie. I think I'm going to take a nap, if that's OK.' I didn't feel superconfident that my talk had done much for her, but I figured I could improve on it later.

When I got home that night (or I should say *morning* – it was nearly 3 a.m.), Natty wasn't there. She had left a message on my slate, which she knew I never brought with me anymore: *Out with Pierce*. It was way past city curfew, and she had explicitly ignored my instructions.

I paced around the foyer and tried to decide what to do. As a minor, Natty didn't have a cell phone, and if I called the police, she'd be in trouble with the law. I looked around her room for Pierce's number. I found a pack of condoms in her nightstand – was my baby sister having sex with this boy? On some level, I didn't even want to know. And then I did finally locate Pierce's phone number in her desk drawer.

He answered sleepily. 'Pierce.'

'Hello, Pierce. Is my sister with you?'

'Yeah, she's here. I'm handing her the phone right now.'

'What?' Natty said.

'Are you kidding me? Where are you? Do you have any idea what time it is?' I wasn't even trying not to yell.

'Relax, Anya. I'm with Pierce –'

'Obviously.'

'I fell asleep here. It isn't a big deal. Nothing happened. I'll be home in the morning.'

'Are you kidding me? You are fourteen years old! You can't up and spend the night at your boyfriend's house.'

She hung up on me. I walked into the living room and threw my phone at the couch, not realizing that someone was lying on it.

'Ow!' Theo yelled. 'What is wrong with you?'

'None of your business.' I didn't want to go into it with him. 'When are you getting a place of your own?'

'When my mean boss gives me some time off,' Theo said.

'Why are you even here? No date tonight?' Theo was popular in New York, to say the least. I didn't know how he found the time, but he was with a different girl every night.

'No, tonight I get beauty sleep.' Theo handed me my phone.

'Lucky you.'

In my bedroom, I didn't even try to sleep. I stared at the ceiling, hoping the cracks in the plaster might offer some insight regarding what I should do. I thought of myself, lying in this same bed at age sixteen, the year everything had begun to go so horribly wrong. What would sixteen-year-old Anya have wanted someone to do for her?

I waited until 5 a.m. to call Mr Kipling. 'I need to find a new school for Natty. Something strict, but with good academics. Something far away from here.'

Mr Kipling was quick. Several hours later, he reported that he had found a convent school in Boston that was willing to take her in the middle of the semester.

'Are you sure about this, Anya?' Mr Kipling asked. 'It's a big decision, and you don't want to be hasty.'

I went into Natty's bedroom and packed a suitcase. I was closing the suitcase when she came through the door. She looked from me to the packed suitcase. 'What's this?'

'Look,' I said, 'we both know that I'm not being a good guardian to you right now. I'm too busy with the club to watch you—'

'I don't need to be watched!'

'You do, Natty. You're a kid, and I'm worried that if I

don't act now, your whole life is going to be ruined. Look what happened to Scarlet.'

'Pierce is nothing like Gable Arsley!'

'I see you making mistakes now that you're with him. I see you heading down a bad road.' I took a deep breath. 'I said before that I didn't want you to end up like Scarlet, but the person I don't want you to end up like is' – it was so hard to admit – 'me.'

My sister looked at me with the saddest expression. 'Annie! Annie, don't say that! Look at the club you made.'

'I didn't have a choice. I got myself kicked out of school. Maybe it seems like my life is working out right now, but I want you to have more options than I had. I don't want you to end up working in a nightclub. I don't want you to have anything to do with chocolate or our rotten Family. I truly believe that you're destined for better.'

Natty wiped her eyes on her sleeve. 'You're making me cry.'

'I'm sorry. This school Mr Kipling found for you has a great science programme, much better than HT's.' I tried to make my voice upbeat. 'And wouldn't it be great to be somewhere no one knew anything about you? A place where no one had any preconceptions.'

'Stop trying to sell me, Anya. Maybe you want me out of your hair. Maybe you want me to be someone else's problem for a while.'

'That isn't true! Do you have any idea how horribly lonely I'm going to be without you? You are my sister and there is no one in this whole lousy dystopia I love more than you. But I'm scared, Natty. I'm scared I'm messing everything up. I don't know the right things to do for you right now. I barely know the right things to do for myself most of the time. I wish Daddy were alive. Or Mom or Nana. Because I'm only eighteen and I have no idea what to say, what you need. What I know is I wish someone had gotten me out of New York City when I was having such a rough time at Holy Trinity. I wish someone had gotten me away from Mr Beery and people like him, and our relatives, too.'

She fought me on the cab ride to Penn Station and at the ticket counter (to the amusement of a youth athletic team – I saw the bag of balls, but could not identify the sport), and now she was still fighting me in the waiting area under the departures sign. A panhandler nudged my sister and said, 'Give her a break.' *Her* was me, by the way, and even the homeless thought I needed defending from the fourteen-year-old haranguer.

'I'm not going,' Natty said. 'No matter what you say, I'm not getting on that train.' She had her arms crossed and her lower lip jutted out. She looked exactly like what she was – a teenager who hated the world and everyone in it. For my part, I suspected that I looked and sounded like a kid pretending to be an adult for a school play.

'You're going,' I said. 'You agreed back at the apartment that you would. Why are you changing your mind now?'

The loudspeaker announced that Natty's train to Boston was boarding. She was crying and sniffling, so I offered her my handkerchief.

She blew her nose and then she stood up straight.

'How would you make me get on the train?' she asked in a calm voice. 'You can't physically force me. I'm taller than you and I'm probably stronger than you, too.'

The jig was up. The lion had realized the impotence of the zookeeper. 'I can't, Natty. All I can tell you is I love you, and I think this is for the best.'

'Well, I think you're wrong,' she said. We stared at each other. I didn't blink and neither did she. A second later, she turned on her heel and stalked off toward the stairway that led to the train.

'Goodbye, Natty!' I called after her. 'I love you! Call me if you need anything.'

She did not reply or even turn her head.

A week later, she called me, sobbing. 'Please, Anya. Please let me come home.'

'What's wrong?'

'I can't do anything here. There are tons of rules and even more because I'm new. If you let me come home, I'll be good, I swear. I know I was wrong before. I shouldn't have stayed out with Pierce. I shouldn't have been disrespectful to you or Mr Beery.'

I steeled myself. 'Give it a couple of weeks.'

'I can't, Anya! I'll die. I will seriously die.'

'Are they doing anything bad to you? Because if they are, you need to tell me what it is.'

She didn't answer.

'Is this about Pierce?' I asked. 'Do you miss him?'

'No! That's . . . You don't know everything. You don't know anything!'

'Give it until Thanksgiving. You can come home for Thanksgiving and then you'll see Leo.'

She hung up on me.

I wished I could see her. I wished the school wasn't so far away or that I hadn't been so busy with the club. If only I knew someone in Boston, I thought.

I did, of course, though I didn't want to have to talk to *him*. I didn't want to have to ask him for anything either.

In point of fact, I didn't even have his cell-phone number.

I got my slate from the drawer. Only people in school used slates, but unlike me, Win was still in school. Although we had never slate-messaged much (no one my age did; SM-ing was something your grandparents or even your great-grandparents did), at that moment, the ancient technology appealed to me. It seemed more respectful, and easier than having to actually speak.

anyaschka66: *Are you there? Do you ever use this?*

He did not reply for nearly an hour.

win-win: *Not often. What do you want?*
anyaschka66: *Are you at college?*
win-win: *Yes.*
anyaschka66: *Boston, right? Do you like it?*
win-win: *Yes and yes. Actually, I have to get to class soon.*
anyaschka66: *You don't owe me anything, but I*

74

*need a favour. Natty's at a new school in Boston, and
I wondered if you could go visit her for me. She
sounded upset the last time we talked. I know it's a
lot to ask . . .*

win-win: OK, *for Natty,* OK. Where is it?*

anyaschka66: *Sacred Heart, on Commonwealth.*

(*'For Natty' – read: not for me.)

The next day, he messaged me again.

win-win: *Saw N. this afternoon. She's definitely
OK. Likes her classes and the other girls. Maybe she's
a little homesick, but she'll live. I let her steal
my hat.*

anyaschka66: *Thank you. Thank you so much.*

win-win: *Not a problem. I should go.*

anyaschka66: *Maybe if you're home for Thanksgiving, you could stop by my club. We could catch
up. Drinks on me.*

win-win: *I'm not coming home for Thanksgiving. I'm
going to visit my girlfriend's family in Vermont.**

anyaschka66: *Sounds fun. I've never been to
Vermont. That's so great. I'm really, really happy to
hear that.***

win-win: *Dad says you're a success. Congrats,
Annie. Sounds like you've gotten everything you
wanted.****

anyaschka66: *Yeah. Well, thanks. Thank you
again for going to see Natty. Have a good*

*Thanksgiving if I don't see you. I guess I probably
won't.*

win-win: *Take care.*

(**Vermont? That was* fast. *Though maybe it wasn't. It had been
about five and a half months since we'd bid adieu. Had I expected
him to become a monk?*)

(***Maybe there was a point to this slate-messaging after all. I
was glad he couldn't hear my voice or see my face as I expressed how*
really, really *happy* I *was for him.*)

(****Suffice it to say, not quite everything.*)

VI

I DELIVER THE WORLD'S SHORTEST EULOGY;
THROW A PARTY; AM KISSED PROPERLY

Two DAYS BEFORE CHRISTMAS, I received a phone call from Keisha, Mr Kipling's wife. 'Anya,' she said tearfully, 'Mr K. is dead.' Mr Kipling had been fifty-four years old. He'd had a major heart attack my junior year of high school. A little over two years later, a second heart attack had finished him off. Mortality rates in my circle were always high, but that year, they had been particularly so. I'd lost Imogen in January, my cousin Mickey in September, and now, Mr Kipling. A loss for nearly every season of the year.

Perhaps this is why I did not cry when Keisha gave me the news. 'I'm truly sorry,' I said.

'I'm calling because I wondered if you might say a few words at his funeral?'

'It's not really my strong suit.' I was not comfortable with public displays of emotion.

'But it would mean so much to him. He was incredibly proud of you and the club. Every single article about you, he saved.'

I was surprised to hear that. For the last nine months of his life, Mr Kipling and I had fought, mainly over my decision to open the club that apparently he'd been 'incredibly proud of.' (There had been other reasons.) However, from my father's death in 2075 until I'd become an adult last summer, Mr Kipling had overseen every financial decision I had made and quite a few of the personal ones. I'm not sure how good his advice was at times, but he had always done his best and had never given up on me even when it seemed that the world was against me. I knew he had loved me. I had loved him, too.

Noriko; Leo, who was finally home from prison; and Natty, who was back from Sacred Heart, accompanied me to St Patrick's. I was the third to speak – after Simon Green and a man named Joe Burns, who apparently had been Mr Kipling's squash partner, but before his daughter, Grace, and his brother, Peter. By the time it was my turn, my palms and armpits were moist. Though it was winter, I was seriously regretting my decision to wear a black sweaterdress.

I brought my slate with me to the podium. 'Hello,' I began. 'I wrote some notes.' I turned on my slate, which seemed to take forever, and glanced over what I had written:

> 1. *Mr K. = Dad's best friend. Joke about how it's hard to be a crime boss's best friend?*
> 2. *Mr K., funny story about his being bald?*

3. Mr K., maybe not the best lawyer, but loyal. Story about that?
4. Mr K. honoured commitments.

And that was what I had. I had written the notes after coming home from a late night at work. They had made sense at the time, but as I stood in St Patrick's, they looked pretty inadequate. I turned off my slate. I would have to speak from the heart, which was an act I tried to avoid.

'I don't know what to say,' I said stupidly. 'He was' – my inane notes ran through my head: *bald? my dad's best friend? a mediocre lawyer?* – 'a good man.' My foot was shaking and I could hear myself breathing. 'Thank you.'

As I walked back down the aisle, I could not look Keisha Kipling in the eye. I sat down in my pew, and Natty squeezed my hand.

After the funeral, Simon Green, who I usually tried to avoid, approached my siblings and me. Natty hugged him. 'He was like a father to you,' she said generously. 'You must be heartbroken.'

'Yes. Thank you, Natty.' Simon took off his glasses and wiped them on his shirt. He nodded toward me. 'Anya,' he said, 'I wondered if I might speak to you a moment.'

I would have preferred not to, but what choice did I have? 'This is hard to say,' Simon said once we were outside.

I crossed my arms. I already didn't like the tone of his voice.

'Mr Kipling left his firm to me, but unfortunately, his

client list is vastly diminished. I don't know if I'll be able to keep it afloat. Of course you can say no, but I wondered if you might have a job for me at the Dark Room.'

'The Dark Room has a lawyer already,' I said. Furthermore, I didn't want Simon around.

'I know. I only meant because your business is so big now. Maybe if it gets any bigger you'll need another lawyer. And a man like Charles Delacroix can't be thinking he'll be legal counsel to a nightclub forever.'

'I've learned it's fruitless to try to speculate about what Charles Delacroix is thinking.'

'OK, Annie. I can see I've made you upset. You can't blame a person for asking.'

I knew I was being unkind. 'Listen, Simon, it's not personal, it's business.'

'Sure, Annie. I get that.' He paused. 'Leo's back from prison, I see.'

This was not said casually, but as a reminder of an obligation I may or may not have had to Simon regarding the circumstances of my brother's return from Japan last Easter. Had Simon spoken bluntly, I would have respected him more. 'If my situation changes, I'll let you know.'

And so I came to the end of 2084. It was tempting to dwell on the lows (the deaths, the loss of Win, the arguments with my sister, etc., etc., etc.), but for once in my life, I chose not to. My portion of tragedy had made my triumphs somehow sweeter. My business was prospering; I had settled relations with Fats and the Family; I was on the right side of the law for the first time in my life; I had more than enough money; I had become a godmother; and I'd become increasingly skilled at wearing heels.

And perhaps this explains why your fun-challenged heroine decided to behave in a way that was entirely out of character: New Year's Eve, I threw a party at the Dark Room.

I posted a sign out front that read: CLOSED FOR A PRIVATE AFFAIR. Then I opened the doors of my club wide and turned the music up loud.

That night was the first time Leo had been at the club. 'What do you think?' I asked him.

He grabbed my head with his hands and kissed me on my forehead, my cheeks, and the top of my head. 'I honestly cannot believe that my tiny baby sister made this herself!'

'I had help,' I said. 'Noriko. And Theo. And Mr Delacroix.'

'You are the most amazing sister. Hey, Annie, can I come work here, too?'

'Sure,' I said. 'What would you want to do?'

'I don't know. I want to be useful.'

I would figure something out. Maybe I could team him up with the meticulous Noriko. I was still thinking about this when Natty grabbed my hand.

'Win's here! I asked him to come. We should go say hi.'

'What? Who's here?' I wasn't sure if I had heard her correctly over the loud music.

'When we were riding back on the train from Boston, I told him he *had* to see your club because it was amazing. I reasoned with him that since it was basically the reason you two broke up, he probably wouldn't have closure unless he did.'

'Natty, you really shouldn't have done that,' I said.

'Truthfully, I didn't think he would come, but he's here now.'

I ran my fingers through my hair. He hadn't seen me since I'd gotten my hair cut.

Natty led me to a table near the windows. Win was indeed there, along with his mother, Mr Delacroix, and a girl about my age. I knew without being told that this was the girlfriend from Vermont. She was *skinny* skinny and *tall* tall with blonde hair that flowed to her waist. Mr Delacroix and Win stood. I smiled (in a way I hoped was) graciously at the table and put on my best hostess voice. 'Mr Delacroix, Mrs Delacroix, so nice to see you again. Win, what a surprise. And you must be Win's girlfriend?' I held my hand out for the Viking to shake.

'Astrid,' she said.

'Anya,' I said. 'Amazing to meet you.'

'This place is so charming,' she said. 'I love it.' Her hand was resting on his thigh. He brushed several long, blonde strands of hair from her face.

'*Charming* is the word,' Mrs Delacroix agreed. The last time I'd spoken to her, she'd seemed nonplussed about the club and her husband's role in it, but she seemed to have made peace with both. 'You've done a wonderful job. You and Charlie both.' She looked at her husband. Mr Delacroix's expression was cryptic, and I did not know him well enough to decipher it. He had not even greeted me when I'd arrived at the table, but had kept his gaze toward the window, as if the real party was going on just outside.

'Thanks,' I said. 'We're proud of it.'

'It's great,' Win said without much enthusiasm. 'I'm glad I got to see it.' He paused. 'You changed your hair.'

'I did.' I put my hand on the back of my neck.

'Well, it suits this club at least,' Win said.

'Drink up,' I told the table. 'And a very happy New Year!'

I walked to the bar. 'Sorry about that,' Natty said. 'So awkward. I didn't know his girlfriend was coming to the city.'

'It was fine,' I said. 'I'm happy he saw the club, and I knew about the girlfriend already.'

Natty was about to speak, but then she shook her head. She ordered two Theobromas for us. 'I was surprised to see Mrs Delacroix here, though. Win says his parents are getting a divorce.'

'Oh, I hadn't heard.' Mr Delacroix was pretty tight-lipped about his personal life.

'Yeah. Win's not that upset. He says it was a long time coming. It was his mother's decision, I guess.'

'You and Win talk a lot?'

'Some. I've always liked him, as you know,' she said. 'And when I see him in Boston, it makes me feel less homesick.' She sipped her drink. 'Thank you for sending him to me, by the way.'

'Natty, I don't know if you'll even be able to answer this question. But do you think Win understands now? Does he understand why I had to do this?'

'I think so,' she said slowly. 'He's moved on, obviously,

and he seems less bitter.' She rested her chin in her hands. 'I thought you'd be with him forever.'

'Well, that's because you were a little kid when he and I met,' I said. 'I've thought a lot about it. The truth is, sometimes too much can happen in a relationship, and then there's nothing anyone can do or say. It's broken.'

'You don't believe that could ever happen between us?' Natty asked.

'Of course not, you goose. You could be awful forever, and I'd still love you. Things are good at the new school?'

She took a long drink, and then she laughed. 'I hate to say it, but you were right. It was getting too serious with Pierce. Once I got away, I could see that, and he started to seem a lot less important.'

'Funny,' I said. 'Maybe if someone had sent me away to school, it would have been the same with Win.'

Natty shook her head. 'Probably not, though. Win's kind of, sort of wonderful, and Pierce is just some dumb boy.'

I laughed at Natty. 'You can't have Win,' I said. 'He's too old for you. Plus, he's dating a Viking.'

'She does look like a Viking. I wouldn't want Win anyway. I would never date the boy who broke my sister's heart.'

He hadn't broken it. I knew that now. If I was honest, I had done it to myself. *(NB: Who needs a heart anyway?)*

It was important for her to know this, so I said it aloud. 'He didn't break it. No one can break your heart except you.'

'Maybe she looks more like an Icelandic princess,' Natty said.

Theo joined us at the bar. 'Who looks like an Icelandic princess?' he asked.

Natty pointed to the Delacroixs' table.

'Stop it,' I said. 'We don't want them to know we're talking about them.'

Natty waved. 'It's fine. They can't hear us. Hi, Icelandic princess!'

'Very pretty girl,' Theo said, 'but you are both wrong. She looks like a mermaid.'

'No date?' I asked him.

He shook his head.

'What? Have you run through every girl in New York? Theo's a big slut,' I informed Natty.

'*Si*. You will have to open a new location in another city so that I can find some new women to date.'

'Yeah, I'll get right on that.'

'Maybe Canada. I would like to see Canada before I die,' Theo said.

'Or Paris!' Natty said with a squeal of delight.

'Unfortunately, chocolate's legal there. What would be the point?'

I excused myself to go talk to the DJ. She'd been playing too many slow, romantic songs. It was a party; I wanted party music. On the way back, I ran into Win, who was by himself.

He didn't look like he wanted to talk to me, but whatever. I still hadn't thanked him in person for going to see Natty. 'Hey, stranger,' I said.

'Hey.' He barely looked at me. Instead, he looked over at the table where his parents and the Viking still sat.

'I wanted to thank you in person for visiting Natty.'

'It's nothing,' he said. 'Her school's not that far from mine.'

'It *is* something,' I insisted. 'You and I didn't exactly end on good terms – so I appreciate you doing this.'

'Doing things for you is a bad habit with me. I should get back.'

'Wait.' I tried to invent a reason to prolong our conversation. 'Win, how do you like school?'

'Good.'

A one-word reply, but I pressed on anyway.

'Astrid is really pretty. I'm happy that you met someone,' I said. 'I hope me and you can be friends someday.'

Silence. 'I don't need a friend like you,' he said finally. He sounded angrier than when we had broken up. 'I should not have come here tonight.'

'Why are you still so angry with me? I'm not angry with you.'

I heard him take a deep breath. 'How about my parents' divorce?'

'That is not on me, Win. Your parents have been unhappy for years. You told me as much yourself.'

'They seemed better after he lost the election. But all that went to Hell after you and your big idea.'

'You can't be serious.'

'I am sorry I ever met you, Anya. I am sorry that I pursued you and that I didn't leave you alone when you asked. I wish I'd never had to move from Albany. You were not worth getting shot for. You were not worth waiting for. You were not worth this trouble. You are the worst thing that ever happened to me. You have been a hurricane in my life and not in a good way!' He was almost screaming at me, but maybe that was the effect of the loud music. The DJ had honoured my request to play party music, and the bass was literally deafening. 'But hey, it's not like I wasn't warned. My father only told me about – I don't know – roughly one million times to stay away from you. So no, I don't want to be friends with you. The best part about breaking up with you is that we *don't* have to be friends.'

And then he left. It would have been pathetic of me to run after him, to insist that he accept my friendship when he clearly thought it was worth so little. Even if I felt like it, I couldn't leave the party I had thrown. I couldn't go home, get into bed, pull the covers over my head, and cry. I put a smile on my face and went back to my friends at the bar.

The DJ announced that there were only two minutes until 2085 would officially begin.

Leo and Noriko came over to our group, and Natty chatted to them about whether they should have another wedding, a real one, now that Leo was out of prison.

With thirty seconds to go, Theo took my hand and looked at me with bright and perhaps slightly intoxicated eyes. '*Abuela* says that it's bad luck not to kiss someone on New Year's.'

'You're such a liar,' I said. 'I'm sure your *abuela* says nothing of the kind.'

'It's true,' Theo said. 'She worries that in New York, I am not getting kissed enough.'

87

I rolled my eyes. 'Then you've not been telling her the full story.'

'12 . . . 11 . . . 10 . . .'

He took my hand and rotated my barstool toward him.

'Life is short, Anya. Do you want to die knowing you had a chance to kiss a sexy Latin man but let it pass you by?'

'What sexy Latin man are you referring to?'

'9 . . . 8 . . . 7 . . .'

He set his hand on my knee. 'Once in your life, *chica*, you should be kissed by a man who knows how to do it properly.'

'6 . . . 5 . . . 4 . . .'

Theo looked at me with his smouldering Jesus eyes, and the Catholic schoolgirl in me crossed her legs.

'3 . . . 2 . . .'

I would be lying if I said it hadn't occurred to me that across the room my ex-boyfriend was being kissed by a *Vikingmermaidicelandicprincess*.

'And 1! Happy New Year! Here's to 2085!'

'All right, Theo,' I said. 'Since it's a brand-new year, you may as well show me what you mean by "properly".'

VIE

I HAVE AN IDEA; EMBARK ON A
RELATIONSHIP FOR DUBIOUS REASONS

I WOKE UP BEFORE DAWN on New Year's Day. An idea had popped into my head and, once it had, that idea would not let me rest.

Theo and I had fallen asleep on the sofa. I unwrapped myself from his arms and went outside to call Mr Delacroix.

'Anya, do you have any idea what time it is?'

'6 a.m.-ish?'

'It's 5:13.'

'You never sleep, so I thought it would be fine.'

'New Year's Day, I might sleep a little. I'd prefer the option at least.'

'Can we meet today? I want to run a business idea by you.'

'Of course. I'll see you at 10 a.m.,' he said.

'You're already awake anyway,' I said. 'Let's say seven?'

'You've gotten to be a huge bully since you've become a success,' he said.

'Theo's coming, too.' I hung up.

I went into the living room and shook Theo awake. 'Happy New Year, *mamacita*,' he said drowsily. He puckered his lips but didn't open his eyes.

'There's no time for that,' I said. 'We've got a meeting to get to.'

The three of us met at the Dark Room, which was a mess owing to the previous night's festivities.

'You are looking terrifyingly bright-eyed,' Mr Delacroix said to me. 'I've seen this look from you before, and it usually means trouble.'

'What is this about, Anya?' Theo asked.

'Well, I was thinking about where the second location should be.'

'Have you gone off Brooklyn again?' Mr Delacroix said. We had been discussing the possibility of a second Dark Room in Brooklyn for a while.

'No. But last night, my brother was saying how he'd like to work for the club, and the day before that, at Mr Kipling's funeral, Simon Green made a similar request.' I looked at Mr Delacroix. 'He wanted your job, actually.'

'He should have it then,' Mr Delacroix said. 'The hours are brutal. And the boss is demanding.'

'Sometimes,' I continued, 'Fats asks me about jobs for Family guys, too. The black-market chocolate business has been bad these last couple of months.'

'Who can say why?' Mr Delacroix asked. 'This isn't your responsibility.'

'Maybe not, but I think about it. And then, last night, I was talking to you' – I pointed to Theo – 'and my sister, and we were joking about Dark Rooms in Canada and Paris – basically places Theo and Natty want to visit. And we had a good laugh. But this morning, I thought, why not? Why open one more location when you can open ten?'

'Oh dear,' Mr Delacroix said.

'Could we do it, Mr Delacroix? Could we have a franchise?'

'You sound like you're asking me for a puppy.'

'I'm not asking your permission,' I said coolly.

'I didn't think you were. But by God, I'd hate to see what you look like when you don't get what you want for Christmas.'

'I've never gotten what I want for Christmas, Mr Delacroix. I'm used to disappointment.'

'What about the year I gave you the machete?' Theo asked.

'Except for that,' I said. 'What I want to know, Mr Delacroix, is if it's possible for us to raise enough money.'

'Yes, but it's not only about the money. It's the logistics – the peculiarities of regional government and laws, the regional scarcity of certain resources and supplies, the particular tastes and habits of the locals, and much more,' Mr Delacroix said. 'Whatever you do, you definitely shouldn't attempt this abroad. Domestic locations only. And technically you don't mean "franchise". You're talking about a chain.'

Chain sounded so much less glamorous. 'What I'm asking you, Theo, is could we use the same menu for all our locations, and could we get enough cacao to supply them?'

'If you wanted Granja to supply it, we would have to get more land, though I could investigate other suppliers,' Theo said. 'As for the menu? Yes, it is refined, and I believe it will translate to many different venues.'

'Anya,' Mr Delacroix said. 'This is a bold proposition, and as such, I approve of it. But you should know it's an enormously risky one, too.'

I shrugged. 'I didn't get in this to be small. You once told me that the only real way to change this world was to be giant.'

'Did I?'

'You did.'

'Sounds like hubris.'

Theo said we needed drinks. He went to get them, leaving Mr Delacroix and me alone at the table.

'We can do this,' Mr Delacroix said. 'And I will help you. But why not sit back and enjoy your success for a while?'

'Because what fun would that be?' I said.

'I don't know. Some girls like hobbies and boyfriends and diversions of that nature.'

'Mr Delacroix, you have to understand. I feel responsibility toward the Family and my family, but even more than that, I believe in what we've done here. I want to make my business large enough to put a lot more people to work. Wouldn't that be a very grand accomplishment?'

'*Grand*. Yes, of course, it would be grand.' He laughed. 'You do sound like me sometimes. A younger – *obviously* – more hopeful, comelier version of me.'

I noticed the dark circles under his eyes, but I didn't think they were the kind that came from one night's lost sleep. Although the gesture was unlike me, I put my hand on his.

'I know we don't normally discuss such matters, but I was sorry to hear about your divorce,' I said.

His eyes flashed anger and he pulled his hand away. 'Is my dirty laundry public knowledge now?' he asked.

'I'm sorry. Win told Natty. She told me.'

'Frankly, Anya, I'd rather not . . .' he said.

'Fine,' I said. 'You are allowed to give me advice. You are allowed to offer opinions on everything in my life, but we can't ever talk about anything to do with you.'

He didn't reply.

'This is ridiculous, Mr Delacroix. You are my friend.'

'Can you be certain of that? Colleague, I will give you. I have many of them. But friend? You cannot be my friend, because I have no friends.'

'Yes! It is not a usual friendship, but it is one. And you are mean to pretend that it isn't. I'm an orphan, alone in the world, and I know very well who my friends are. So, yes, we are friends, Mr Delacroix, and as your friend, I am allowed to offer sympathy when I can plainly see my friend is upset.'

He stood. 'If that's all, I should go. I will begin looking for investors.'

On his way back to the table, Theo passed Mr Delacroix. 'Bye, Delacroix,' Theo called, but Mr Delacroix did not reply. 'Where is he going?'

'To get investors.'

'Right this moment? It's New Year's Day.'

I shrugged.

Theo set the drinks on the table. 'We are doing this, then?' Theo clinked his glass to mine, and then he leaned across the table to kiss me.

'Whoa, Theo,' I said, pulling away.

'What?'

'Last night was last night, and this morning is this morning.'

Theo took a drink. 'As you like,' he said. 'Let's go eat. The club doesn't open for hours, and I am sick to death of macaroni and peas.'

Toro Supper Club was in a ground-floor apartment in a housing project in Washington Heights. A leather-skinned gentleman with a jet-black curly moustache poked his head out the window and called, 'Theo, my man! Good to see you!'

'Dali, I brought Anya with me!' Theo yelled from the street.

'It's freezing out there,' Dali said. 'Come inside.'

Dali greeted Theo by kissing him on both his cheeks. 'Anya,' Dali said, 'I am an admirer of your club, but Theo didn't say you were such a beauty.'

For New Year's, the supper club was serving breakfast, brunch, or maybe it was indeed a late supper for those who hadn't yet made it home from the prior evening's merriments. The scent emanating from the kitchen was familiar. It only took me a moment to place it. 'Theo, how in the world did you find out how to get *mole* in Manhattan?' I asked.

'*Mole* contains cacao, and Granja supplies it,' Theo said. 'Besides, I am very popular in this city.'

94

The restaurant only had three tables, and two of them were filled by the time we walked in. There were blue-and-white-checked tablecloths and votive candles in blue glass holders. A dried rose with a bent neck stood in a vase by the fireplace.

The *mole* was perhaps not quite as good as it had been at Granja Mañana, but it was close. The flavour was delicious and spicy. My eyes began to water.

'Anya,' Theo said, 'you are crying. You really must have been starving.'

'It's the heat. I'll be fine.' I waved my hand in front of my face. 'I like the heat.'

I ate three more bowls. I hadn't realized how hungry I was. Theo laughed at me as I sat and contemplated whether to go on to a fourth bowl.

'I can't do it,' I said finally. I pushed the bowl away and tried not to belch. I was so warm and satisfied; I barely knew what to do with myself.

We couldn't get a cab, so we walked the long way back to the club. It took hours, but we were young and strong and had the time to spare.

'It's not the safest walk,' I warned him. 'But it's daytime, and I do have my machete.'

By the time we reached the southernmost side of Central Park, it had begun to snow. I was a little cold, so when Theo put his arm over my shoulder, I let him.

'Theo,' I said guiltily, 'aren't we better as friends?'

'Who says we will not be friends because we kiss each other in the park every now and again?'

I leaned in to kiss him but then I stopped myself. 'You need to know: I don't love you that way.'

'What does it matter? I do not love you either. Let us have some fun together. I like you. You like me. No one has to say A-M-O-R or anything *estúpido* like that. We are both good-looking and alone. So why not?'

Why not indeed?

My breath probably stunk of chicken *mole*, but what difference did it make? Theo didn't worship me. He didn't think I was a princess. That is to say, he knew my breath did not always taste of mint chewing gum and cinnamon. I leaned over and kissed him hard. It is nice, on occasion, to kiss someone because he is cute and because it is fun and because it feels *so good*.

VII

I ACQUIRE TWO ADDITIONAL ROOMMATES

IN THE MONTHS SINCE SCARLET had had her baby, I'd seen her only a handful of times. Though she had attended the opening of my club, she'd left early, before any of the fun started. She had missed my New Year's party because she'd spent the holiday with Gable's parents. In an attempt to be a good godparent, I'd gone to Midnight Mass with her and Felix. But that was it. We didn't have school to keep us together, and she lived a lot further away than she used to – sixty-two more blocks.

A couple of days after Easter, I found her sitting on the couch in my living room with Felix in her arms. She looked the same, pretty as ever, though she was skinnier than she had been before she'd had the baby. A fine wrinkle had taken up residency between her eyebrows. 'Gable's gone,' she said. 'His parents blame me, and I can't stay there anymore.'

'Where did Gable go?' I asked.

'I don't know,' she said. 'We were fighting constantly. He hated his job at the hospital. His parents had been pressuring us to get married, but neither of us wanted to do it. And now he's gone.'

'Scarlet, I'm sorry.' I was sorry for Felix, if not particularly for Scarlet. I was sorry about the situation, but I wasn't surprised. Given enough time, Gable Arsley always managed to live up to his last name.

'Could we stay here for a little while? I don't want to live with my parents, and I can't be at Gable's with his mother hating me so much.'

'Of course you can stay here.' Though truthfully, there were a lot of people currently in residence at my apartment: Noriko, Leo, Theo, and Natty when she was home. 'You can use Natty's room while she's away.'

'Also, I need to find work. I've been auditioning for plays a little bit. I've come close to getting cast a couple of times—'

'Scarlet! That's great.'

'But with Gable gone, I know I can't afford to wait around anymore. I need to figure out how to make money now.' She made a face. 'I hate to ask, but would you give me a job at the club? A hostess or a waitress or whatever. I know I'm not qualified for anything else. If I had a job with tips and flexible hours, I could still audition now and then.'

I sat down next to Scarlet. I was still awkward around Felix, but he climbed into my lap anyway.

'Good,' Scarlet said. 'Sit on your godmother. You're getting too heavy for me, Felix.'

'Hi, Felix,' I said.

'Hi,' he said.

'Oh, he's talking now,' I said. 'Hi,' I said again.

He waved and laughed at me.

'The club can definitely take on another waitress, but won't that be weird for you? I mean, I wish I had something better to offer you.'

'There aren't exactly a ton of jobs in this city, and I'm not proud. I can't afford to be.'

'Who will watch Felix while you're at work? I'm not here a lot.'

'No, I would never ask you to do that. My father can. Dad always tries to help. It's really my mother who disapproves of me, which is why I can't live there either.'

'I'll go back to Gable's apartment with you to get your stuff and Felix's, if you want.'

She laughed. 'I'm about to sound terrible. I know I've already asked you for so much. But would you . . . would you mind going alone? I don't want to bring Felix back to Gable's parents' place. Everyone is so upset. I don't want him in the middle.'

At that moment, Theo came into the living room. 'I will watch the baby,' he said, 'and then you both will go.' He must have been eavesdropping.

He walked over to the couch and scooped up Felix from my lap. 'See. *Los niños*, they love me.' Felix was grabbing Theo's moustache, which he had grown in the months since he'd moved to New York.

He offered Scarlet his hand. 'We have not met. I am Theo.'

99

'Scarlet,' she said. 'And he's Felix.'

'Ah, the best friend. I am Anya's boyfriend.'

Scarlet looked at me. 'What? Since when do you have a boyfriend?'

'He's not my boyfriend,' I said.

'My English is not perfect,' Theo said. 'I only mean I am a boy and I am her friend.'

'I don't understand,' Scarlet said. 'Is he your boyfriend or isn't he?'

I sighed. 'Who needs such labels? We should leave if you want to do this tonight.' I turned to Theo. 'Also, Scarlet's going to be your new waitress.'

'Wait? What?' Theo said. 'You are not bad to look at, but do you have any experience?'

'I'm a fast learner,' she said with a smile.

Scarlet unlocked the door to Gable's parents' apartment. 'Maybe they won't be home,' she said.

We went inside and no one was there. Scarlet told me to pack up the bedroom while she packed up the nursery. I threw her clothes into a suitcase and her make-up and jewellery into a box. I was nearly finished when I heard the door to the apartment open.

'Scarlet?' a woman called. I recognized the voice as Gable's mother.

'In the nursery,' Scarlet replied.

I set the suitcase and the box by the front door and went to wait just outside the nursery door. I thought there could be trouble so I wanted to keep close.

'You can't take our grandchild away!' Gable's mother yelled.

'I'm not taking him away. I would never do that. But we can't live here anymore. It isn't good for anybody. And it doesn't make sense now that Gable is gone.'

'Gable will come back,' his mother said. 'He's upset.'

'No,' Scarlet said, 'he's not coming back. He told me he wasn't, and I believe him.'

'Gable is a good boy,' his mother insisted. 'He wouldn't leave the mother of his child.'

'He did,' Scarlet said. 'It's been a month.'

I was mildly shocked that Scarlet had waited an entire month before she'd told me about Gable leaving.

'Well, you can't take my grandson,' Gable's mother repeated. 'I won't let you. I'll call the police.'

I went into the nursery. 'Actually, she has every right to take your grandson.'

'What is *she* doing here?' Gable's mother was no great fan of mine.

'Scarlet is the mother, and the city doesn't automatically recognize grandparents' rights,' I said.

'Why should I believe you?' Gable's mother asked. 'You're no lawyer. You're some trashy girl who owns a club.'

'The reason you should believe me is because trashy girls like me have hard lives.' I got right in Gable's mother's piggish face. 'I've bounced around family and juvenile courts since I was a kid, and I know everything about everything when it comes to who gets custody of whom.'

'It's all your fault!' Gable's mother yelled at me. 'If you hadn't poisoned him—'

'I didn't poison him. He ate bad chocolate. And your son was a terrible boyfriend, so it comes as no surprise that he's a terrible father and fiancé. Come on, Scarlet. We're leaving.' Gable's mother was blocking the door so I moved her out of the way.

It took forever to get a cab and almost as long to cram Scarlet's possessions into the trunk and backseat. We rode uptown in silence. 'Thank you,' she said, as the cab rounded the park. 'I really appreciate you coming with me.'

'I'm glad you called, though I can't believe you waited a month to tell me Gable had left.'

'Truthfully, I've been kind of mad at you,' she said.

'Why?'

'I guess it's not entirely your fault, but we haven't seen each other that much, and I'd read about your club in the paper and how well everything was going for you, and I'd feel pretty bitter. Like, I'd always tried to be a good person and a good friend and look how my life has turned out.'

'You can't think that way.'

'Most of the time I don't, but sometimes. And then I'd get mad because I felt like you'd moved on without me. And I felt like you had amazing new friends and you didn't want me around.'

'Scarlet, I've been busy, that's all, and I know it's difficult for you to make plans with the baby. If you had needed me, I would have been there.'

Scarlet sighed. 'I know, but that's why it's hard to be friends with you, I guess. Sometimes I would like to know that

I'm needed, too. I mean, have you even missed me? We've spoken like three times this whole year.'

I put my arm around her. 'Scarlet, I'm sorry I'm not more . . . I'm sorry I don't wear my heart on my sleeve.'

'No, you definitely don't. At one point, I actually made a promise to myself that I wouldn't call you again until you called me. Do you know how long that went on?'

I didn't want to.

'Four months.'

'I'm sorry. I'm a bad friend.'

'You're not. You're the best friend. You're my best friend. But you do have your faults.'

'*I know.*'

'Oh, don't have hurt feelings. What I actually wanted to say is I realize that I was being silly before. We may not see each other as much as we used to, but there is no one else I would have wanted to be with me tonight. And isn't it funny? You can lose a boy – God knows we've both lost a few of those – but even if I wanted to, I know I could never lose you.'

I EXPAND; RECONSIDER MY BROTHER; LISTEN TO THEO EXPOUND ON THE DIFFICULTIES OF A LONG-TERM RELATIONSHIP WITH . . . CACAO

For the first six months of 2085, Mr Delacroix courted new investors, and Theo and I travelled across the United States in pursuit of perfect locations for the Dark Room. When we were on the road, Noriko and Leo managed the New York club. Though I'd travelled abroad, I had never been anywhere in America except Manhattan and seventy-five square miles around Manhattan, and it interested me to see how people lived in other places. In an error particular to youth, I had the impression that everyone lived as I did: they dwelled in apartments, rode buses, and traded at the market on Saturday. In fact, this was not the case. In Illinois, there were still grocery stores. In California, fruit and flowers grew everywhere. (My nana would have loved it.) In Texas, everything smelled like fire. In Pennsylvania, Theo and I visited a ghost town with the motto 'the sweetest place on earth'. Hershey, Pennsylvania, once had a chocolate factory and a chocolate-themed amusement park, too. I wouldn't have believed it if I hadn't seen first-hand the ancient statue of an anthropomorphized milk-chocolate bar. He was googly-eyed, grinned maniacally, and wore white gloves and saddle shoes. I suppose he was meant to appeal to children, but I found him terrifying. Still, a chocolate amusement park! Reader, can you imagine?

By July, Mr Delacroix and I had raised enough money for the club to expand to five more locations: San Francisco, Seattle, Brooklyn, Chicago, and Philadelphia. 'Congratulations, Anya,' Mr Delacroix said after the last set of contracts had been executed. 'You are officially a chain, coming soon to five locations across this great country of ours. Is it everything you hoped? Are you an entirely new woman?'

'I'm the same,' I said. 'I wish it was ten locations, though.'

'You *would* say that. I wonder what makes Anya Balanchine keep running so hard?' he asked.

'The usual,' I said lightly. 'Trying to shake off that huge chip on my shoulder caused by the death of my parents. Never feeling like there was enough love for me. Wanting to prove wrong everyone who tried to take me down or who got in my way. I think of the teachers, the boyfriends, the *semya*, the cops, the DAs. So many people to thank.'

'*Acting* DA,' he said. 'Try to be a little happy, would you? Try to enjoy this moment.'

'That's not my nature, colleague,' I said with a smile.

The night after the last deal closed, Noriko and Leo threw a small dinner party to celebrate the expansion of the business. I don't know if it was his stint in the psychiatric prison or Noriko's influence, but Leo was a new man since he'd been released. For one, he suddenly had skills: he knew how to open a wine bottle, how to sear a fish, how to hang curtains, how to fix our sink. He made friends with the other people who lived in our building – perhaps I'm antisocial, but aside from a grunt of greeting, I had never even spoken to *any* of our neighbours in the eighteen and a half years I had resided there. Leo seemed more capable to me (more capable *than me* in certain ways) and less a child who needed my care and watch. When he got frustrated, which was rarely, Noriko would put her hand on his back, and in a moment, he would be calm again. (Natty joked that Noriko was the Leo-whisperer.) There had always been conflict between my brother and me, but for the first time in my life, I felt like I could appreciate him as a person.

One other thing: Noriko and Leo loved home improvement. I'd come back to find that they had painted the walls a dusky purple, or reupholstered our old sofa in grey wool. Our apartment became, for the first time since my parents had died, a home.

At the dinner party, the guests included Lucy, Scarlet, Felix, Theo, Mr Delacroix, and Mr Delacroix's new girlfriend, Penelope, who had a shrill voice that made everything she said come off as annoying. Penelope ran her own very successful public-relations firm, as she would tell me no fewer than ten times that night. She was nothing like Win's mother, the pretty dark-haired farmer.

Everyone assumed that Theo and I were a couple, but I never called him my boyfriend. Aside from that one time with

Scarlet, he didn't refer to himself that way either. I liked his company, liked his teasing, liked that he smelled of cinnamon. I liked him and I liked myself when I was with him. By my nature, I was reserved, and by his nature, Theo was the opposite. People seemed to like me better when they met the two of us together; his warmth and good cheer buoyed me. However, I didn't want to possess him; I didn't even expect him to stop dating other people (I knew that he had). My heart did not break when we were apart, though I was always glad to see him when we were reunited.

However, I understood why people could have come to the conclusion that Theo was my boyfriend. We were together for work, and we even – Nana would be horrified – lived together. I had not meant to live in sin and I didn't really like the idea of it. But, well, Theo had come to New York in the middle of an emergency, and he had never moved out.

(NB: Looking back, I probably should have made him.)

After the dinner party, I told Noriko and Leo to go to bed, that I would clean up. Noriko went, but Leo stayed behind to help me. 'Annie,' Leo said when we were almost through drying the dishes, 'what would you think about Noriko and me going to San Francisco to start up the new club?'

'Are you unhappy in New York?' I asked.

'Of course not, Annie. I love it here. New York is my home. But I really, truly want to do this.'

'Why?' I carefully hung the kitchen towel over the back of the chair.

'I guess I want to leave my mark the way you have in New

107

York. I can do it in San Francisco, if you'll let me. I know I've made huge mistakes in the past and that you had to fix them for me. But I'm smarter now, Annie. I don't make as many mistakes.'

'What about Noriko?' I asked. 'How does she feel about this plan?'

'She's excited, Annie. She's so smart and she has great ideas. She makes me feel smarter, too.' I am embarrassed to admit this, but I truly had worried that once Noriko's English improved, she would lose interest in and possibly even leave my brother.

I looked at Leo. His face, which I knew so well, was a little boy's and a grown man's at the same time. I knew it cost him every time he had to ask me for anything. 'If I agree to this, I'll have to treat you as I would any employee. If it doesn't work out, I'll fire you and Noriko both.'

'I know, Annie! I wouldn't expect any different. But nothing will go wrong.'

'Well,' I said, 'I guess the only problem is how much I'm going to miss you.' I had liked coming home to the apartment to find him and Noriko there.

Leo hugged me ferociously. 'Thank you for trusting me! I won't let you down. I swear I won't.' Leo hugged me again. 'Wait, I had one other thought. What would you think about us taking Simon Green to San Francisco with us? We need a lawyer, and I know Simon could use the job.'

Leo was clearly a better person than I. Frankly, it didn't seem like the worst idea I'd ever heard, and it would, at the very least, separate Simon Green and me by the width of a continent. 'It's up to you, Leo,' I said. 'San Francisco is your show, and you and Noriko should hire who you want.'

The three of them left about a week after my nineteenth birthday. I cried at the airport, I don't know why. I had not known that I was going to, but then the sight of my brother and his wife, who I'd grown very fond of, filled me with unexpected emotion. Leo reminded me so much of my father. Everything I'd sacrificed to try to keep him safe suddenly seemed worth it.

'I'll be fine, Annie,' Leo said.

'I know,' I said.

'You'll never stop worrying about me, will you?'

'That's the thing, Leo. I have. That's why I'm crying. I'm relieved. I really do believe you'll be fine.'

With Leo and Noriko gone, Theo and I could not be out of town at the same time – I had to oversee the New York club, which was the headquarters for the business, and Theo was busy setting up the kitchens of the other locations. Consequently, I saw less of Theo in the second half of 2085 than I had in the first. He called me one October night from a hotel room in Chicago. 'Anya, I miss you. Say you miss me.'

'I miss you,' I said with a yawn.

'You do not sound like you miss me one bit,' he said.

'I'm just tired, Theo. Of course I miss you.'

'Good, then you must come home with me for Christmas,' he said.

'I don't know. Natty and I always spend the holidays in New York.'

'She will come, too.'

'Airfare is expensive.'

'You're a rich lady. You and I fly all the time for work now anyway.'

'Doesn't everyone in your family hate me for stealing their beloved Theo away?'

'No. They will rejoice to see you. You have not been to Chiapas in almost two years. Besides, the *mole* we have at Dali's is good, but it is not up to the standard of the *abuelas*'.'

'You're relentless,' I said.

'That's how you have to be when you farm cacao. Cacao is a demanding plant, as you well know. Too much water, there is mould. Too little water, she dries out and dies. You cannot simply shower her with affection either. She needs to be left alone sometimes to grow. If you make it too easy for her, she won't produce a strong crop. Sometimes, you do everything right and she still is not satisfied. You remind yourself not to have hurt feelings – for that is just how she is. But she is worth the effort – I tell you, Anya, she is. Get everything right and you are rewarded with an uncommon sweetness, a rich flavour that you can't find anywhere else. Growing cacao has made me relentless, as you say, but also patient and deliberate. Everything worth loving is difficult. But I get off the subject. You will go with me to Chiapas for Christmas, yes? My *bisabuela* is not getting any younger, and you have often said you wanted to show Natty my farm.'

I RETURN TO CHIAPAS; CHRISTMAS AT GRANJA MAÑANA; A PROPOSAL AKA THE SECOND-WORST THING EVER TO HAPPEN TO ME IN A CACAO FIELD

THE YEAR HAD PASSED QUICKLY, painlessly, and without the tears, blood, and tragedy I had come to expect from this life. The worst I was willing to say about 2085 was that it had left me weary from work. (The worst I was *unwilling* to admit about my actions that year was that it might have been a mistake to date Theo.) The last week of December, I left my club in the capable hands of my staff, and along with Theo and Natty, boarded a plane to Chiapas.

The first time I had gone to Mexico, it was under an assumed name as a mustachioed passenger on a cargo ship. Needless to say, travel was smoother this time. For years, I had dreamed of having Natty in Chiapas, and it was a joy to see it through her eyes. She remarked upon the pure air and cerulean skies, the flowers in their surreal shapes and colours, the chocolate shops right out in the open. I loved introducing her to Theo's family: his mother, Luz; his sister Luna; his brother, Castillo, the Priest; and of course, his two *abuelas*. (His other sister, Isabelle, was spending the holidays in Mexico City.) The only sadness was that the older of the two *abuelas*, his *bisabuela*, was unable to leave her room. She was ninety-seven years old, and they did not think she had much longer to live.

When I arrived, Luna walked right past her brother to embrace me. 'Why have you waited so long to visit?' she asked. 'We have missed you terribly.'

'Hey, Luna,' Theo said. 'Your loving brother is here, too.'

Luna ignored him. 'And this must be Natty. The smart one, yes?'

'Most of the time,' Natty said.

Luna whispered conspiratorially to my sister, 'I am the smart one in my family, too. It is a terrible burden, no?' Luna turned to her brother and me. 'Nice of you both to show up *after* the big cacao harvest. I could have used your help a week ago.'

Natty and I had just set our bags in our room when I was told that Bisabuela wanted to see me. I changed into a dress and went up to her room, where Theo was already by her side.

'Ahn-juh,' she said in a scratchy voice. Then she said something in Spanish, which I could not understand. My Spanish had become rusty. She wagged a knotted finger at me, and I looked to Theo for help.

'She says she is happy to see you,' Theo translated. 'That you look very well, neither too plump nor too slim. She is sad it has taken you so long to come back to the farm. She wants to say again that she is sorry about what happened with Sophia

112

Bitter. She – Nana, I am not going to say that!'

'What?' I asked.

Words were exchanged between Theo and his great-grandmother. 'Fine. She says we are both nice Catholic kids, and she doesn't like us living in sin. And God doesn't like it either.' Theo's checks turned as red as an overripe strawberry.

'Tell her that she misunderstands,' I said. 'That you and I are only friends. Tell her that it's a very large apartment.'

Theo shook his head and left the room. I took Bisabuela's hand. 'He is only my friend. It's not a sin.' I knew this was not quite true, but I felt fine about a lie that would make a sweet old lady feel better.

Bisabuela shook her head. *'El te ama, Ahn-juh. El te ama.'* She clapped a hand to her heart, then pointed to the door by which Theo had just exited.

I kissed her wrinkled cheek and pretended I had no idea what she was saying.

I had been too worried to truly appreciate my last Christmas at Granja. I had been on the lam and torn from everyone I loved. But this Christmas, with Natty there and my worries at a record low, I allowed myself to drink in Theo's family.

We exchanged presents in the morning. Natty and I had brought silk scarves for the Marquez women. For Theo, I had purchased a new leather suitcase, which I had already given him before we'd left. He travelled so much for the Dark Room that I thought he would find it useful. My present from Theo was a sheath for my machete, with ANYA BARNUM, my one-time

113

alias, burned into the side. 'Every time I see you pull that machete out of your backpack, I laugh,' he said.

Christmas dinner was turkey *mole* and *tres leches*. Natty ate so much she fell asleep – siesta was a sacred tradition at Granja. While my sister napped, Theo asked if I wanted to take a walk around the cacao orchard.

The last time Theo and I had walked these fields, we'd been attacked by an assassin come to kill me. (As absurd as it sounds to report such an incident, this had been my life.) Theo had been gravely injured, and I'd cut off someone's hand. Two years later, I could still remember the sensation of swinging a blade through flesh and bone.

Still, the field did not have only bad associations for me. It was where Theo had taught me about cacao, and if I hadn't come here, I never would have opened the Dark Room.

I saw a cacao pod with signs of rot. Out of habit, I drew my machete and sliced it off.

'You have not lost your touch,' Theo said.

'Guess not.' I resheathed my machete.

'I'll sharpen it for you before we leave,' Theo said. He slipped his fingers through mine, and we walked in silence for a while. It was almost sunset, but I was glad to be outside with the last rays of warm Mexican sun on my skin.

'Are you glad you came?' Theo asked me.

'I am. Thanks for making me. I needed to get out of the city.'

'I know you, Anya,' he said. 'I know you better than you know yourself.'

We walked a bit further, stopping every now and then to

tend the cacao. When we came to the end of the field, Theo stopped.

'We should turn around,' I said.

'I cannot,' he said. 'I must speak.' But then he did not speak.

'What is it, Theo? Out with it already. I'm getting cold.' In December, the weather in Mexico abruptly turned from pleasant to frigid. He grabbed me by the leather belt that strapped my new machete sheath to my waist. He undid the buckle.

'What are you doing?' I asked.

He took my machete out of the sheath. 'Get your hands off my machete,' I said, giving him a playful smack on the wrist.

'Hold out your hand,' he said.

He turned the sheath over and a small ring – a silver band with a white pearl – fell out of the case and into the palm of my hand. 'You did not look close enough,' he said.

I stood there, dumbfounded. I sincerely hoped it was not what it looked like. 'Theo, what is this?'

He grabbed my hand and forced the band over my knuckle. 'I love you, Anya.'

'No, you don't! You think I'm ugly. We fight all the time. You don't love me.'

'I tease, I tease. You know this is my way. I *do* love you. I have never met a person I love as much as you.'

I began to back away from him.

'I think we should be married. We are the same, and Bisabuela is right. It is wrong for us to spend our lives together, as

115

we have been for the past year, and not be married.'

'Theo, we can't get married just because we've offended your great-grandmother.'

'That is not the only reason, and you know it. I love you. My family loves you. And no one will ever have more in common with you than me.'

'But, Theo, I don't love you, and I never claimed that I did.'

'What does that matter? You lie to yourself about love. I know you, Anya. You are afraid of being hurt or of being controlled, so you tell yourself you are not in love. You are afraid of happiness, so you destroy and vex her whenever she arrives.' He took my hand. 'Have we not been happy this year?'

'Yes, but . . .'

'And is there anyone you prefer to me?'

'No, Theo, there's no one I prefer.'

'Of course there is not. So marry me, Anya. Give yourself over to the happiness.' He put his arms around me.

'Theo,' I said, 'I don't want to marry you. I don't want to marry anyone. Look at my parents. Look at Win's parents.'

'We won't be like them. I can see you as a little old woman and me as a little old man. We cook and we tease each other all day long. And we are happy, Anya. I promise you that we are happy.'

I could tell he wasn't listening to me. I didn't know how to make him understand. I felt trapped, tricked, and fooled by him. But I also didn't want to lose the little traitor either. I looked at him. What was wrong with me anyway that this handsome, funny boy was not enough? 'Theo, let's give it time,' I said.

'Do you mean an engagement before the wedding?'

'I'm still very young. I need time to think.'

'You are not young,' he said. 'You have never been young. You were born old and you have known your own mind as long as I have known you.'

'Theo,' I said, 'even if I did love you, I don't believe love is enough of a reason to get married.'

Theo laughed at me. 'What is enough of a reason then? Tell me.'

I tried to think of one. 'I don't know.' The ring, with its too-tight band, had started to hurt my finger. When I pulled it off, it flew from my hand, landing somewhere in the dirt. I got on my hands and knees and began combing through the soil, looking for it. 'Theo, forgive me. I think I lost your ring!'

'Calm down,' he said. 'I see it.' He had sharp eyes from years of tending cacao. In a second, he had located the ring. 'Not hard to find a pearl in the dirt,' he said.

He tried to hand it back to me, but I would not accept it this time. I kept my fists closed. 'Theo, please,' I said. 'I'm begging you. Ask me some other time.'

'Admit that you love me. I know that you love me.'

'Theo, I don't love you.'

'Then what have we been doing for the past year?'

'I don't know,' I said. 'It was a terrible mistake. I like you so much. I like kissing you, and I couldn't be more grateful to you. But I know I don't love you.'

'How do you know?'

'Because I . . . I have been in love. And it is not what I feel for you.'

'Do you mean with Win? Why are you not still with him if you love him so much?'

'I wanted other things, Theo. Maybe love is enough for some girls, but it isn't enough for me.'

'You leave Win, the boy you claim to love, because you say that love is not enough. You have friendship and work and fun with me, but that is not enough for you either. You don't want love, but then you do. Has it occurred to you that nothing will ever satisfy you?'

'Theo, I'm only nineteen. I don't have to know what I want.'

Theo set the ring on the palm of his hand and contemplated it for a moment. 'Maybe we break up? Is that what you want?'

'No. I'm saying . . . What I'm saying is I can't marry you *right now*. That's all I'm saying.' It was selfish and weak, but I didn't want to lose him. 'Let's forget this ever happened. Let's go back to New York and back to the way we were.'

Theo stared at me and then he nodded and put the ring in his pocket. 'Someday, Anya, you will be old, old like your nana and my *bisabuela*. You will be sick and you will need to rely on someone other than yourself. And you may find yourself sorry that you sent everyone who tried to love you away.' He offered me his hand, helped me up off the ground. I brushed the dirt from my dress, but because the ground was damp, most of it would not come off.

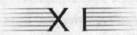

I ALMOST FOLLOW IN MY
FATHER'S FOOTSTEPS

WHEN I WAS TWELVE, I had discussed with Scarlet what would happen if a boy (perhaps a prince) proposed marriage and you were put in the awkward position of having to reject him. 'He'll probably disappear the next day,' Scarlet had said. In any case, the discussion had given me the false idea that a no might convey the power of magical banishment. And wouldn't that be for the best? Because how could a boy be expected to stick around after he'd offered you his heart and you'd said, *Thanks for your heart, but I'd prefer a different heart. Actually, I'd rather not have a heart at all.*

When we returned to New York, I half expected Theo, who I had always known to be proud, to move out or even leave the country. Of course, that was impractical – he lived in my apartment, and we ran a business together. Instead, we both went on as if nothing had changed, and that was awful.

He did not bring up the proposal, though I felt it hanging in the air above us like a rain cloud in August. Maybe he was being patient. Maybe he thought I would change my mind. I wanted to say to him, *Please, my friend. Go and be free. I release you. I owe you so much and I don't want to cause you unhappiness. You deserve more love than I can give you.* But I was too cowardly, I guess.

Occasionally, his insults felt less playful and more pointed than they had in the past. Once, when we'd been arguing over the minimum amount of cacao a certain drink required, he told me that I had 'an ugly heart to match my hair'. In moments like this, I felt we were on the verge of having the argument that would lead to the final act.

By March, the first of the new wave of Dark Rooms was ready to open. The location was in Williamsburg, Brooklyn, and it had been quite easy for us to get the place going once we had the money – the laws and many of the logistics were the same as those for the Manhattan club, and travel by the L train, though it only ran once every other hour, was not difficult. The new club was in a building that had once been a Russian Orthodox cathedral. Though my cousin Fats had run a speakeasy out of a church for years, this was *my* first 'holy' location. Perhaps I should have paid greater consideration to the spiritual issues, but I didn't – it was not my faith, and as I have already mentioned, I had more or less given up on organized religion during that period of my life. In its favour, the site was central and picturesque, with yellow brick walls and copper-helmeted domes in the Russian style. In truth, the

Russian part gave me pause more than the cathedral part, as I still did not wish to associate the club with my Russian crime family. But the Dark Room was so popular in Manhattan that I thought the potential association wouldn't be much of a hit. Plus, the price was right.

I was getting dressed for the opening of the new club when my cell phone rang. It was Jones. 'Ms. Balanchine, there's a body outside the Manhattan club. The police have already been called, but I think you should come down, too.'

The police were slow in those days, so I was not surprised to find that the body had not been attended to by the time I arrived. An overweight man lay facedown on the steps. I could not see any obvious trauma to the body. Even from behind, he looked familiar. I knew you weren't supposed to touch a body at a crime scene, but I couldn't help myself. I bent down and I lifted the big onion-shaped pate, which reminded me of the domes of the Brooklyn club. The head was still unnaturally warm in my hands.

It was my cousin Fats, the boss of the Family.

I was not an observant Catholic anymore, but I crossed myself.

I instructed Jones to cover Fats and then to erect velvet ropes, routing our customers around my cousin's body. While I waited for the police to arrive, I went inside to call Mouse, who in a relatively short time had managed to become Fats's second-in-command. 'Mouse, Fats is dead.'

Mouse, like me, was not a crier. She was silent for several moments, which I knew to be her way of coping with hardship.

'Are you still there?' I asked.

'Yes, I was thinking,' she said in a voice that sounded as calm as milk. 'It must have been the Balanchiadze. Look at the timing. They knew you were opening the second Dark Room location, and they must have decided to make a statement by killing Fats. It's only a theory, but Fats had been fighting with them for months. He was trying to protect your business.'

'Why didn't he come to me?'

'He wanted to keep you out of it, Annie,' she said. 'There will be a scramble to see who leads the Family now that Fats is gone. I wonder . . .'

'Yes?'

'Maybe it should be you? Everyone in the *semya* respects you so much.'

'I can't do that, Mouse. I have a job and I have no interest in running the Family.'

'No, you wouldn't. Why would you?'

'I know you and Fats were close,' I said. 'Will you be OK?'

'I'm always OK,' she said.

The police didn't arrive to claim Fats's body until 8 p.m., a full three hours after Jones had reported the death. They tossed Fats into a black bag, and I was told that that concluded the investigation.

'Do you want to look for evidence?' I said to one of the police officers. 'Maybe ask me a couple of questions?'

'You telling me how to do my job now, missy?' the police officer said. 'Look, Fats Medovukha was a high-level gangster. There's no crime here. It was only a matter of time before he

122

ended up with three bullet holes in his chest. We've got *real* situations, and a force that's about forty per cent of the size required to deal with all of them.'

I felt angry. I knew the same sentiments had been expressed when my father had died. My cousin couldn't help that he'd been born a Balanchine any more than I could. 'He was my cousin,' I said. 'People cared about this man.'

'Oh, so you knew the deceased, did you? Maybe you want us to investigate you?' the police officer said. 'The victim is usually close to the perpetrator.'

'I've got friends, you know. Bertha Sinclair comes to my club every week.'

The police officer laughed. 'You think she isn't aware that your cousin was killed? She's the one who told us to bring the body to the morgue and consider this matter closed.'

I was four hours late for the Brooklyn launch. When I finally arrived, the party was in its denouement. It looked like it had been a good party, but I was in no mood for partying anyway.

'What happened?' Theo asked me.

I shook my head and said I would tell him later.

I went to get myself a drink from the bar. I needed to clear my head. Mr Delacroix sat down next to me.

'Where were you?' he said.

I related my evening. At the end, I asked, 'If this had happened when you were DA, would you have acted as Bertha Sinclair has? Would you have tossed Fats's body in a bag and told me there wouldn't be an investigation because

123

my cousin was a bad guy from a bad family?'

'I'd like to tell you that I definitely would have investigated, but that isn't true,' Mr Delacroix said after a beat. 'The decision would have depended on what else was happening in the city at the time.'

'What about me? If I died, would anyone bother to investigate?'

'Anya, you're important now. You own a business and you bring a lot of money into this city. Your death would not go unnoticed.'

I felt a little better.

'For the city, the problem is not your cousin's death, but who will succeed him. We like to know with whom we'll be dealing. Did your friend have any thoughts about that?'

I shrugged.

'Well, someone will run the Family and it would probably be wise of you to take an interest. You don't want them to choose someone whose interests run counter to your own.'

I hadn't thought of it that way.

'Anya,' Mr Delacroix said, 'if Mouse is right and the attack was meant as a warning to you, perhaps you should reconsider getting personal security—'

'Mr Delacroix, we have discussed this matter before, and my position hasn't changed. I would rather die and know I walked this city and this planet as a free person. I have nothing to hide, and I don't require security.'

Mr Delacroix smiled at me. 'This seems noble but wrongheaded to me. You are indeed a free person, as you say. I certainly cannot control what you do. I can only offer you my advice. I don't think hiring security would take anything away from you or your accomplishments. But let's not discuss it any further.' He clinked his glass to mine. 'Brooklyn came out rather well, don't you think?'

The next day, I was summoned to a meeting at the Pool, which was the Balanchine Family's headquarters. I knew it was a sign of respect that I had been asked as I was not technically Family anymore. I had tried to avoid interacting with the Family in the years since I had opened my club. However, this would no longer be an option with Fats dead. Mr Delacroix was right when he said I should take an interest in the person who would be installed as the head of the Balanchine Family.

When I got to the Pool, Mouse was waiting in the lobby. 'Everyone's downstairs.'

'Am I late?' I asked. 'Your message said four.'

'No. You're right on time,' she said. 'Let's go.'

The place seemed unnaturally quiet to me, and I began to wonder if I should have brought security. In the past, Mr Kipling had usually accompanied me to important Family meetings. Maybe it had been foolhardy to go alone, and without telling anyone where I would be either. I stopped at the top of the flight of stairs.

'Mouse, I'm not about to be ambushed, am I?' I asked.

She shook her head. 'Don't you think I have your back?'

In the swimming pool, the Balanchines were seated around the table. I recognized perhaps half of them. There were always new faces, though. Turnover was high among the Balanchines – someone was always dying or going to prison.

125

Everyone stood when I walked in, and I noticed that the only place left was at the head of the table. I looked at the empty chair and wondered what was meant by it.

What else was there to do? I sat down.

A third or fourth cousin of mine named Pip Balanchine was designated the Family's spokesperson. (I had many cousins, but I remembered Pip because he was the one with the moustache.) 'Thank you for coming, Anya. Two years ago, you gave your approval to Fats Medovukha to run the Family. At that time, many of us felt you should be made head of the Family. As you may remember, I was one of those people.'

'Yes,' I said.

'We are deeply saddened by Fats's passing. At the time of his death, he was having an argument with Ivan Balanchiadze. We believe this is why he was killed. The dispute involved the Dark Room.'

'I'm sorry to hear that.'

'Fats Medovukha believed in you and your cause, and he was willing to die for both. Since Fats's murder, we've been discussing the situation. What we believe is that Ivan Balanchiadze and the Russian side of the Family is the past. You, Anya, are our future. We believe that nothing short of legalization is the key to our survival.'

A man in a purple suit spoke: 'Many of us have wives and children, and we're tired of having to look over our shoulders and of wondering when the law is going to catch up with us.'

Pip Balanchine continued. 'We ask you today what we should have asked you two years ago. Anya, will you lead the Balanchine Family into the twenty-second century?'

I did not want to lead this Family.

And yet . . .

As I looked down the long stone table at the pasty complexions and light eyes that recalled my father's, my brother's, and my own, an unfamiliar feeling began to stir within me.

Obligation.

I felt an obligation to these men (and women, though mainly there were men). That I had been born a Balanchine had been the defining circumstance of my life. The name Balanchine had attached to me and defined me as violent, wild, bad, lazy, angry, and difficult. These Family men were as blameless as I had been in the face of this birthright. I knew I had to help them. If it was within my power to help them, I could not say no.

I looked over my shoulder at Mouse, who stood behind me like a loyal consigliere. Her eyes looked hopeful and expectant.

'I cannot officially run the Family and run my business,' I said. 'I wish I could, but I can't.

'However, I want to do everything I can to help you. Your words, Pip, have moved me, and I will not abandon you. I want to give even more Balanchines jobs, working for the clubs. I want to cut off our dependence on the Balanchiadze chocolate supply altogether. We can leave the black-market chocolate business to some other family, and together we can channel our efforts into legal revenue sources like cacao and medicinal chocolate.'

The Balanchines were nodding.

'But who will run the Family?' the man in the purple suit asked. 'Who will ensure your plans are executed?'

'Perhaps one of you,' I began, but, as I was saying this, I had a better idea. Why not the slim-shouldered, resilient girl standing behind me? Mouse had been my only confidante at Liberty, and, at significant personal cost, she had even helped me escape. She had been mute, bullied, homeless, and cast out by her family. No one had overcome more or complained less than she had. No one had been more loyal to me. I trusted her like a sister. Of course it should be Mouse. I only had to convince the Family to my way of thinking. 'Though I wonder if you would consider appointing Mouse to run the Family in my absence. I could consult with her on every decision. I know she isn't a Balanchine, but she was Fats's right hand and my loyal friend from prison, and I trust her to be my eyes and ears. Believe me when I say – no person has been a better listener or a more reliable friend to me than Mouse.'

I turned to look at Mouse. Her eyes were bright. 'Is this all right?' I mouthed.

She reached for the notepad that used to hang around her neck. Back in the day, that notepad had been the only way she could communicate. 'Yes,' she said.

'This *is* an intriguing proposition,' Pip said. 'We will need to vote.'

'I assumed as much,' I said. 'But whatever the outcome, I will do what I can to help you. I am a Balanchine and my father's daughter.'

I stood, and the Family stood with me.

The following day, Mouse came to the Manhattan club, trailed by Pip Balanchine and a woman I did not know. Mouse informed me that the vote had been unanimous. As improbable as it was, a once-mute girl from Long Island had become the head of the Balanchine crime family. She bowed her head when she entered my office. 'I await your instruction,' she said.

Over the next two months, we reduced the amount of chocolate supply that came to America. We reassigned dealers to new positions driving trucks or working security. The ones who didn't want these jobs were given retirement packages, which was pretty much unheard of in organized crime. (In the Family, death was usually the sole retirement option.) We used the existing Balanchine labour force to move cacao and other supplies around the country to new locations.

During this period, the Balanchiadze were silent. Perhaps they thought we were still reeling from Fats's death. 'We should not take their silence as acceptance,' Mouse advised. 'They will strike when they are ready. And I will be vigilant.'

'Drink with me,' Mr Delacroix said one night at the club. 'You are never around these days, and I almost feel as if I'm having a sighting of the Loch Ness monster.'

I shrugged. I had not told him about my new responsibilities. I had thought my life was full when I'd just been running the club, but it had become ridiculously so now that I was shadow-running an organized-crime family.

'I don't know if you've heard, but word on the street is that Kate Bonham has become the new head of the Balanchine crime family.'

'Oh?'

'Well, it's an interesting choice on many levels. She's not a Balanchine. She's a girl. She's only twenty years old, and she was at Liberty. Did you know her, Anya?'

I said nothing.

'I recognized her name, of course. I may be old, but my memory is long. And I kept very good tabs on you that summer of 2083. Kate Bonham went by the name Mouse back then, and I think she might even have been your bunk mate at Liberty. What an extraordinary coincidence that Anya Balanchine's bunk mate should become the improbable head of the Balanchine crime family.'

I wasn't fooling him. I never had.

'I assume you know what you're doing. I assume you don't require any help. I might renew my request that you hire security, but I suppose you'll do exactly what you want to no matter what I say.'

'How's Win?' I asked. I had not uttered my ex-boyfriend's name in months, and that bantam proper noun felt strange on my tongue, as if I were speaking a foreign language. 'It was his birthday a week or two ago, no?'

'A change of subject. You suppose the way to my heart is through questions about my boy. It is a cheap manoeuvre, though I will allow it.' He crossed his hands over his knee. 'Goodwin says he wants to go to medical school. I rather like this profession for him, don't you?'

130

'That's nothing new. Even senior year of high school, he wanted to be a doctor.'

'Well, I suppose you know my son better than I.'

'I used to, Mr Delacroix. A long time ago, I was considered an expert in the field, but then I broadened my interests.'

XII

I RECEIVE AN UNEXPECTED VISITOR;
A STORY IS TOLD; A REQUEST
IS RENEWED

IN NEW YORK AT LEAST, April is not the cruellest month. The snow melts, heavy coats and boots are returned to closets, and perhaps best of all, I could walk home from work again. Sometimes Scarlet and I walked together, and it was almost like we were at Holy Trinity.

Theo was in San Francisco, helping my brother set up the kitchen there. We had argued the entire winter about subjects including frozen peas; his flirtation with Lucy, the mixologist; winter coats; his sister Isabelle; and even the temperature I kept the apartment. I wanted him to move out though I did not know how to make him go. Sad to say, but I had begun to anticipate his absences. Maybe it wasn't his fault. Maybe I was, by nature, a solitary creature.

I was leaving the Dark Room early, around 11 p.m., when a black car pulled up to the kerb. Not for the first time, I wondered if I was about to be shot, if this was how it was going to end. *(But we are only on page 133 of the third volume of my life, so surely this could not be the end. Unless, reader, you believe in Heaven – I am not always certain that I do.)*

The car door swung open, and a man in a dark suit leaned out. 'A ride, Anya?' Yuji Ono asked. His tone was familiar, as if it had been days and not years since I had last seen him.

I hesitated. I slowly (and I hoped subtly) reached for my machete.

Yuji Ono laughed. When he spoke, his voice was scratchier than I remembered. 'Do you think I have come to kill you? I have brought no weapon aside from Kazuo, who is sleeping back at the hotel and who is, in truth, a pacifist. Besides, had I wanted you dead, I would not have come to see you in person. I would have sent someone to do the job. You'd think even a nascent head of a crime family would understand how these acts are accomplished.'

'What do you want from me?'

'A conversation. I think you owe me as much. You refused me once and therefore you are still in my debt.'

Despite Yuji's association with Sophia Bitter, at this point I had no particular reason to think he wished me dead. I had indeed declined his marriage (business?) proposal three winters ago and though I hadn't entirely understood his conduct in the years since, I could not say for certain that he was my enemy. Besides, I was curious. 'Come into my office,' I said, pointing toward the club.

He leaned further out of the car into the light, and I noticed that dark circles masked his eyes and that he seemed slimmer than the last time I'd seen him. Was it my imagination or did he seem to be considering the four flights of stairs that led to the entrance of the club? 'I would very much like to see the Dark Room, but I have been travelling,' he said after a pause. 'I am tired. Might we see the club tomorrow after our conversation? Assuming you survive it, that is.' He smiled a bit wickedly at me.

The truth was, if Yuji had wanted me dead, I would have been dead long ago. Besides, I had had so much good fortune in the past two years that I had truly begun to believe I was charmed and that nothing would ever go wrong for me again. (*NB: Famous last words.*)

And so I got into the car.

I instructed the driver to take us to my building. When we arrived, Yuji struggled to get out of the car and the walk from the street to the lobby seemed to fatigue him. Though he tried to conceal it from me, his breathing was shallow and laboured.

I took a better look at him under the lights of the elevator. He was still handsome, but his body, which had always been thin, was skeletal. The skin of his face was nearly transparent, and I could make out disturbing patches of blue veins below the surface. His eyes were bright, though perhaps too bright.

The last I had heard from Yuji had been a letter that had accompanied ashes that had turned out *not to be* my brother's. In the letter, he had mentioned that he was in poor health, but that was years ago. Still, this did not look like a healthy man to me, or merely a sick one either. I had watched my nana die, and I knew what dying looked like.

'Yuji, you're dying,' I said tactlessly.

'I thought I was hiding it rather well,' he said with a laugh. 'You're still blunt. I'm glad of that. I had worried that now that you were grown, your rough edges would have been sanded away. But yes, it is true. The elephant in the elevator is that I am dying. As are we all, though I am sure that is a cliché.'

'How? Why?'

'Everything will be revealed. Let's sit down first. Now that my secret is out, I don't have to pretend that I do not fatigue easily these days, my old friend.'

I was not sure that we were friends.

I deposited him on my living-room sofa, and then went to the kitchen to get him a glass of water.

'How long do you have left?'

'The doctors say a couple of months, perhaps a year. I could linger. I would rather not linger though.'

'No.' My grandmother had lingered.

'Come closer to me.'

I did. He took my hand. His fingers were long and bony and cold. He had lost a finger years ago, but he no longer bothered with the prosthetic. I was not sure why this disturbed me, but it did.

I had so many questions to ask him. Why was he dying? Why had he claimed those ashes were my brother's? What was his relationship to Sophia Bitter? Why was he here now? But it didn't seem like the right time. It was a great shock to see Yuji Ono in such a state of physical collapse. Once upon a time, I had thought of him as almost superhuman.

'Anya, I want to begin by telling you that I have watched

your career with great interest. In opening the Dark Room and its sister locations, you have done everything I hoped you would do and more than I ever dreamed. I do not take credit for you, but I am gratified by the small ways in which I may have set you on the road to this success.'

I knew Yuji didn't give such praise lightly. 'Thank you. I have never entirely understood what happened between us. But I do know that you saved my brother's life, possibly twice. And you saved my life once. And you sent me to the cacao farm. If I hadn't gone there, I might never have started the business. And you were always so tough on me. You were the first person who insisted I had a responsibility to learn the business. I didn't see it at the time, but you were a true mentor to me.

'And I have often been sorry about the way we parted in Chiapas,' I said. 'You were – I believe now – trying to protect me and my siblings when you proposed marriage.'

'You get ahead in the story, Anya. It starts a long time before that.'

'Tell me, then.'

'I will. But know that I did not come here only for storytelling. My tale will end with a request. Though you did once make a promise to me, you are a free person, and it is up to you whether you will honour my request. You have paid me back with what you have accomplished. If you refuse me, you needn't fear for your life. I will leave New York, and I can assure you that you will never see me again.'

YUJI'S STORY

Where does a story ever begin, Anya? If you are a self-centred person, I suppose it begins with your birth. If you are other-directed, maybe it begins with your first love.

I have always tried to present a strong face to you. You may not recognize the boy I am about to describe.

When I was twelve, my father sent me to an international school in Belgium.

School life was miserable for me. I was too timid and – dare I say? – too Japanese for my classmates. I didn't understand how to respond to teasing and so I didn't. This made the situation worse. My grasp of the language was poor, and I began to stutter out of nerves. This also made the situation worse. I was frustrated by my inability to get my classmates to like me. I had been well liked at my school in Japan. If you are a person who has always been liked, it is hard to understand why you have, without changing a thing about yourself, suddenly become unlikable. It is equally difficult to turn the tide in your favour when those around you find you to be deficient.

I ate alone in the dining hall or in the library. One day – I had been there about two months – a girl sat down across from me and started talking.

'You are not bad-looking,' she said in a flat, light

German accent. 'You should use that. You are tall. I bet you could join a sport if you like. Join a sport and then they will leave you alone. You'll have a team behind you.'

'G-g-go away,' I said.

She did not move. 'I am only trying to help you. Your English is bad, but it won't be so forever. You need to talk to people. You could talk to me. There are many reasons that I think we should be friends. I'm Sophia, by the way.' She looked at me. 'Here is where you introduce yourself. Sophia Bitter. Yuji Ono.' She held out her large, sweaty hand. The nails were bitten down to the quick.

I looked up at her. At that age, she was a tall, gangly, hairy creature. All eyebrows, limbs, nose, pimples, and greasy hair. Her best feature was her large, brown, intelligent eyes.

'How did you lose your finger, by the way?' I wore leather gloves to cover my prosthetic and I didn't think anyone knew. She tapped on my metal finger with her hand.

'How do you know about that?' I asked.

She raised one of her caterpillar-like eyebrows. 'I read your school file.'

'That is private.'

She shrugged. Sophia cared nothing about privacy.

I told her the story. Perhaps you know it, perhaps you don't. I had been kidnapped when I was a boy.

They had sent my father my right pinkie finger as proof of life.

'The gloves are a mistake,' Sophia said. 'They make you seem affected. No one would make fun of a prosthetic, trust me. These people are as phony as they come.'

'If you know so much, why don't you have any friends?' I knew Sophia Bitter to be as much an outcast as I.

'My problem is I'm ugly,' she said. 'But you can probably see that for yourself. Also, I'm rude, and smarter than everyone here. People like you if you're smart, but not too smart. My family comes from chocolate, too. I'd guess we've both been sent to this school to try to throw some lacquer on the dirt.'

I had never met anyone like her. She was sarcastic and daring. She didn't care what people thought. She could be mean, but I didn't mind that very much at first. I had been raised around people who were polite even as they stabbed you in the back. She became my closest and indeed my only friend. There was nothing in my life that I did not wish to discuss with her.

I took her advice in most areas, and my school life did improve. I took up football, made other friends, stopped wearing the gloves. My English improved. By the time I entered the upper school, other girls began to take notice. I was asked to a dance by a girl named Phillippa Rose. Phil was very popular, very pretty. I was excited and I said yes without talking to Sophia first.

I informed Sophia that night when we were studying. She grew very quiet. 'What's the matter?' I asked.

'Phillippa Rose is a dirty *Schlampe*.' Her words were venom.

'What does that mean?'

'It means what you think it means.'

I said meekly that Phil seemed very nice to me. 'Do you have a reason for saying this about her?'

Sophia snorted as if it should be obvious. You must understand that Sophia thought everyone was against her.

'Sophia, I did not ask her. She asked me.' I looked at my hands. 'Did you want me to ask you?'

'No. Why would I want that? I'm disappointed that you would choose to socialize with such a fake person. I thought you were better.' She stood up and left.

The next time I saw her, she did not mention Phil, and I thought the matter had been forgotten.

The day before the dance, Sophia was not in classes. I went to the dormitory to find her. The girl who lived across the hall from her told me she had gone to the infirmary with a case of food poisoning.

I went to the infirmary to see her, but she wasn't there either. The poisoning was so severe she had been moved to a hospital.

As the hospital was off campus, the school would not let me visit her until the next evening. When I got there, she was hooked up to an IV. She had been vomiting the entire night. She looked very pale, very weak, but her eyes were sharp. 'Sophia,' I said, 'I was worried about you.'

'Good,' she said. 'That was the point.'

'There is no one in the world more important to me than you, except for my family,' I said. You must remember, I was a boy far from home, and when we are far from home, friendly intimacies seem even greater.

She smirked at me. 'Silly boy,' she said. 'Your dance is tonight, is it not? You're missing it.'

'I don't care,' I said.

Her father was a lesser chocolate manufacturer in Germany – you know this, I imagine. But the way he got into the business was as a chemicals manufacturer. From the time she was a little girl, Sophia Bitter knew a lot about poison.

Yuji began to cough. His face was turning blue. 'Should I call a doctor?'

He shook his head. In a minute or two, though it felt much longer, he was fine.

'What exactly is wrong with you?' I asked.

'We will come to that part of the story soon.'

'Did Sophia poison herself so you wouldn't go to the dance with that other girl?'

141

'Very good, and yes.'

'Were you angry?' I asked.

'I wasn't. I understood her. I was young, and at the time, I took it as a sign of the great love she had for me. I felt – and still feel to an extent – that that kind of loyalty should be prized.'

I cannot say that I was swept-off-my-feet in love with Sophia. Perhaps I am incapable of that kind of love. But I know that we would have done anything for each other and that she knew my secrets and fears, and I, hers. We were intimate in every way two people can be intimate.

We graduated from school. My father had died and I went to take over the Ono Sweets Company. She left to make a name for herself at the Bitter factory. The reason the Bitters had always struggled is because their chocolate tasted rotten. An education in chemicals is not necessarily the optimal background for making quality chocolate. She hatched a plan to distinguish the Bitters by making inroads into the American territory. Since the death of Leonyd Balanchine it was known that the American chocolate business was weak, and Ivan Balanchiadze, who is a loathsome man, had all but washed his hands of the American operation. Your father and my father had been friends, so Sophia asked my counsel. I suggested that she arrange a meeting with Mickey Balanchine, who had been a handful of years ahead of us at school. It seems they hit it off, and the next time she called me, she told me they were engaged.

It was, I believe, a political marriage on both sides. Your cousin probably believed he was strengthening his position in your family with a strategic alliance.

'I have a thought, Yuji,' she said to me one night when I was in Germany. 'What if I create a small incident in America?'

'An incident?'

'Timed with my arrival, there could be a problem with the American Balanchine supply. I sweep in as Mickey's fiancée and suggest replacing the Balanchine supply with Bitter chocolate.'

'What kind of problem?' I asked.

'The kind I'm good at making.'

'Innocent people could die,' I said.

'No one will die. We'll tip everyone off before it comes to that.'

I thought it was too risky. And as I mentioned before, your father and mine had been friends. I had no particular interest in seeing the American Balanchines brought down.

'I need your help. Please, *meine Süßer*. I can't do this alone. It will be your wedding present to me.'

I did not refuse her.

A month or so later, she called me. 'It is done, Yuji.'

I came to New York for her wedding.

'It's ridiculous,' Sophia said. 'Mickey is an idiot. I can't stand these people. I detest this country. A couple of years will pass. I'll divorce him. I'll marry you. I'll run the Balanchines and the Bitters. We'll have everything we always wanted.'

You might wonder if I was sad to see my dearest friend married to another man.

I should have been, I suppose.

But I happened to meet the daughter of Leonyd Balanchine that afternoon. I speak of you.

We had met once before but you had been a little girl then. At the wedding, you were almost an adult – a young adult, at least. Very tough. I liked you. And Sophia's poisoning of the Balanchine supply had had an unintended effect. It had made you the star of the American Balanchines. Everyone that afternoon was watching you. Could you feel their eyes?

That night, I had a thought. Wouldn't it be better to make you the head of Balanchine Chocolate in America? Let Mickey and Sophia run the Family for a couple of years on an interim basis and then, when you were old enough, you'd take over. My gut said that you would be a strong business partner. A stronger business partner than Sophia even – although she was smart, she was ruthless and selfish, too. These are weaknesses in business.

I did not express this to Sophia. I knew what her reaction would be.

I tried to express myself to you, but you were, of

course, very young. You had your boyfriend – is he still your boyfriend? You had high school and a complicated family life.

Sophia teased me about my interest in you, but I did not much care. I made up my mind to help you where I could. I took in your brother. I helped you get out of New York.

And here is where the situation gets complicated.

Sophia was unhappy with how long Yuri Balanchine was taking to die. She wanted to speed the process along. She wanted to clear the way for Mickey to be the head of the Family. However, many in your Family had become interested in you becoming the head of Balanchine Chocolate. I was not the only one who saw your father in you. Sophia felt that Mickey had been in error when he'd gone to you to ask you to run the business with him. I'm not sure if she knew that this had been my suggestion.

Sophia had begun to resent you, to see you as a rival not only in the Family but, I believe, for my affections and Mickey's. You were probably unaware of this. That is how Sophia is. She keeps her resentments secret.

I thought I knew a way to keep you out of harm's way and to keep Sophia at bay.

I decided to propose marriage.

I have thought about that day for a long time.

Looking back, I did everything wrong.

I tried to make a deal with you, but I wish I had

spoken from my heart. I wish I had said, *You may be young, but I see so much potential in you. I believe in you. I want to do what I can to keep you safe. I know I ask a lot, but I will give a lot in return. I believe we could be great partners. I believe we could love each other*. Maybe your answer would have been the same, but still, I wish I had been more candid.

I did not tell Sophia that I had proposed to you, but she found out anyway. She had become friends with Theobroma Marquez's older sister, and I imagine that is the way the news travelled. I had never seen her so angry. 'How can you betray me this way?' she screamed. 'I will tell the police about what you did for Leo and Anya, too. I will make it so you can never come to America again. You will never see Anya Balanchine, you weak-minded fool.'

Forgive me, Anya, if I did not intercede enough. I was hurt by your response to me. Perhaps I lied when I said I did not love you.

But let us back up. Something had happened while your brother was in Japan. He fell in love with my sister.

Noriko is actually my half-sister, by my father's mistress. I don't know if she knows this. We never speak of it, and I know that people believe mistakenly that she is my cousin or even my niece. But my father let me know that she was my responsibility. With Sophia on a rampage, I was worried about what she might do to Leo and Noriko. I decided to hide them. I contacted Simon Green. I knew of his background and I knew that he would help me and be discreet.

The best option was to let Sophia think she had been successful, and so that was what I did. I sent you ashes. I wrote you a letter saying I had seen your brother's body.

You drove her out of the country later that year. She went to Germany. And then she came to me in Japan.

She said that she had forgiven me, but I believe she paid one of my servants to poison me. She wanted me to suffer because I did not love her enough. No one could, Anya.

I grew very sick. I thought it was an infection I had caught during my travels.

I had a heart attack. And then another. My organs shut down.

I was alive, but not by much.

Meanwhile, you had opened the Dark Room in New York. I hoped I would get well enough to see your club for myself, and now I have. I am glad I can tell you how proud I am of you in person, Anya. You have done what none of us have been able to. You have made chocolate legal.

I still had so many questions for Yuji.

'Anya, I do not regret anything I ever did to help you, even if it cost me my life. My only regret is that I didn't do more for you. You are the future of our industry. And that is why I have come.

'I will die, Anya, and soon. When I do, I want you to run Ono Sweets Company. I want you to open legal cacao bars across Japan.'

'But how, Yuji?'

'I am sorry I cannot get down on one knee. I am sorry I am not young and healthy. I am going to ask you a question I asked you a very long time ago. I want you to marry me before I die. I have six months, perhaps a year, and when I am gone, everything will be yours. Then you will be able to turn my company into a company of tomorrow. There are many people in our world who are threatened by what you do, Anya, including people in the Russian part of your Family. These people can only function in a world where chocolate is illegal. They fear change. If you become the head of Ono Sweets Company, you can more easily fight against them.'

'Yuji, I . . .' I didn't know what to say.

'Build an empire with me,' Yuji said. 'Every resource I have, my employees, my money will be at your disposal. Every enemy of yours will become mine for as long as I'm alive. Every enemy of the Balanchine family will be an enemy of the Ono family even long after I am dead.

'Years ago, when your father brought you and your sister to my family's estate in Japan, he wanted to form an alliance between our two families. My father did not agree to it. He had his reasons, but I believe he lived to regret it.'

'Yuji, what were those reasons?'

'The Russian Balanchines thought your father had made

148

the wrong decisions. He had been trying to steer the business in a more ethical direction, changing cacao suppliers and improving conditions in the factories. It made your father many enemies.'

'That's why he was killed?' I had lost my father because of a dispute involving cacao suppliers.

'Yes, I believe so, though it is only a theory and I cannot say for certain. But I worry for you, Anya. The Balanchiadzes are ruthless and you are their enemy.'

'You think I am in danger?'

'I know it. But once you have my influence and resources, they will be more cautious when it comes to you.' He took my hand. 'I am so proud of you,' he said. 'I am sorry I cannot be here to turn my company around myself. I could simply leave you in charge without marrying you, but mine is a family business and the only way they will respect you is if you are considered to be an Ono.'

'Yuji, I don't love you. Not that way.'

'But you don't love anyone else either?'

I thought of Theo, but the situation did not seem worth mentioning.

'Am I right? Win Delacroix is in your past, and there is no one else right now?'

'If you knew he was in my past, why did you ask about him before?'

'Because I wanted to see your eyes. I wanted to be certain.'

The last time Yuji had asked me for my hand in marriage, I had been sure that I could only love Win.

Yuji offered me his hand. 'We both go into this with our

149

eyes open. There are many worse reasons to make a marriage.' He looked at me. 'Besides, I have very little time left on this earth. I would not mind spending it with you.'

I told him I needed to think, and then I walked him out to his car.

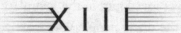

XIII

I HAVE THOUGHTS; I AM MOSTLY WRONG

I COULD NOT SLEEP that night.

I thought of Win and how much I had loved him and how much he had claimed he loved me and how that still hadn't been enough to make him understand why I had to open the club.

I thought of Theo and how well he understood both my business and me. I thought of how very, very much I liked him. I thought how it had made me feel petty and mean that I couldn't seem to love him the way he loved me, the way I had loved Win. *What is so great about you that you turn down a perfectly good boy's love?* I asked myself.

I thought of how I'd tried the entire winter to end my relationship with Theo. I thought this would certainly be one way of ending it.

Mostly I thought of Yuji, who had saved my life and my

brother's life. I thought of the good the union would do my business and the many people I was responsible for.

I thought that Yuji did not have very long to live.

I thought how, when he died, it wouldn't hurt much because I had never loved him in the first place.

I thought of the many people who married and ended up divorced or miserable. I thought of Win's parents and my parents.

I thought, romantic love is not a very good reason to marry anyway. People change; love dies. You might, for instance, find yourself standing in a nightclub on New Year's Eve, with the boy you loved saying that he wished he had never met you. That sometimes happened.

Family. Obligation. Legacy. The more I thought about it, the more these seemed like good and practical reasons to wed.

I thought I was grown-up.

I thought I knew what I was doing.

These were a few of the lies I told myself.

I ATTEND A GRADUATION

'H OW CAN YOU EVEN CONSIDER THIS?' Theo yelled. It was three weeks later, and he had returned from San Francisco to find me packing my bags and making preparations to leave for Japan with a stop in Boston. As hard as it was for me to believe, Natty was graduating from high school and she would be giving the valedictory speech at Sacred Heart.

Theo removed the clothes from my suitcase and threw them across the room.

'Stop that,' I said.

'I will not. I should go even further. I should tie you up or lock you in a closet. You are making a terrible mistake.'

'Theo, please, you're my dearest friend.'

'Then, as your friend, I am not happy for you,' he said. 'You should not leave me for someone you don't love.'

'Love has nothing to do with this.'

'What is the reason, then? You are richer than your father. You have done everything you wanted. You cannot owe this man your heart.'

'I'm not giving him my heart. Only my hand.'

'We are happy, Anya. We have been happy for over a year. Why do you wish to make someone else your husband?'

'We have not been happy. We have been arguing for months. And our being unhappy has nothing to do with this anyway. I am marrying Yuji Ono because I have to. No, because I *want* to.'

'Yuji Ono ruined my cousin Sophia.'

'That isn't true.'

He changed his tone. 'Anya, *por favor*. We must discuss this. If you still wish to marry Yuji Ono, then do it. But do not be hasty. Why must you rush?'

'He is dying, Theo. And he wants me to inherit his business so that I can do for Ono Sweets what we have done in New York.'

'*Puta*,' Theo spat.

'*What?*'

'It means "whore".'

'I know what it means. Are you calling me a whore?'

'I am calling you a person who chooses money over love. That is a whore.'

'I don't love you, Theo. I don't know how else or how many times I can say this. And even if I did love you, I'm not sure it would be enough.'

Theo muttered something in Spanish.

'What?'

154

'You are a sad person, Anya. I pity you.'

My phone rang. 'That's my cab,' I said. 'I'm leaving.'

He didn't reply.

'Congratulate me. I would congratulate you.'

'You cannot honestly think that. Sometimes I feel I have never known you at all.' He left my room and then I heard him leave the apartment.

I picked up my rumpled clothes and jammed them back into the suitcase. I would be lying if I told you my spirits hadn't also been slightly rumpled by Theo's words.

As I went into the hallway, Scarlet came out of her bedroom – she and Felix were now using Noriko and Leo's old room. Scarlet was still in her Dark Room uniform from the night before. She must have fallen asleep in it. About a month ago, Scarlet had been cast in a play. Something experimental in a black-box theatre. Something for no pay. Her character was called Truth. Between her job and the play, I barely saw her despite the fact that we lived together. 'Anya!' she said. 'Wait.'

'Are you going to try to stop me and tell me what a terrible person I am, too?' I asked.

'Of course not. How could I judge anyone, especially you, my darling? I wanted to say be safe and call me when you can.' She put her arms around me. 'Also, wish Natty a happy graduation for me.'

Two years ago, I had graduated in a room with a broken-down air conditioner. In contrast, Natty graduated in a garden on the most perfect day in May. Navy-blue and white ribbons hung from the awnings and the trees. Roses were in bloom and their scent perfumed the air. The church kept peacocks, and there were peacock feathers strewn about the grounds, which I found strange but charming. Natty, who had cut her hair into a short bob, was tall and lovely in her pale yellow cap and gown. Next year, she would be going to the Massachusetts Institute of Technology. Her valedictory speech was about water and the importance of developing new divining technologies. I loved watching the way other people listened to her. My sister was going to be someone.

People clustered around her after the graduation was over. I was milling about toward the back of the crowd when I felt a hand on my shoulder.

'Annie,' Win said. 'How are you?'

I knew Natty had invited him – they had been friends in Boston, and it did not escape my notice that their friendship had outlasted my relationship with Win – and so I was not surprised to see him. He was wearing a light grey three-piece suit. The pants were cut very slim, and he was as handsome as ever. I offered him my hand, and he shook it. 'It is good to see you,' I said.

He was carrying a peacock feather and he smelled like citrus and musk. 'How are you?' we both said at the same time.

I laughed. 'You first. Your dad says you are still thinking about medical school?'

'I can see exactly what type of conversation this is going to be. Yes. Yes, I am.'

'What would you rather talk about?'

'Anything. The weather,' he said.

'It's a perfect day for a graduation.'

'Your hair.'

'I'm thinking about letting it grow out.'

'Though I don't have a vote, I would approve of such a plan.'

I picked up the peacock feather. 'What's this?' I asked.

'I'm not sure. Maybe I'll write my novel with it,' he said.

'Oh yes?' I asked. 'What will it be about?'

'Hmm. Bad girl meets good boy. Ambitious father gets in the middle.. Girl chooses business over boy. That kind of thing.'

'I think I've read that story before,' I said.

'That's probably because it's a cliché.'

'What happens in the end?'

'The girl marries someone else. That's what I've heard.' He paused. 'Is it true?'

'Yes,' I said, looking away. 'But it isn't what it looks like.'

'Will it look like you walking down an aisle?'

'It will.'

He cleared his throat. 'Well, you have always known what you want. You have always known your own heart.'

'Have I?'

'I think so,' he said. 'I . . . I made a mistake two years ago in trying to tell you what to do. I still think I was right, but the reason I liked you in the first place was because you were so independent, so stubborn, and so much yourself. One cannot change Anya Balanchine's mind about anything. I was wrong even to try.' He looked at my sister, who was talking to one of her teachers at the podium. 'You must be so proud.'

157

'I am.'

'You did everything right, Anya. I know she thinks so, too.'

'I did my best, but I'm sure I made mistakes. I'm glad we are finally talking like this,' I said. 'I've missed you.'

'Really? I wouldn't think you missed anyone. You look straight ahead into the future, and you don't look back. Besides, I know you haven't suffered for company these last two years. Theo Marquez, Yuji Ono.'

'You haven't either! Natty says you have a different girlfriend every time she sees you.'

'That ought to make you feel important. I'm serious about no one.' He looked at me. 'You ruined me,' he said in as playful a way as it is possible to make such a remark. 'I was hoping I'd see you today. I've had something I've wanted to say to you for a while, but then the years pass, and things go unsaid. The truth is, I read about your club sometimes.'

'You do?'

'I like to keep up. But that's the context, not the point. What I wanted to tell you is how very proud of you I am.' He took my hand in his. 'I don't know if it will even matter to you, but I wanted to have said it.'

I was about to reply that of course it mattered to me, but at that moment, Natty joined us. 'Win,' she said, 'come to lunch with us!'

'I can't,' he said. 'Your speech was great, kid.' He took a small box out of his pocket and handed it to her. 'For you, Natty. Congratulations again.'

He embraced Natty and then shook my hand. Natty and I watched him walk away. I was still holding his peacock feather.

I almost called after him, but decided not to.

At lunch, Natty unwrapped Win's gift. It was a small silver locket in the shape of a heart. 'He still sees me like a little kid,' she said. She stuffed the box into her purse. 'What did you two talk about today?'

'Old times,' I said.

'Fine. Don't tell me,' she said. 'Are you sure you don't want me to come with you to Japan? You *are* getting married.'

'It's going to be more like a business meeting.'

'That's the saddest thing I've ever heard.'

'Natty. I've decided.' I took out my calendar. 'You have camp' – she was a counsellor – 'and then college. I'll be back in September to help you set up your dorm room, OK?'

'Annie, I'm worried about you. I don't think you know what you're getting into.'

'I do, Natty. Listen, people get married for many different reasons. There are only two things that matter to me in this world, and the first is my family – you and Leo – and the second is my work. I'm not romantic, so getting married for a reason other than love doesn't matter as much to me as it might to someone else. What's making me feel bad right now is you looking at me with that tragic expression.'

'You *are* romantic. You loved Win.'

'I was a teenager then. It was different.'

'You're still a teenager until August,' she reminded me.

'Technically.'

Natty rolled her eyes. 'Even if it is a sham, take pictures, would you? The way things are going, it might be my only chance to see you in a wedding dress.'

XV

I CONTINUE TO EXPERIMENT WITH
ANCIENT FORMS OF TECHNOLOGY;
DISCUSS THE USE AND MEANING OF LOL

WHEN I ARRIVED IN TOKYO, an entourage of ten representatives of the Ono Sweets Company met me. All wore dark suits. Two women carried signs that said BALANCHINE. After a great deal of bowing, I was presented with a bouquet of pink tulips, a basket of oranges, a box of Ono candies, and a silk purse that contained several pairs of elaborately embroidered socks.

'Is Ono-san's house close by?' I asked one of the women.

'No, Anya-san, we have to go into Tokyo. There, we will take the bullet train to Osaka.'

I had been to Japan as a child, but I didn't remember much about it. Physically, the urban parts were not unlike New York, I suppose, though the train (and the air) was much cleaner. At first the view consisted of the familiar grey and neon flashes of a vertical city: red signs indicating stores or bars or girls; impressive steel-and-glass balconies with unexpectedly old-fashioned clothes lines strung across them. I find such views relaxing as they remind me of my home and indeed, I fell asleep. When I awoke, we were speeding through a green swirl of forest. Too much nature makes me anxious; I fell asleep again. When I next awoke, the view had shifted once more: ocean, modest skyscrapers. This was Osaka.

We drove in long black cars with tinted windows to the Ono estate. I could not shake the feeling that I was in a funeral procession.

Finally we came to a gate with two iron doors mounted in stone walls. A guard waved us through.

The Ono house was two storeys high, with dark walnut siding and a grey tile roof. It sprawled across the land, low but somehow muscular. A member of the entourage explained that the house was in the traditional Japanese style. There were canals along the perimeter, several ponds, and groomed trees. When we reached the house entrance, I knew to take off my shoes. Perhaps that explained the gift of socks.

Kazuo, Yuji's bodyguard, told me that my luggage would be brought to my room and that dinner was laid out for me if I was hungry – I wasn't. 'May I say hello to Yuji?' I asked. I was told he'd already retired for the evening.

A female house servant dressed in a maroon kimono led me down a hallway. The hallways ran along the perimeter of the building. The servant slid open a door that also acted as a wall.

I went into the bedroom, which had tatami mats on the floor and walls, but a Western-style bed. The room had a distant view of a pond. A cat roamed the grounds, and I

161

wondered if she was a descendant of the cat Natty and I had met on our visit over a decade ago. Or perhaps it was the same cat? Cats live a long time, sometimes longer than people.

I unpacked my suitcase and then lay down on the bed. Silly to say, but it began to seem of pivotal importance that I find out the weather for tomorrow, my wedding day. I turned on my phone, but it wouldn't work. I turned on my slate; slates were said to be more reliable than phones when you were travelling. A message came up on the screen.

win-win: *Anya?*

anyaschka66: *I'm here.*

win-win: *I hoped you might be using your slate since you were travelling abroad. You're in Japan, right?*

anyaschka66: *Yes.*

win-win: *That means you're getting married tomorrow.*

anyaschka66: *Are you going to try to stop me?*

win-win: *I'd never try to stop you from doing anything anymore. I'm slow, but I learned my lesson.*

anyaschka66: *Smart boy.*

win-win: *I was thinking that it was nice seeing you at Natty's graduation, though.*

anyaschka66: *Yes.*

win-win: *This is tiring. Why did our grandparents ever like doing this? Why didn't people pick up phones?*

anyaschka66: *They had a lot more acronyms than us. My nana used to tell me them sometimes. She won a speed-texting competition when she was* *fifteen or maybe sixteen. OMG. LOL.*

win-win: *I know OMG but what's LOL?*

anyaschka66: *Laughing out loud.*

win-win: *So you don't need that one much.*

anyaschka66: *What's that supposed to mean?*

win-win: *You're kind of serious. You're kind of a funeral of a girl.*

anyaschka66: *I'm funny.*

win-win: *Not LOL funny.*

anyaschka66: *LOL.*

win-win: *Wait, are you actually laughing out loud?*

anyaschka66: *I'm not laughing out loud. Probably no one is EVER laughing out loud when they write LOL. Actually, I'm ROTFL.*

win-win: *What's that one?*

anyaschka66: *I'll tell you the next time I see you.*

win-win: *When will that be?*

anyaschka66: *Maybe not for a long while. I'll be based in Japan for the next several months at least, though I'll be travelling to the other club locations, too. I will be in Boston briefly for Natty's freshman orientation at MIT.*

win-win: *Look me up if you have time. I'll congratulate you on your marriage, and I can help you and Natty if you need a big, strong man to move boxes or whatever.*

anyaschka66: *Who's this big, strong man you're talking about?*

win-win: *LOL.*

163

anyaschka66: *I should go. I'm getting married in the morning.*

win-win: *OMG.*

anyaschka66: *Look at you, using those fancy acronyms.*

win-win: DDT YLRPANG IS IMY IHTYMYO IKIDHARBIDWAETHY ITIMSLY IDHMR

anyaschka66: *Now you're making stuff up.*

win-win: *All of it stood for something, I assure you.*

anyaschka66: *I don't think a one of those acronyms has any chance of catching on.*

win-win: *Congratulations, Annie. Congratulations, my old friend. I'm serious. Be well and be safe and no matter what happens to either of us in life, let's promise never to go so long without talking again. LOL.*

anyaschka66: *I think you might be misusing LOL, Win. Unless you meant that last part as a joke.*

He must have already turned off his slate, because he did not reply. I turned off my slate and got into bed.

I could see that peacock feather sitting on my suitcase across the room. I felt as if the eye was looking at me, and so I got out of bed and tucked the feather into the sheath of my machete.

That night, I did not sleep. It may have been the jet lag.

It may just have been the jet lag.

XVI

I BELIEVE MYSELF TO BE MAKING A CAREFULLY CONSIDERED AND CALCULATED DECISION; I IMMEDIATELY EXPERIENCE REGRETS; I DO MY BEST TO IGNORE THEM

WHEN I AWOKE IN THE MORNING, I had not even slept an hour. My skin was puffy, my vision was blurred, my hands were sweaty, and my head throbbed.

A woman from Yuji's staff dressed me in a kimono made from cream-coloured silk with the lightest pink cherry blossoms embroidered into the hem and sleeves. My hair had grown long enough to accommodate the traditional topknot style. Gold ornaments on surprisingly sharp daggers were stuck into the buns. My face was powdered white, my cheeks were powdered pink, and my lips were painted blood red. Finally, a heavy silken hood was draped over me. I felt like I was in a costume, but maybe every bride feels this way no matter what the circumstances of her nuptials are.

The thong sandals I was wearing forced me to take very small steps. I shuffled over to the bathroom. I closed the door behind me. I lifted the kimono and strapped my machete under it. Better to be safe than sorry, I thought. I looked in the mirror, and I fluffed out my kimono.

We were married in a Shinto shrine. I didn't understand most of what was said. I nodded when I was asked, uttered the occasional *hai* when it seemed appropriate. We drank sake from small ceramic cups, and an atonal guitar provided the accompaniment. We performed a ceremonial act with tree branches, and then the service was over. Less than a half-hour, I'd say.

I looked into my husband's eyes.

'What are you thinking?' he whispered.

'I can't believe I've – we've – done this.' I was about to faint. They'd wrapped the kimono too tight, and the weight of the fabric was causing my machete to jab me in the thigh.

He chuckled and seemed less ill than he had in some time.

'Suddenly you're looking healthier,' I said.

'Are you worried that I will live?'

'Yuji, of course not.' But it had honestly not occurred to me that he might get better.

I was beginning to feel rather unwell myself. I wanted to be back in New York. I told my 'husband' that I needed to lie down. He took me to a room reserved for married couples that was near the shrine.

Kazuo trailed us. He called to Yuji in Japanese.

'Kazuo wants to know if I am sick,' Yuji translated. 'For once, it is Anya,' he called merrily to Kazuo.

Yuji and I went into the marital suite. I lay down on the bed. Yuji sat nearby, watching me.

What had I been thinking? How had I convinced myself that this made sense?

I had married a man I barely knew.

I had married him!

I could not unmarry him either.

This was it. This had happened. This was my first marriage.

Natty and Theo and everyone else who'd tried to warn me off this had been right.

I was hyperventilating.

'Calm yourself,' Yuji said gently. 'I will die as promised.'

I started to cry. 'I don't want you to die.'

I was still hyperventilating.

'May I loosen your obi?' he asked.

I nodded. He untied my kimono, and I began to feel better. He lay beside me. He looked at me, then he touched my face.

'Yuji, do you think I am a bad person?'

'Why?'

'Because you know I don't love you. In a sense, I am marrying you for your money.'

'The same could be said of me. You are on the verge of being richer than I am, no? The truth is, I do not think of you in terms of good or bad.'

'How do you think of me?'

'I remember you as a child, playing in the garden with your sister. I remember you as a teenage girl, angry and reckless. I see you now, as a woman, usually so sturdy and strong. I like you best now. I like you better than I have ever liked you before. It is a shame we have had to do everything in the wrong order, but those are the lives you and I have. I

167

would have liked, if I were young and strong, to have courted you, to have made you love me above all others, to have wooed you and won you. I would have liked to have known that when I died, Anya would be inconsolable.'

'Yuji.' I turned on my side so that I could face him. My kimono fell open and I pulled it closed.

He grabbed the obi and wrapped one end around his hand. 'I wish I could make love to you.' He pulled me toward him by the belt.

My eyes widened. I was not such a fallen creature that I would make love to a man I barely knew, even if he were my husband.

'But I cannot. I am too weak. Today has been very tiring.' He looked at me. 'I am pumped full of drugs and nothing works as it should.'

He was a ridiculously beautiful man, and the sickness had made him almost unbearably so. He looked like a charcoal drawing of a man. In death, he was blacks and whites.

'I think I could have loved you if we'd met when I was a few years older,' I told him.

'What a pity.'

I pulled him to me. I could feel his bones coiling and creaking around me. He must have weighed less than me, and he was terribly cold, too. We were both tired so I pulled open my kimono and then I sealed it so we were both inside.

'This life,' he said when we were eye to eye. 'This life,' he repeated. 'I will have more reason to miss it than once I thought.'

In the morning, he was gone. Kazuo explained that Yuji had needed to return to his own room on account of his health and that we were to meet him at the Ono Sweets factory later that day.

Back at the house, I changed out of my wedding kimono, which I had been wearing for almost twenty-four hours, and into my regular clothes. The servants were even more deferential than they had been before, but I almost did not know to whom they were speaking when they called me Anya Ono-san. I did not take his name, if you were wondering, but my Japanese was insufficient to explain to the servants that despite what it looked like, I was still Anya Balanchine.

Yuji, accompanied by an even larger entourage of businesspeople than had been at the airport, was waiting for us at the Ono Sweets factory in Osaka. For the first time since I'd arrived, Yuji wore a dark suit. I associated him with that suit and I found it comforting to see him in it again. He introduced me to his colleagues, and then we toured the plant, which was clean, well lit, and well run. There was no telltale scent to indicate that chocolate was being concocted. Their main product appeared to be *mochi*, a gummy, rice-based dessert.

'Where's the chocolate?' I whispered to Yuji. 'Or do you import it the way my family does?'

'Chocolate is illegal in Japan. You know that,' he replied. 'Follow me.'

We separated from the main group and took an elevator down to a room that held a furnace. He pressed a button on the wall. The wall disappeared, and we entered a secret passage that led to a room smelling distinctly of warm chocolate. He pressed another button to close the door.

'I have spent 200 million yen building this underground factory,' Yuji told me, 'but, if everything progresses as I hope, soon I will have no need for it.'

As he led me through the secret factory, I noticed that the workers, who were dressed in coveralls, sanitary masks, and gloves, were careful not to make eye contact. The factory had state-of-the-art ovens and thermometers, thick metal cauldrons and scales, and along the walls, bins of unprocessed cacao. As a result of Theo's teachings, I knew this cacao to be subpar. The colour was bad, and the odour and consistency were off.

'You can't make cacao-based products with this,' I told him. 'You can bury low-quality cacao in conventional chocolate with enough sugar or milk, but you can't make high-per centage cacao products with this. You must change suppliers.'

Yuji nodded. I would need to call Granja Mañana to see if they could supply Ono Sweets as well.

We left the secret factory and went upstairs to meet with Yuji's legal adviser, Sugiyama, who explained some of the challenges of opening a Dark Room-like club in Japan. 'An official from the Department of Wellness will need to place a government stamp on every product, verifying the cacao content and the health benefits. This requires much money,' the adviser said.

'At first,' I said, 'but then you'll save money. You won't have to run a secret factory, for instance. And if your business is anything like mine, you were paying off officials before.

Now you'll be paying off different officials instead.'

Sugiyama did not look at me or acknowledge that I had spoken. 'Perhaps we are better off as operations stand, Ono-san,' he said.

'You must listen to Anya-san,' Yuji said. 'This is what I want, Sugiyama-san. This is how it must be. We will no longer be a Pachinko operation.'

'As you wish, Ono-san.' Sugiyama nodded to me.

Yuji and I went outside to wait for a car. 'These people are hopelessly conservative, Anya. They resist change. You must insist. I will insist as long as I am able.'

'Where are we going now?' I asked.

'I want to show you where the first cacao bar could be, if you approve. And then I want to introduce you to the world as my wife.'

Though we planned to open five locations in Japan, the location Yuji had selected for the flagship was an old, abandoned teahouse in the middle of the most urban part of Osaka. As soon as you passed through the grey stone front you were in another world. There were sakura trees and a garden with a few stalwart purple irises that had not yet resigned themselves to the despotic weeds. Everything was hopelessly overgrown. The feeling was unlike our location in New York, but it could be lovely. Romantic even.

'Do you think this will suit?' Yuji asked me.

'It is very different from New York,' I said.

'I want a place that will operate in the daylight,' he said. 'I am so tired of the darkness.'

171

'Originally I wanted to do that, too, but my business partner talked me out of it. He said the club should be sexy.'

'I see his point. But the Japanese are different from the Americans. I think we will be better in the daylight here.'

'It can't be called the Dark Room then.' I paused. 'The Light Bar?'

He considered my suggestion. 'I like this.'

About fifteen minutes later, several members of the media arrived along with Yosh, Yugi's company's publicist, who translated for me the parts of the press conference that were in Japanese.

'Ono-san, it's been months since anyone has seen you,' one of the interviewers noted. 'Rumour has it you are ailing, and you do look very lean.'

'I am not ailing,' Yuji said. 'Nor did I summon you here today to discuss my health. I have two announcements to make. The first is that my company will undergo a dramatic reorganization in the months that follow. The second is to introduce Japan to this woman.' He pointed to me. 'Her name is Anya Balanchine. She is the president of the renowned Dark Room cacao club in New York City, and she has done me the great honour of becoming my wife.'

Flashbulbs went off. I smiled at the reporters.

The story went global. In certain parts of the world, both my name and my husband's were notorious, and it was noteworthy, I suppose, that two organized-crime families should have merged. In reality, our families had joined years before, when Leo had married the illegitimate Noriko.

I knew without him having to say it that Yuji wanted to see at least one of the clubs open before he died. And though I was only a bogus wife, I wanted to make him happy. For the rest of the summer, Yuji and I worked to launch the Light Bars. It wasn't easy – the cultural and linguistic barriers could not be overstated. I worried for Yuji's health. He was as tireless as a dying man can be.

About a week after my twentieth birthday, the first Light Bar opened. The mood of the place was more like an upscale teahouse than a nightclub. When you entered, a carpet of rose petals led you to the main room. Tiny Christmas lights hung everywhere in messy strings, and column candles in hammered silver cans lit the wrought iron tables, which were each canopied by diaphanous white fabric. Yuji and I had made it the most romantic place imaginable – the irony being that the two people who had created it had not been in love.

His heart was incredibly weak by this point and he was not able to stay at the opening long. 'Are you happy?' I asked him on the ride back to his estate.

'I am,' he said. 'Tomorrow, we will return to work. Maybe I will live to see Tokyo, too.'

That night, I went down the hall to Yuji's room. He often couldn't sleep through the night. I made sure his light was on before I knocked.

'Yuji,' I said, 'I'm going home to help my sister move into her dorm, but I'll return in two weeks. I'd invite you to come along with me, but in your condition . . .'

Yuji nodded. 'Of course.'

'Please don't die while I'm away.'

'I won't. Do you want to know a secret?' he asked.

'Always from you.'

'Go to the window and look by the koi pond,' he said.

I obeyed. Yuji's grey cat was sitting next to a black cat on the bench. The grey cat licked the black cat's cheek. 'Oh! They're in love, aren't they? How do you think they met?'

'There's a farm not so far down the road from here. I suppose he might be from there.'

'Or maybe he's a city cat,' I said. 'Come to the country for the girl of his dreams.'

'I like your way better.' He was smiling to himself.

He patted the spot next to him in bed, and I lay down beside him.

'How do you feel?' He hated the question, but I wanted to know.

'I feel happy that I have been able to push Ono Sweets into the new era. It's 2086, Anya. We must be ready for the twenty-second century.'

'How is your heart?' I specified.

'It beats. For now, it beats.' I lay my hand on his chest, and he flinched slightly. 'Am I hurting you?'

'It's fine.' He inhaled. 'No, it's good. The only people who touch me are doctors so I appreciate the change.'

'Tell me a story about my father,' I said.

Yuji thought for a moment before he spoke. 'When I was introduced to him, it was not long after the kidnapping. I was wary of strangers. I think I have told you this before.'

'Tell me again.'

'He was an enormous man, and I was terrified of him. He got down on his knees and held his palm face up the way you would when approaching a timid animal. "I hear you have an interesting battle wound, young man. Would you like to show it to me?" he asked. I was embarrassed to be missing a finger, but I held out my hand to him anyway. He looked at it for the longest time. "That is a scar to be proud of," he said.'

Yuji held out his hand to me, and I kissed it in the broken place. Years earlier, my father's hand had touched that hand, too.

'I am glad I will always be your first husband,' he said.

'And last,' I said. 'I don't think I am built for marriage or for love.'

'I'm not certain you are right. You're still so young, and life is usually long.'

He fell asleep shortly after that. His breathing was laboured, and beneath my hand, his heartbeat was so weak that I could barely make it out.

When I awoke the next day, the bed was soaking wet. So as not to embarrass Yuji, I tried to slip away without him seeing me. He awoke shivering and sat straight up.

'*Sumimasen*,' he said, bowing his head. He rarely spoke in Japanese to me.

'It's fine.' I looked him in the eye. I remembered that Nana had always hated when people didn't look her in the eye.

On the sheets, the urine was spotted with blood.

'Anya, please go.'

'I want to help you,' I said.

175

'This has no dignity. Please leave.'

But I did not leave.

His eyes were wide and panicked. 'Please leave. I don't want you here.'

'Yuji, you are my husband.'

'It is only a business arrangement.'

'You are my friend, then.'

'You do not have to do anything for me. I do not expect this kind of service from you.' He shook his head.

I went over to him. 'This is nothing to be ashamed of,' I said. 'This is just life.' I helped him out of bed and to the bathroom, where I drew him a bath. I barely felt his weight.

'Please leave me,' he whimpered.

'I won't,' I said. 'Not because of our arrangement, but because of everything you've done for me. You saved my brother's life. You smuggled me out of the country. You told a silly teenage girl to demand more of herself. Even now, you offer me everything you have. Helping you when you are sick hardly makes us even.'

He bowed his head.

I helped him out of his damp clothes and into the bath. I ran hot water over a tough, natural sponge and washed his back. He closed his eyes.

'Many months ago, I was even sicker than I am now. The pain was worse. They were still trying to cure me then, but I knew it was hopeless,' he said. 'I asked Kazuo to kill me. I handed him my father's samurai sword. I said, "You must cut off my head so that I can die with some honour." Tears in his eyes, he refused. He said, "You have time. I will not steal that

176

time from you. Use your time, Ono-san." He was right. I began to think of what I wanted to do with the end of my days. Yours was the face that kept coming back to me. And so when I was well enough, I went to America to see if I could convince you to marry me. I was not sure that you would.'

'I honour my debts.'

'But I had another plan for if you hadn't come. My alternate plan was to track down Sophia and murder her. I hate her for doing this to me.'

'I hate her, too.' I wrung out the sponge.

'Promise me you will kill her if you ever see her again.'

For a moment, I considered his request. 'I won't do that, Yuji. I'm not in the murder business and neither are you.'

We had been raised like wolves, Yuji and I. He thought it was perfectly fine to ask me to kill for him, but too much of an imposition to ask for help into the bath.

═XVII═

I BRIEFLY TEND TO BUSINESS AT HOME;
LIFE GOES ON WITHOUT ME

A<small>ND THEN I WAS BACK IN BOSTON</small>. I was relieved to be among English speakers again and to be with Natty, though nothing I did that weekend felt quite real. It was strange to be among people my age, people who were still in school, people who hadn't married or run businesses. The resident adviser at her dorm was a goofy, cute, dark-haired boy named Vikram. He shook my hand and promised to take good care of my sister. 'How long are you in Boston, Natty's sister?' he asked. 'I could show you some cool places.'

I showed him my wedding band. 'I'm married, and I've already seen some places.'

'You have been so quiet this weekend,' Natty said. We were lying on her bed, which we had just outfitted with fresh white sheets.

'I'm jet-lagged,' I said.

'I could have managed myself. You didn't have to come.'

'Natty, I would never miss this.' I rolled over and kissed my sister on her smooth, pink cheek.

Toward the end of the weekend, I turned on my slate. I thought about contacting Win, but I didn't. It would have seemed disloyal to Yuji, though I'm not sure why I felt that way. Win had not been my boyfriend for over two years now, and I doubted he ever would be again. It would have been pleasant to see him, though.

I stopped in New York and then San Francisco on my way back to Japan. In New York, I found that Theo had moved out of the apartment. When I went into the office, he did not ask about my marriage. He was all business.

'Anya, Luna says that you require more cacao to supply the five new locations in Japan. At first I didn't know if we could do it – Granja Mañana is only so big, you know? But then she researched the matter and found that we could buy a derelict coffee farm about fifteen miles away from Granja Mañana. I need to know if you are serious about needing that cacao.'

'I am serious,' I said.

'*Bueno*. We will do this then.' He smiled at me, but it was not a warm smile. It was a professional one. And then Theo left. It was as if we had never meant anything to each other.

I had wondered if he might quit or go back to Mexico. He hadn't, and I admired him for it. He had taken an apartment across town. My fallen-woman status wasn't enough reason for him to leave the Dark Room. He loved our business. He loved what we had built even though he hated me.

With Theo gone, Scarlet was happy to have my apartment to Felix and herself. 'I suppose some year we'll have to get our own place,' she said as we sat in the living room.

'Why?'

'To prove I'm a grown-up, something like that. I mean, I can't be thirty and living in my best friend's apartment. And I've been on the Upper East Side my whole life. It might be nice to see another part of town. Also, I don't know anyone who lives up here anymore.' She'd been doing more theatre, and she reported that most of her friends lived downtown or in the boroughs.

'Do you hear from' – I lowered my voice in case Felix was listening – 'Gable?'

'He sends some money, not that often, and he sent a football for Felix's second birthday. An *adult* football.' She rolled her eyes.

'I guess he was thinking ahead. Felix'll be using that in about ten years.'

'He'll be using that *never*.' She scooped the toddler up from the floor where he was playing with blocks and wearing a tiny kimono I'd bought in Japan and said to him, 'Mama doesn't want a big, dumb football spoiling that handsome face.' Felix kissed her and then he kissed me.

'He kisses everyone,' Scarlet explained. 'He's very into kissing.'

'So were you.'

'Shut up,' Scarlet said, laughing. 'Anyway, what's better than kissing? I'm *still* into kissing.' She sighed. 'God, I miss kissing.'

Felix kissed her again.

'Thank you, Fee. So, Anya my darling bestest friend, should we discuss the fact that you're married?' Scarlet asked.

'There's not much to report,' I said.

I had lunch with Mouse. As the new locations of the Dark Room had begun to open across the country, we'd managed to convert almost ninety per cent of the Balanchines to legal employment. We toasted to our successes and talked about old times.

'I ran into Rinko,' she said. 'Do you remember her?'

'Of course I remember her.'

'Well, she didn't even recognize me. I was introduced to her as Kate Bonham, Balanchine crime boss, and she didn't even register that I was Mouse, the girl she had tormented for three years at Liberty. I thought surely she'd connect you with me, but she didn't.'

'Is she still in coffee?' I asked.

'She is. The coffee people are having a rough time of it.'

'Those Rimbaud laws are as stupid on coffee as they are on chocolate.'

'I know it,' Mouse said.

'Anything else we should discuss?'

'Well, the Russians have been silent a while. I don't necessarily like it or trust it. However, I've heard that they're channelling their excess supply to other families and to other countries. So maybe they've made peace with the fact that the Balanchines are out of the chocolate business.' She took a drink. 'Maybe knowing that messing with Balanchine means messing with Ono was enough to calm everyone down. Who knows? I doubt it though. We'll definitely hear from them again.

'Congratulations on your marriage, by the way,' Mouse said. 'I was going to get you a present, but I wasn't sure what you'd want.'

'What to buy for the *mafiya* daughter entering an inevitably tragic marriage of convenience.'

'It's hard, right? She's the girl who has everything.'

'I guess what I'd like is for no one in this Family to have to take a job dealing illegal chocolate ever again.'

'I'm trying, Anya.'

'I know you are.'

We shook hands. Neither of us was the hugging kind.

'Anya, wait. Before you go. Thank you.'

'For what, Mouse?'

'For recommending me to Fats. For trusting me with so much more than anyone ever had. For never asking me what my crime was. For everything, my whole life really. I don't think you have any idea how much you've saved me.'

'Loyal friends are hard to come by, Mouse.'

The last person I saw before I left town was Mr Delacroix. He took me out to dinner to celebrate my marriage. A restaurant had opened across the street from the Dark Room. There had not been a new restaurant on that block for a decade.

Mr Delacroix was contemplating a run for mayor. He had gotten quite a bit more popular since helping me open the Dark Room. If he did run, I knew it would mean that he would have to leave the business.

'I'm not certain married life agrees with you,' he said. 'You look very tired.'

'The travel.' I used my standard excuse.

'I suspect it is more than that.'

I gave him my haughtiest look. 'We don't speak of our personal lives, colleague,' I said.

'Fine, Anya.'

The waiter offered us dessert. I declined, but Mr Delacroix ordered the pie. 'If you were my daughter –' he said.

'I am not your daughter.'

'But let us suspend disbelief and imagine that you are. You remind me of her a bit, you know. If you were my daughter, I would tell you to let go of any guilt you might be feeling. You made a decision. Maybe it was right; maybe it was wrong. But the decision is done. There is nothing you can do now except continue moving ahead.'

'Have you made decisions you regret?'

'Anya. Look who you are talking to. I am the king of regrets. But I might very well be mayor in two years. Life is turnabouts, my dear. Look at us. Wasn't I the worst enemy of your seventeenth year of life? And now I am your friend.'

'I wouldn't overstate matters, Mr Delacroix. It has already been established that we are colleagues, nothing more. I saw your son at Natty's graduation, by the way.'

'I know.'

'You always know everything.'

'Win told me. He said, "I am glad you helped her open the business, Dad," or something to that effect. He said that – wait for it – he had been wrong. My jaw nearly dropped to the floor. One is never prepared for one's son to say something so shocking as, "Dad, you were right." '

'Well, isn't that good news come too late?' I twisted my wedding band around my finger.

'My dear, it is never too late. Now won't you finish this pie of mine? And please get a good night's sleep. You have a long flight tomorrow.'

'Mr Delacroix,' I said, 'if you do decide to run for mayor, you will have my complete support.'

'You have decided you won't miss me at the Dark Room.'

'No, it isn't that. I would miss your counsel more than I can say. However, I'm willing to sacrifice you to the greater good. In these years we have worked together, you have steered me right every time. Whenever I would listen, that is. And having seen the Bertha Sinclairs of this world in action, I would rather back you.'

'Thank you, Anya. The support and compliments of a colleague are always appreciated.'

XVIII

I MOURN AGAIN

In osaka, the end of September was the height of typhoon season, and my flight was delayed by weather for several days. When I finally arrived, the rains were pummelling the ground and the sole view from my window was a curtain of rain. Normally such a vista might have soothed me, but, on this occasion, it did not. Based on my conversations with Yuji's bodyguard and Yuji himself, and based on what was and was not being said, I had begun to be frightened that I would not see my husband before he died.

I went straight to his room. He was hooked up to an oxygen tank. He hated such measures, so I knew the end must be near. Every time I saw him, there was less of him. I had a strange thought: if Yuji did not die, perhaps he would simply disappear.

'I promised not to die while you were away,' he said.

'It looks as if you barely kept that promise.'

'How was America?'

I told him of my adventures, eking more excitement and humour out of my travels than there had actually been. I wanted to amuse him, I suppose. He reported the progress that had been made with the Japanese clubs. We spoke of our parents, none of whom were living. Without thinking, I asked him to say hi to my mother, my father, and my nana if he happened to see them in Heaven.

He smiled at me. 'I think you know I am not going to Heaven, Anya. One, I am not a good man. And two, I don't believe in such a place. I didn't know you believed either.'

'I'm weak, Yuji,' I said. 'I believe when it is convenient for me to believe. I don't want to think that you might end up nowhere, in some black void.'

The rain cleared, and though his doctor was against it, he wanted to go for a walk. The grounds of the estate were lovely, and despite the humidity, I was glad to be outside.

The act of walking and talking soon proved too much for Yuji Ono, and even with his oxygen tank in tow, he quickly lost his breath. We stopped at a bench by a koi pond. 'I do not like dying,' he said mildly after his breathing had regulated.

'You say that as if you're speaking of a food you dislike. I do not like broccoli.'

'I don't remember you being funny,' he said. 'It is my upbringing. We are taught to keep much inside. But I don't like dying. I would rather be alive to fight, to plan, to plot, to connive, to win, to betray, to eat chocolate, to drink sake, to tease, to make love, to laugh my head off, to leave my mark on this world . . .'

'I'm sorry, Yuji.'

'No. I don't want your pity. I only want to tell you that I don't like it. I don't like the pain. I don't like the affairs of my physical body being a matter of daily discussion. I don't like looking like a zombie.'

'You're still handsome,' I told him. He was.

'I'm a *zombie*.' He smiled at me crookedly. 'We should be like the fish,' Yuji said. 'Look at them. They swim, they eat, they die. They don't make such a production of these little things.'

Yuji passed early the next morning. When Kazuo told me, I bowed my head, but I did not allow myself to cry. 'Was it peaceful?' I asked.

Kazuo did not reply for a moment. 'He was in pain.'

'Did he have any last words?'

'No.'

'Did he have any message for me?'

'Yes. He wrote you a note.'

Kazuo handed me a slate. Yuji's stroke was very light. I squinted to make it out before realizing the message was in Japanese. I handed the slate back to Kazuo. 'I can't read this. Would you translate for me?'

Kazuo bowed deeply. 'It does not make much sense to me. I am very sorry.'

'Try. If you don't mind. Maybe it will mean something to me.'

'As you wish.' Kazuo cleared his throat. 'To my wife. The fish does not die with regrets because the fish cannot love. I die with regrets, and yet I am glad I am not a fish.'

I nodded.

I bowed my head.

I had not loved him, but I would miss him terribly.

He had understood me.

He had believed in me.

Is this better than love?

And maybe fish do love. How could Yuji even know?

Perhaps it was a sign of denial but I had not brought black clothes to Japan. One of the maids lent me a *mofuku*, a black mourning kimono. I put it on, then looked at myself in the mirror. I seemed older than twenty, I thought. I was a widow and maybe this was how widows looked.

The funeral began like any funeral. I had, at this point, been to more than my share. This one was in Japanese, but it doesn't particularly matter what language a funeral is in. The tiny room had light pine walls, like the interior of a poor man's coffin, and was so packed with Yuji's colleagues and relatives that I could not even see who was in the back. Incense was burning on the altar, and the air smelled sickly sweet, of synthetic frangipani and sandalwood. (No matter how old I get, I will never stop associating the scent of frangipani with death.) Orchids leaned in a blue vase, and a white lily floated in a shallow wooden bowl.

People say that the dead at funerals look peaceful. It's a nice sentiment, if untrue. The dead look dead. Perhaps the body is peaceful – it does not cough or wheeze or argue or move – but it is a husk, nothing more. The body that had once been Yuji Ono was dressed in his wedding clothes. The hands were clasped over his favourite samurai sword and had been positioned so that his amputated finger was not in view. The mouth had been forced into a strange almost-smile, an expression Yuji had never worn in life. This was not Yuji to me, and this was not peace.

The priest signalled us to come and leave incense at the altar. After that, people went to view the body, though there was not much to see. He was a layer of wasted flesh over a pile of bones. Sophia's poison had killed him leisurely and dreadfully.

Though it was customary to acknowledge the widow, a woman with a shroud of black hair and a wide-brimmed, charcoal-coloured hat walked right past me on her way to the altar. She was taller than almost anyone at the funeral.

Even from behind, the woman appeared overcome. Her shoulders shook, and she was whispering. I thought she might be praying, though I could not make out the words or the language. She lifted her hand and moved it in a way that could have been the sign of the cross. The longer I regarded her, the more her hair seemed to take on the waxy quality of a wig. Something was off. I stood and walked the three steps to the altar. I meant to set my hand on the woman's shoulder, but I caught her hair instead. The black wig slipped down to reveal brown hair.

Sophia Bitter turned around. Her large dark eyes were red and her eyelids were swollen like lips. 'Anya,' she said, 'did you imagine I wouldn't come to the funeral of my best friend?'

'I did actually,' I said. 'Seeing as you killed him, good manners would dictate that you should sit this one out.'

'I don't have good manners,' she said. 'Besides, I only killed him because I loved him.'

'That is not love.'

'And what would you know about love, *liebchen*? Did you marry Yuji for love?'

I pushed her against the casket. We were attracting the attention of other funeral-goers.

'He betrayed me,' Sophia insisted. 'You know that he did.'

I felt my fingers begin to spread toward my machete. I thought of Yuji asking me to kill her, but for better or for worse, I was still not the murdering kind. Sophia Bitter had committed atrocious acts, but in my memory flashed a picture of the girl Yuji had described. Sophia had once been young and unpopular and embarrassed. She had thought herself ugly, though she couldn't have ever been more than plain. She had murdered perhaps the only person in the world who had loved her. And for what? For power? For money? For chocolate? For jealousy? For love? I know she told herself it was for love, but it could not have been.

'Go,' I said. 'You've paid your respects, for what they are worth, and now you should leave.'

'I will be seeing you, Anya. Good luck opening the rest of the clubs in Japan.'

'Is that a threat?' I imagined her making a disturbance at one of our openings.

'You're a very suspicious young woman,' she said.

'Probably so. If we were in America, I'd have you arrested.'

'But we are not. And poisoning is the perfect crime. It takes patience, but it's so very hard to prove.'

'By the way, what are your plans after the funeral?'

'Will we be having lunch?' she asked. 'Girl talk and chocolate. Unfortunately, I leave tomorrow. You are not the only one with a business to run, though you act as if you are. This leaves no time for you and me to catch up. What a pity.'

'I feel so sorry for you,' I said. 'He loved you, and you killed him, and now no one will ever love you again.'

Her eyes turned black with hate. I knew even as I was saying it that nothing except the belief that others found her pitiable could have had such an effect on that woman. She lunged toward me, but I wasn't scared of her. She was weak and stupid. I called Kazuo over and asked him to show her the door.

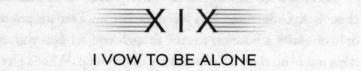

XIX

I VOW TO BE ALONE

T**HOUGH IT WAS THE MIDDLE** of the day, I went back to Yuji's house to my room to sleep. I was psychically tired, if not physically so. I lay down on my bed, not even bothering to remove my black kimono.

When I awoke, it was past midnight, and the room felt cramped and musty. My clothes reeked of incense, and I craved a walk, a bit of fresh air. Though I was not particularly concerned for my safety, I strapped my machete underneath the kimono.

I took the same stone path I had travelled with Yuji not so many days earlier. I arrived at the koi pond and sat down on the ancient stone bench. I watched the orange, red, and white fish as they swam and jumped about. I contemplated these fish. It was so late – were these a peculiar breed of party fish? When did fish sleep? *Did* they sleep?

I loosened my kimono, which the servant had tied too tightly.

I looked at my hands and at my wedding band. So much for that experiment, I thought.

There was much moonshine that night, and I was able to see my reflection in the water. I looked at Anya Balanchine as the fish swam across her face. She seemed on the verge of tears, and I hated her for that. I took off my wedding band and threw it at her. 'You chose this,' I said. 'You don't get to feel sad.'

I was twenty years old. I had married and now I was a widow. In that moment, I determined that I would never marry again. I did not like the jewellery that said you were owned, the pretentious pageantry of weddings, or the fact that joining your life to someone meant inviting sadness in your door. For love or for any other reason, I was not for marriage, or perhaps marriage was not for me.

The business had made sense with Yuji, but the whole arrangement had become so complicated. I could see no reason to join my life to anyone else's in the future. If you married for love, you always fell out of love (cf. my parents, Win's parents). If you married for business, the relationship refused to stay business. Furthermore, I had worked hard, made tough choices, and built something other than a starry-eyed teenager's house of dreams. I did not wish to inherit anyone else's history and mistakes, nor did I wish mine on anyone. Besides, who could I be with who wouldn't judge me? Who would ever understand why I had done all these things I'd done? I sat on that rigid stone bench in a foreign country in the middle of the night, and I thought, Why on earth would I ever get married again?

So I determined to be alone. Maybe occasionally, I would take a lover. (The Catholic schoolgirl in me was scandalized by the thought; I told her we'd been thrown out of Catholic school so she should shut up.) Theo had effectively been my lover, and look how well that had worked out. *Definitely* better to be alone. I would fill my spare time with productive hobbies. I would take up reading like Imogen, go to cooking school, learn to dance, volunteer with orphans, become a more involved godparent to Felix. I would write my memoirs.

(NB: Even many years later, it is hard for me to admit this. Marrying Yuji Ono, despite the good it had done the Dark Room, would probably go down as the worst mistake of my life. As anyone who has read these accounts knows, I have made many. That night, I was not quite ready to admit that the error had been mine and not perhaps the institution of marriage itself.)

In the middle of having these thoughts, I felt something hit me in the back, underneath my left shoulder blade. It felt wrong, but that said, it did not feel significant either. It felt blunt, of medium size, harmless. It felt like a softball or a grapefruit. But when I looked down, my chest was pierced by the sparkling tip of a blade. Suddenly, the blade retracted and I began to bleed. It did not hurt much, but this was just adrenalin. I tried to retrieve my machete from beneath my kimono, but the garment was so voluminous, I could not reach it quickly. As I turned my neck to see what was coming, the blade penetrated again – this time, somewhere in my lower back. I tried to stand, but my right foot gave out, and I fell, slamming my chin and neck on the stone bench. Above me, Sophia Bitter held a sword. The look in her eye said she would not stop until I was dead.

How had she broken in to the estate? Who else was with her? I did not have even a moment to contemplate. I wanted to live. I needed time to get to my machete, so I decided to talk to her. 'Why?' My voice was barely more than a whisper – I had injured my larynx when I'd fallen into the bench. 'What have I ever done to you?'

'You know what you've done. I would rather poison you, but I have neither the time nor the access. I'll have to make do with this.' She drew back the sword and she raised it in the air.

'Wait,' I whispered as loudly as I could. 'Before you kill me . . . Yuji said to tell you something.' It was a pathetic ploy on my part, and I had almost no faith that it would work.

She rolled her eyes but lowered her weapon. 'Speak,' she said.

'Yuji told me—'

'Louder,' she said.

'I can't. My throat. Please. Closer.'

She crouched down so that we were eye to eye. I could feel her breath on my cheek. The scent was slightly acrid, like she had been drinking coffee. I thought of Daddy making coffee for my mother on the stovetop. *Oh, Daddy, it might be nice to see you again.* I felt my eyelids start to drop.

'Speak,' she repeated. 'What did Yuji say?'

'Yuji said . . . He was so handsome, wasn't he?'

Sophia slapped me across the face, but I didn't even feel it. 'Stop stalling!'

'Yuji said that the fish have no regrets because . . .'

'You are not making any sense.'

I was about to pass out when I felt something tickle my thigh. Of all things, it was the peacock feather I'd put in my sheath – Win's feather. Get the machete, I thought. Machetes are meant for chopping, not piercing, and my injuries had left me at a serious disadvantage. But I knew this was my only chance.

I wrapped my fingers around the machete. I pulled up my arms as high as I could, and I thrust forward, piercing what I hoped would be her heart. I withdrew the machete. She fell over into the koi pond, and strangely, I remember feeling guilty for the disturbance it would mean to the fish.

Sophia Bitter had once given me good advice. What had she said? *It isn't tough to have injured someone if you ought to have killed them.*

I tried to scream for Kazuo, but my voice would not work. I could tell I was bleeding out fast, that if I did not get medical attention soon, I would die.

I tried to stand, but I could not. My left leg felt dead. I did not have time to be scared. I dragged myself by my hands along the stone path. It was perhaps a thousand feet back to the house, and I knew I was leaving a trail of blood behind me.

My heart was beating faster than I can ever remember it having beaten. I wondered if it might give out.

When I was about halfway there, a man with a hook for a hand came out of the bushes. I knew him. My advantage, in that moment, was not that I would be able to outrun anyone, but that I was level with the ground.

'Sophia!' the man called.

Obviously she did not reply.

I saw him look at the bloody trail, but he did not pause to consider that it led toward the house and stopped. At that moment, Yuji Ono's cat began walking on the path in the direction of the koi pond. Upon spotting me, the cat paused – I worried that she might come over – and then she miaowed, attracting the man's attention. She continued walking to the koi pond, and he followed her.

I pulled myself to Kazuo's room. The adrenalin had begun to wear off and the pain was nothing short of excruciating. I scratched at the door. Kazuo was a light sleeper, and he was immediately on his feet.

'Sophia Bitter is dead. Her bodyguard is on the estate. There may be others, I don't know. Also, I may need to go to the hospital,' I managed to say.

I had always thought I'd die young. I thought I'd die because of something to do with crime and chocolate, but it was Sophia's love (and my own poor choices) that had done me in.

Sweet Jesus, I thought just before my heart stopped, Sophia Bitter had really loved Yuji Ono. It almost made me laugh: some people never got over their high-school boyfriends.

THE AGE OF LOVE

HAVING VOWED TO BE ALONE,
I AM NEVER ALONE

When I awoke, I was in a hospital bed. Without knowing why, I could tell that this was different from any other time I had been injured. I was not in pain, but my body had a peculiar, ominous numbness to it.

The miniature nurse said something encouraging in Japanese. It seemed like she was saying, 'Yay, you are not dead!' But I couldn't tell. She scurried out of the room.

Moments later, a doctor came in, and with him were Mr Delacroix and my sister.

I knew whatever was wrong with me must be serious if Natty had been summoned to Japan. She took my hand. 'Anya, you're awake, thank God.' Her eyes filled with tears. Mr Delacroix stayed in the corner, as if he were being punished. It did not strike me as particularly odd that he had come, as there was business to attend to in Japan. With me indisposed, either he or Theo would have needed to make the trip.

I tried to speak, but there were tubes in my throat. I pulled at them, and the nurse grabbed my hand.

'Do you remember what happened to you?' the doctor asked. It was a relief that he spoke English.

I nodded because that was the only response I could make.

'You were attacked and stabbed.' He showed me a diagram: I was represented by a one-dimensional cartoon girl with an intimidating series of red Xs to indicate areas of trauma. The girl looked as if she had made many mistakes.

'The first wound went from under your shoulder blade, penetrating through your chest, to below your collarbone. Along the way, it grazed the wall of your heart. The second wound penetrated your lower back, severing nerves along the left side of your spinal column. That is why you can't feel your left foot.'

I nodded – same reason as before.

'Luckily, the wound was very low. A bit higher and your entire leg might not work. A bit more central, and you might have been paralysed entirely. The other good news is that your right foot should work perfectly, and it is likely that you will be able to walk normally again but no one can say how long that will take.'

I nodded though I considered rolling my eyes to mix it up.

'When the wall of your heart was damaged, it set off a series of cardiac incidents. We had to perform heart surgery to repair the wall and to return your heart to normal function.

'You've broken your ankle, so you will notice that your foot is in a cast. We suspect you tried to stand at some point after you were stabbed, and you must have twisted your foot.'

I had not noticed, but now I saw that it was. It didn't seem to make much difference as my foot apparently didn't work anyway and obviously this was only one of many problems.

'Also, your larynx was badly bruised, but as you are intubated, we can't yet know the outlook for this injury.

'You are on a morphine drip, and your pain should be manageable for the time being. I don't want to sugarcoat the situation, Ms Balanchine. You have a long recovery ahead of you.'

He probably didn't need to say that last sentence. The fact that it had taken over two minutes to deliver a cursory description of my injuries was a pretty good sign that I would not be up and about for a while.

'I'll leave you to your friends,' the doctor said, and then he left.

Natty sat down on my bed and immediately began to cry. 'Annie, you almost died. Does it hurt?'

I shook my head. It didn't. That would come later.

'I'll stay with you until you're well,' she said.

I shook my head again. I was glad to see her, but even in my current condition, I could think of nothing worse than her staying with me when she was supposed to be at college.

Mr Delacroix came over to my bedside. He had not spoken once during this scene. 'I am, of course, attending to the openings of the Japanese clubs while you are out of commission.'

I wanted to say thank you, but I couldn't.

He looked at me with eyes that were steady and

unemotional. He nodded and then he left.

Natty kissed me, and though I had been awake for less than a half-hour, I fell asleep.

And now a small irony: I, who had only recently vowed to be alone, was never alone. I had never been so humbled. I could do nothing for myself. I could not get to the bathroom without assistance. I could not eat without help. Moving my right hand to the level of my mouth would reopen the stitches in my back and chest, and so I was encouraged to stay very still. I was worse than a baby, because I was so unwieldy and not adorable in the least.

I could not bathe. I could not brush my hair. I could not walk across the room, obviously. My ribs had been broken during the surgery to repair my heart, so those hurt, too. For a while, I was considered too fragile even to be placed in a wheelchair. I did not see the outdoors for weeks. It hurt to talk so I avoided it, but it hurt more to write. So I whispered. But what was there to say? I did not feel clever anymore. I did not care about the news from home. I did not care about the Family or the clubs.

I had been in the hospital before; I had been sick before. But this was not comparable in any way to those other occasions. I could not do anything except lie in bed and stare out the window. There was no revenge to be plotted. I had killed Sophia Bitter and I was tired.

The police came to see me. As Sophia had attacked me, the case appeared fairly cut-and-dried to them. We were both foreigners, *gaijin*, and so no one much cared what her, or for that matter, my reasons had been.

After a week or so of being tended to, I no longer had much in the way of self-consciousness. Who cared if my breasts were exposed when they re-dressed the stitches on my chest? Who cared if my hospital gown fell open when the bedpan was slipped below me? Who cared if I could not do anything without the assistance of at least one other person? I gave myself over to it. I did not fight with anyone like my nana had. I smiled sweetly and let myself be attended to. I was like a broken doll. I believe the nurses liked me very much.

Although I had stopped caring about most everything, my one concern was Natty. She had been a superb advocate in those first days. Though I was broken, I was no longer in danger of dying. I wanted her to return to college.

'I have a nurse and I don't like you to be away from school,' I managed to say in as cheerful a voice as I could muster.

'But you'll be so lonely,' Natty said.

'I am not lonely, Natty. I am never alone.'

'That's not the same thing, Argon, and you know it. You almost died. The doctors say you have months of recovery ahead of you. You can't travel, and I won't leave you here.'

I tried to sit up in bed but couldn't. 'Natty, I don't find it relaxing to have you here. I find it relaxing to know you are at college, learning important things.'

'This is ridiculous, Annie. I will not leave you!'

From the darkest corner of the room, Mr Delacroix spoke: 'I will stay with her.'

'What?' Natty said.

'I will stay with her, and then she will not be alone.'

205

Natty stood very tall. Her particular facial expression, a daunting combination of queen and gangster, was one I had seen many times before – on my nana. 'With all due respect, Mr Delacroix, I'm not going to leave my sister with you. I don't even know you that well, and what I do know, I am not sure I much like.'

'Trust me, Natty,' Mr Delacroix said. 'This is for the best. I will stay with her. I am already seeing to business in Japan.' He took off his jacket and set it on the chair, as if to indicate that he was planning to stay awhile. 'Do you remember the year she went to Liberty?'

'Yes, that is precisely what makes me not like you,' Natty said.

'Essentially, she traded her freedom so that you could go to genius camp in Amherst, and I was able to strike that deal with Anya because of the great love she had for you. And what she wanted that year is not dissimilar from what she wants right now. Respect her wishes and leave. You may call me as much as you like, and I will bring her home to you when she is safe to travel in the summer.'

Natty turned to me. 'You would rather him stay with you than me? You would prefer Win's awful father, who we used to hate? I mean, even his son, who is the nicest boy in the world and who gets along with everyone, hates him.'

Of course I would rather have had Natty, but more than that, I wanted her back at school. 'Yes,' I said. 'Besides, shouldn't he have to do something for me for once in his life?'

Natty turned to Mr Delacroix. 'If she takes even the slightest turn for the worse, you need to contact me immediately. You need to come see her at least once a day and make sure she is being taken care of. And I expect reports, too.' She left the room in a huff, and three days later, she was back at MIT.

'Thank you,' I told him later that day, or maybe it was the next. I slept a lot, and the days often blended together. 'But you don't have to check on me so often. I do have nurses. I'll be fine, and I can't very well get myself in any trouble in the condition I'm in.'

'I promised your sister,' Mr Delacroix said. 'And I am a man of my word.'

'No, you're not.'

'Anya,' Mr Delacroix said, 'would you like to go over some business details with me? The Light Bar in Hiroshima is—'

'I don't care. I'm sure whatever you decide will be fine.'

'You have to try.'

'Try to do what? I don't have to do anything except lie here, Mr Delacroix.'

They were weaning me off morphine that week, and this turned out to be the kind of adventure best experienced in solitude.

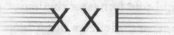

XXI

I AM WEAK; REFLECT ON THE
TRANSFORMATIVE NATURE OF PAIN;
DETERMINE THAT MY CHARACTER IS BUILT

Mʀ DELACROIX CAME EVERY DAY and usually for several hours.
I am certain I was terrible company. One day in late October,
he brought a chess set with him.

'What is this?' I asked. 'Do you think I want anything to
do with games?'

'Well, I am bored with you,' he said. 'You don't wish to
discuss the business and you say nothing even slightly amusing,
so I thought at least we could play chess.'

'I don't know how to play,' I said.

'Grand. That gives us something to do then.'

'If you're so bored with me, perhaps you should go back to
America. You must have business there.'

'I promised your sister,' he said.

'No one expects you to honour your promises, Mr Delacroix. Everyone knows what you are like.'

He propped a pillow behind my head. Sitting up was uncomfortable for me, but I tried not to complain. 'Is this OK?' he asked gently.

I gritted my teeth and nodded. There was not a single part of me that felt or operated as it once had.

I thought about Leo, when he'd been in the crash, and Yuji, and of course, my nana. I had not been patient enough with any of them.

He set the chessboard on my bed tray. 'Pawns move forward. They seem boring but the game is won or lost on pawn management, which is something a politician like myself knows perfectly well. The queen is very powerful. She can do anything she wants.'

'What happens if she's hurt?'

'The game goes on, but it's much more difficult to win. It's best to watch your queen.'

I cupped the black queen in my hand. 'I feel so stupid, Mr Delacroix,' I said. 'You told me to hire security over and over again. If I'd listened, I wouldn't be in the situation I'm in. You must be glad to be right.'

'In this instance, I am not glad in the least to be right, and you shouldn't blame yourself. You would not be you if you didn't insist upon doing things your way.'

'My way is seeming fairly stupid at this point.'

'That's in the past, Anya,' he said in a matter-of-fact voice. 'We are where we are. Sophia Bitter was a psychopath, and I am astonished that you managed to survive. Now the knight is perhaps the most difficult piece to master. He moves in an L.'

'How do you know the knight's a he?' I asked. 'There could be anything under that armour.'

He smiled at me. 'Good girl.'

At the end of November, I checked out of the hospital and moved back to Yuji Ono's house. A nurse came with me, and she set me up in Yuji's old room, which was the most convenient room in the house. I tried not to think of the fact that the last inhabitant of this room had died slowly and painfully.

By December, I was moving around with a walker. By February, I had crutches. By the middle of March, my cast came off, revealing a spectacularly lifeless foot in sickly shades of yellow, green, and grey. Structurally, it did not look sound either: the arch was flat, my ankle was as skinny as my wrist, and my toes curled strangely and uselessly. I looked at those toes and wondered what purpose they had ever served. I would rather have avoided the spectacle of my foot, though this was not an option – I had to look at it constantly, because it didn't work! When I set my foot down, I could not feel the ground. They gave me a brace and a cane. I lurched around like a zombie. It is beyond boring to have to instruct your brain to move your leg and then your leg to move your foot and then to have to check to see where the ground is with every step.

As for the rest of my body? It was not what I would call attractive. Thick pink scars snaked up the middle of my chest, under my shoulder, down my lower back, across my neck, down my leg and foot, under my chin. Some of the scars were from the attack; some were from the measures the doctors had taken to save my life. What I looked like was a girl who had been stabbed by a maniac and had heart surgery, which is exactly what I was. When exiting the bath, I tried not to consider myself too closely. I took to wearing long, loose, high-necked dresses, which Mr Delacroix said made me look like a frontierswoman.

The truth was, the scars did not bother me very much. I was far more self-conscious about the fact that my foot didn't work properly and far more annoyed by the constant pain I was in due to the nerve damage I'd sustained from being stabbed in the spine.

Pain . . . for a long time, that was all I could think about. The person known as Anya Balanchine had been replaced with a body that hurt. I was a throbbing, aching, monstrous, cranky ball. It did not make me pleasant to be around, I am sure. (I am not what you would call an upbeat person to start with.)

As I was afraid of slipping and falling, I stayed indoors a lot that winter.

I took up reading.

I played chess with Mr Delacroix.

I began to feel ever so slightly better. I even considered turning on my slate, but I decided against it. In my current condition, I did not wish to hear from Win. I did however speak to Theo, Mouse, and Scarlet on the phone. Sometimes, Scarlet would put Felix on the line. He wasn't that great a conversationalist, but I liked talking to him anyway. At the very least, he never asked me how I was feeling.

'What's going on, kid?' I said.

What was going on was that my three-year-old godson had a girlfriend. Her name was Ruby, and she was an older woman – four. She'd proposed marriage, but he wasn't sure he was ready. She was nice most of the time, but boy, could she be bossy. He wasn't entirely sure, but he suspected he might have been tricked into marrying her already. There had been an ambiguous incident involving a kiss in a coat cubby and what had been either the loan or the gift of a can of clay. As he somewhat lacked for vocabulary, this story took about an hour to tell, but it was fine. I had time.

And then, because the world is relentless this way, it was spring.

The sakura trees on Yuji's estate bloomed, the ground thawed, and I began to fear falling less. There were even signs of life in my dead foot, and I could more or less make myself end up where I wanted to go, though it took a million years.

I sometimes walked the path to the pond where I had been attacked. The trip that had taken me less than five minutes a half-dozen months ago now took me forty. The fish were still alive. The blood had been scoured away. There was no evidence that I had killed someone there and had almost been killed myself. The world is relentless in this way, too.

More often than not, Mr Delacroix came with me. Still, we did not speak much of business, which is what we had always spoken of before. Instead, we talked of our families: his son, his wife, my childhood, his childhood, my mother, my father, my siblings, my nana. He had been orphaned when he was young. His father, who had been in coffee, had killed himself when the Rimbaud laws went into effect. He was adopted when he was twelve by a wealthy family, fell in love with a girl at fifteen – his ex-wife, Win's mother. He was heartbroken over the divorce and he loved his wife still, though he accepted that he was at fault and held out little hope that there would be a happy ending in his future.

'Was it the club?' I asked him. 'Is that why you divorced?'

'No, Anya. It was much more than that. It was years of neglect and bad choices on my part. You have a thousand chances to make something right. That's a heck of a lot of chances, by the way. But they do run out eventually.'

Mr Delacroix encouraged me to venture from Yuji's estate, even for an afternoon, but I was reluctant. I preferred hobbling around where no one could see me. 'Some day you'll have to leave here,' he said.

I tried not to think about that.

The second to last Sunday in April, Mr Delacroix insisted we go out. 'I have a reason you can't argue with.'

'I doubt that,' I said. 'I can argue with anything.'

'Have you forgotten what today is?'

Nothing came to mind.

'It's Easter,' he said. 'The day even lapsed Catholics like you and me manage to darken the church's door. I see you are more lapsed than I thought.'

I was beyond lapsed. What I truly believed was that I was beyond redemption. Since the last time I'd gone to Mass with Scarlet and Felix, I'd killed a person. There was no point in believing in Heaven if you were certain the only place you could end up was Hell. 'Mr Delacroix, you can't have found a Catholic church in Osaka.'

'There are Catholics everywhere, Anya.'

213

'I'm surprised you go even on Easter,' I said.

'You mean because I am so evil, I suppose. But sinners especially deserve their annual portion of redemption, don't you think?'

The courtyard had granite statues of the Virgin Mary and Jesus. Both had Japanese features. Usually, Jesus reminded me of Theo, but in Osaka, he looked more like Yuji Ono.

The liturgy was the same as it was in New York – mostly Latin, though the English parts were in Japanese. It was not hard for me to follow. I knew what was being said, and I knew when to nod my assent, whether I meant it or not.

I found myself thinking of Sophia Bitter.

I could still see her face when I'd plunged that machete through her heart.

I could smell the scent of her blood mixed with mine.

If given the chance, I would kill her again.

So I probably wouldn't be going to Heaven. No amount of church or confession could fix me anymore. The Easter service was lovely though. I was glad to have gone.

We both decided to skip confession. Who even knew if the priest spoke English?

'Do you feel renewed?' Mr Delacroix asked me on the way out.

'I feel the same,' I said. I wanted to ask him if he'd ever killed anyone, but I doubted that he had. 'When I was sixteen, I used to feel like I was so bad. I went to confession constantly. I always felt like I was failing someone. My grandmother, my brother. And I had bad thoughts about my parents. And of course, the usual impure thoughts that teenage girls are wont

214

to have – nothing that awful. But in the years since, I've actually sinned, Mr Delacroix. And I can't help but laugh at that girl who thought she was so terrible. She'd done nothing. Except maybe having been born to the wrong family in the wrong city in the wrong year.'

He stopped walking. 'Even now, what have you done really?'

'I'm not going to list everything.' I paused. 'I killed a woman.'

'In self-defence.'

'But still, I wanted to be alive more than I wanted her to be alive. Wouldn't a truly good person have let herself die by that koi pond?'

'No.'

'But even if that is true, it wasn't like I was blameless. She didn't choose me at random. She chose me because she perceived that I had stolen something from her. And I probably had.'

'The guilt is pointless, Anya. Remember: you are as good as you are tomorrow.'

'You can't honestly believe that?'

'I have to,' he said.

One day toward the end of April, I asked him, 'Mr Delacroix, why are you still here? You must have business in the States. When we left, you were discussing a run for mayor.'

'My plans changed,' he said. 'It hasn't been ruled out.'

We had arrived at the pond, and he helped me to the bench.

'You know, perhaps, that I had a daughter once?'

'Win's sister, who died.'

'She did. She was very pretty, like you. She was sharp-tongued, like me. And also like you. Jane and I had her when we were young, still in high school, but luckily Jane's parents had money so it did not affect our lives as dramatically as it might have in the absence of money. My daughter got sick. It was exhausting for everyone. My ex-wife, my son. Alexa fought very hard for a bit over a year, and then she died. My family was not the same. I could no longer be at home. I did things I'm not proud of. I forced them to move to New York City so that I could take the job in the district attorney's office. I thought it might be a fresh start, but it wasn't. I could not bear to be with my wife or my son because it made me too unhappy.'

'That is a very sad story,' I said.

'Would you like it to get even sadder?'

'No. My heart is damaged. It probably can't take such a narrative.'

'My son, in the year 2082, moves to New York City, and within a week of starting a brand-new school, within a week of what was meant to be our fresh start, he manages to fall in love with a girl who is a ringer for his dead sister. Not particularly in looks, but in behaviour, in manner. She has that rare kind of sturdiness that even grown women rarely have. If the boy notices this, he never mentions it, seems blissfully unaware. But the first time I meet her, I am shocked.'

'I couldn't tell.'

'I am very good at concealing what I am feeling.'

'Like me.'

'Like you. And I have questioned the motivations for my behaviour when you and my son got together. And lately, in my old age, I have even come to regret it.'

'You? Regrets?'

'A few. And so it is 2087, and I find myself with a second chance. Theo was willing to come to Osaka, but I wanted to do it myself. Helping you has felt redemptive to me. It was a redemption I did not even think I had a right to hope for.'

'Because I remind you of your daughter?'

'That, yes. But because of yourself, too. You are in my life. I called you my colleague, but you were right to say you were my friend. I felt as if the whole world had given up on me after I lost that election, but you, who had every reason to be cruel to me, had not. Do you remember what you said to me?'

I did. 'I said I hadn't counted you out. You'd been such an enormous annoyance to me. How could I have counted you out? I was being nice, by the way,' I said.

'Be that as it may, it came at a time when very few people were being nice to me, and, well, your friendship in the years since has meant more to me than perhaps I can even express. I am a hard person to know. And so I am here because I must be here. I am here because I know what you are like. I know that you wouldn't have asked for the help you needed. You're a proud, stubborn thing and I could not leave you in a foreign country, broken and alone. Long ago, you did me a good turn, and despite what you or the world might think of me, I pay my debts.'

It had begun to rain so he helped me off the bench. He offered me his arm and I took it. The path was slick with moisture, and it was hard for my damaged foot to negotiate.

'You're doing much better,' he said. 'Just go slow.'

'I have no choice but to go slow.'

'It is nearly summer, Anya. You are much better than you were, and the business with the Light Bars is about concluded. I think we should both return to New York.'

I did not reply for a moment. The world that I had left, with its stairs and buses and boys and plots and gangsters, seemed too much to even consider.

'What is it?' Mr Delacroix asked.

'Mr Delacroix, if I tell you something, will you promise not to judge me? I feel weak saying this but I am scared to go back. The city is so difficult to manage. I do feel better, but I know I will never be the same. I don't want to face the Family or the people in the business, and I do not feel strong enough to go back to my life yet.'

He nodded. I thought he would tell me not to be scared, but he didn't. 'You have been terribly hurt, I can understand why you might feel that way. Let me think of a plan.'

'I didn't mean that you had to do anything about it. I only wanted to say how I was feeling.'

'Anya, if you tell me a problem, I will try my best to fix it.'

The next day, he proposed a solution. 'My ex-wife, Ms Rothschild, has a farm outside Albany, in a town called Niskayuna. You might remember that she is a farmer by trade?'

I did. Win used to help her out. The first time I met him, I remembered thinking that his hands didn't look like a city boy's.

'The farm is incredibly peaceful. And Jane would be delighted to host you and your sister for the summer. You could rest up, relieved from the burden of city life. I will visit you when I am able. And then at the end of the summer, you'll go back to New York City a new woman, I feel quite sure.'

'And she isn't angry with me because of the club?'

'That was years ago, and she blames me, not you, for anything that might have happened. She was always appalled by my behaviour where you were concerned, as you have probably guessed. If you're worried about Win being there, I believe he's undertaking a pre-med programme in Boston. He won't be in Niskayuna for more than a couple of days at the end of August, at the most.'

'Good.' I was in no condition to see him.

'So you'll go?'

'I will,' I said. 'I've always wanted to get out of the city for the summer.'

'Have you never gone away?' he asked.

'One year, I came close to going to Teen Crime Scene Summer, a programme for budding criminologists in Washington, DC, but I struck a deal with the acting district attorney that landed me at Liberty Children's instead.'

'I imagine the experience was character-building for you.'

'Oh, it was. Enormously.' I rolled my eyes. 'Though I have had no shortage of character-building experiences in my life.'

'At this point,' he said, 'I think we can safely consider your character built.'

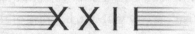

XXI

I EXPERIENCE THE SUMMER LIFE; EAT A STRAWBERRY; LEARN TO SWIM

THE HOUSE IN NISKAYUNA was white with grey shutters. In the back was a deck, and the Mohawk River streamed pleasantly by. To the side was farmland – I could see peach trees, corn, cucumbers, and tomatoes. The place looked like summer to me, but not the kind of summer I had ever known. Summer as I had imagined other, more fortunate people lived it.

Ms Rothschild greeted me with a hug followed immediately by an expression of concern. 'Oh my dear, you are nothing but bones.'

I knew it was true. At my last doctor's appointment, I had weighed less than I had at twelve years old. I was skinny like someone with a disease.

'Looking at you, I want to cry. What may I feed you?'

'I'm not hungry,' I said. The truth was, I had lost my appetite since I'd been injured.

'Charlie,' she said to her ex-husband, 'this situation won't do.' She turned to me. 'What are your favourite foods?'

'I'm not sure I have any,' I said.

She looked at me with an appalled expression. 'Anya, you *must* have a favourite food. Please, explain. What did your mother make for you?'

'At home, you know, my parents died when I was pretty young, and my nana was sick, and I was responsible for the meals, so I basically made whatever came out of a box or a bag. I'm not that into food, and I guess, um, that's why I've kind of quit eating. It doesn't seem worth the bother. For a while I liked *mole*, but now it kind of has bad associations.' I was rambling.

'Don't you even like chocolate?' Ms Rothschild asked.

'It's not my favourite. I mean, I get it, but it's not my favourite.' I paused. 'I used to like oranges.'

'Unfortunately, I'm not growing them right now.' She furrowed her brow. 'It would take me three months to get a crop going, but by then, you'll be gone. The Friedmans down the road might be growing them, so maybe I can arrange a trade. In the meantime, how about a peach?'

'I'm really not hungry,' I said. 'Thank you for the offer. I've been travelling a long time. Would you mind showing me to my room?'

Ms Rothschild barked at her ex-husband to get my suitcase. She linked her arm through mine. 'How good are you with stairs?'

'Not great.'

'Charlie said that might be the case. I have a room for you

on the ground floor. It's my favourite bedroom and it looks out on the deck.'

She led me into the bedroom, which had a wide wooden bed with a white cotton cover on it. 'Wait,' I said. 'Is this your room?' It looked suspiciously like a master bedroom.

'This summer, it's yours,' she said.

'Are you sure? I don't want to take your bedroom. Mr Delacroix said something about a spare room.'

'The bed's too big for me anyway. I'm sleeping alone these days and probably indefinitely. When your sister comes, she can share the room with you, if she likes. It's big enough. Or she can take a different one upstairs.'

She kissed me on the cheek. 'Tell me if I can get you anything,' she said. 'I am glad you've come. The farm likes visitors, and so do I.'

The next day, Mr Delacroix left for the city, and my sister arrived.

My sister was not alone, though I suppose this should not have come as a surprise.

'Win,' I said. 'They didn't say you were coming.' I was sitting at the kitchen table. I did not get up. I didn't want to have to walk in front of him.

'I wanted to come,' he said. 'I've always liked this house, and the summer programme I was supposed to go to didn't end up working out. Natty said she was coming, so I thought I'd make the trip with her.'

Natty hugged me. 'You look awful, but at the same time, you look so much better,' she said. 'Both awful and better.'

'A mixed review,' I said.

'Show me where the bedroom is. Win's mom said we could share. It will be like when we were little.' Win was still watching us, and I didn't want to have to rise from the table in front of him. I didn't want him to feel sorry for me, I guess. 'Win can show you,' I said. 'It's the master. I'll be along in a minute. I want to finish my water.'

Natty considered me. 'Win,' she said, 'could you leave Annie and me alone for a second?'

Win nodded. 'Nice seeing you, Annie,' he said casually as he left.

She lowered her voice. 'Something is wrong. What is it?'

'Well, I move like an old woman and it's actually kind of hard for me to get up from this chair without my cane, which I left over there.' I pointed to the cupboard. 'And I get . . . well . . . well, I get embarrassed.'

'Annie,' she said, 'you're being silly.' She took two graceful, easy steps, grabbed the cane, and handed it to me.

She offered me her arm, and I awkwardly shuffled to my feet.

'Isn't this place beautiful?' she said rapturously. 'I'm so glad to be here. Isn't Win's mom so pretty and nice? She looks like him, no? Aren't we lucky?'

'Natty, you shouldn't have invited Win.'

She shrugged. 'It's his mother's house. Of course he was going to come. Besides, it was his father who invited him, not me, so I assumed it was fine with you. Aren't you two thick as thieves now?'

Mr Delacroix, I thought, *et tu, Brute*?

223

'Win already knew I was coming, and he asked me if *I* wanted to travel with *him*, not the other way around.' She paused to look at me. 'Seeing him won't be awful for you, will it?'

'No, of course not. It'll be fine. You're right. I don't know what my problem was back there. I suppose I was surprised. The truth is, he's like a different person and so am I. And those new people don't even know each other.'

'So no chance that you'll try to rekindle the romance? It is very romantic here.'

'No, Natty. All that is done. And I have no interest in romance with anyone at the moment. Possibly ever.'

She looked like she wanted to say something more, but she bit her tongue.

We ate dinner on the porch, though I was still not hungry. Despite what I had said to Natty, I felt angry at Mr Delacroix for inviting me, angry at Win for coming, and angry at Natty for not knowing enough to tell Win to stay in Boston. I excused myself before dessert, which was peach cobbler, and went to bed.

As would become my custom, I woke at dawn to drag myself around the farm. I knew I needed to exercise, but I didn't want anyone to watch me. Then I limped over to a deckchair and lay down with a book.

Every day, Win and Natty went on excursions, like kayaking, trips to the farmers' market, and horseback riding. They tried to include me, but I resisted activities.

One afternoon, they came home with a carton of strawberries from a nearby farm. 'We picked these for you,' Natty said. Her cheeks were ruddy, and her long black hair was so shiny and glossy that I thought I could practically use it as a mirror. The truth was, I couldn't remember her ever having been prettier. Her prettiness struck me as aggressive and almost offensive. It was a reminder of how *not pretty* I looked at that moment.

'I'm not hungry,' I said.

'You always say that,' Natty said, popping one into her mouth. 'I'll leave them for you then.' She set them on the table next to my chair. 'Can we get you anything else?'

'I'm fine.'

She sighed and looked as if she might argue with me. 'You should eat,' she said. 'You won't get well if you don't eat.'

I picked up my book.

Later that afternoon, just before sunset, Win returned to the deck. He took the carton of strawberries, which I had not touched. We had not spoken much since he'd arrived. I didn't think he was avoiding me, but I really was awful company and I did nothing to encourage conversation. 'Hey,' he said.

I nodded.

He was wearing a white shirt. He rolled up the sleeves. He took a single, perfect red strawberry from the carton. He carefully removed its leafy crown. He got down on one knee by my chair. He placed the strawberry in the centre of the palm of his hand, and without looking at me, he held out his hand to me, as if I were an old dog that might turn on him. 'Please, Annie, have this one,' he said in a soft, pleading tone.

'Oh, Win,' I said, trying to keep my voice light. 'I'm fine. Really, I'm fine.'

'Just the one,' he implored. 'For old times' sake. I know you aren't mine and I'm not yours, so I probably don't have a right to ask you to do anything. But I hate seeing you so frail.'

This might have hurt my feelings, but it was said in an incredibly kind way. Besides, I knew how I looked. I was bones and messy hair and scars. I wasn't trying to starve myself in some dramatic fashion. I was tired and I hurt and that took up the time I used to devote to feeding myself. 'Do you truly think that one strawberry will make a difference?'

'I don't know. I hope so.'

I leaned my head down and took the strawberry from his hand. For a fraction of a second, I let my lips rest on his palm. I took the strawberry in my mouth. The flavour was sweet, but delicate and strange, wild and a bit tart.

He took his hand back and closed it with resolve. A second later, he left without another word.

I picked up the carton, and I ate another strawberry.

The next afternoon, he brought me an orange. He peeled it and offered me a single section in the same way he had offered me that strawberry. He set the rest of the orange on the table and then he left.

And the afternoon after that, he brought me a kiwi. He took out a knife and removed its skin. He cut it into seven even slices and set a single one on his hand.

'Wherever did you get a kiwi?' I asked.

'I have my ways,' he said.

And then he brought me an enormous peach – pinkish orange and perfect, without a single bruise. He took a knife from his pocket. He was about to cut it, but I put my hand on his. 'I think I'll eat the whole peach, but promise not to watch me. I can tell it's going to be messy.'

'As you wish,' he said. He took out his book, and he began to read.

The juice ran down my chin and hands, as I had expected. The peach was pulpy and so good I almost felt emotional as I ate it. I laughed for what felt like the first time in months. 'I'm so dirty,' I said.

He took his handkerchief from his pocket and handed it to me.

'Was this from your mother's orchard?'

'Yes, it seemed a particularly good peach, so I saved it for you. But as for the rest, I take Natty, and we trade my mother's crops at the other farms.'

'I didn't know this many kinds of fruit could grow in the same season?'

'See for yourself. You could come with us,' he said. 'It would mean leaving this chair, though.'

'I am attached to this chair, Win. We have a relationship.'

'I can see that,' he said. 'But Natty and I wouldn't mind having your company if the chair could spare you. Your sister is worried about you.'

'I don't want anyone to worry about me.'

227

'She thinks you are depressed. You don't eat. You don't much want to go anywhere. You are so quiet. And of course there's the matter of this chair.'

'Why doesn't she say this to me herself?'

'You're not the easiest person in the world to talk to.'

'What do you mean? I'm easy to talk to.'

'No, you're not. Once upon a time, I was your boyfriend, or have you forgotten?' His hand was hanging over the side of his chair and his fingertips grazed mine. I moved my hand.

Suddenly, he stood and offered me his hand. 'Come with me,' he said. 'I want to show you something.'

'Win, I'd like to but I move pretty slow now.'

'It's summer in upstate New York, Annie. Nothing moves very fast.' He offered me his hand.

I looked at the hand, then I looked at the boy attached to it. I was a bit scared. In those days, I didn't like to go places I hadn't been before.

'You still trust me, don't you?'

I grabbed my cane from under my chair and then I took his hand.

We walked maybe a half-mile, which was a long way when your foot did not move without a reminder.

'Are you sorry you asked me to come with you yet?' I asked.

'No,' he said. 'I am sorry for quite a few things when it comes to you, but not this.'

'Sorry you ever met me, I suppose.'

He did not reply.

I was out of breath. 'Are we almost there?' I asked.

'Only about another five hundred feet. It's in that barn right up there.'

'Is that coffee I smell?'

Indeed, Win had taken me to a coffee speakeasy. On the back counter, an antique espresso machine steamed and chirped, blithely unaware that it was in the process of manufacturing a drug. The top of the machine was a dented copper dome that reminded me of a Russian cathedral. Win ordered me a cup, and then he introduced me to the owner.

'Anya Balanchine?' the owner said. 'Naw, you're too young to be Anya Balanchine. You're a bona fide folk hero. When are you going to do for coffee what you did for chocolate?'

'Well, I—'

'I'd like to stop running my coffee shop from a barn someday. Free coffee for Anya Balanchine. Hey, Win, how's your dad?'

'He's running for mayor.'

'Give him my regards, would you?'

Win said he would, and the owner led us over to a wrought-iron table for two by the window.

'People are impressed with you in these parts,' Win said.

'Listen, Win, I'm sorry if I've ruined your vacation. I didn't know you'd be here. Your dad said you'd only be staying for a couple of days in August.'

Win shook his head, then stirred cream into his espresso. 'I'm glad to see you,' he said. 'I hope I'm a little helpful to you.'

'You are helpful to me,' I said after a while. 'You have always been helpful to me.'

'If you wanted more, all you would have to do is ask.'

I changed the subject. 'You are a senior next year, and then medical school?'

'Yes.'

'So you must have taken pre-med. What's my prognosis?'

'I'm not a doctor yet, Anya.'

'But looking at me, what do you think? I would like an honest opinion of what a person sees when he or she looks at me.'

'I think you look as if you've been through something unimaginably terrible,' he said finally. 'However, I suspect if I met you today, if I were walking into this coffee shop, having never seen you before, I'd walk across this room and if no one was sitting across from you and maybe even if someone was, I'd take off my hat and I'd offer to buy you a cup of coffee.'

'And then you'd meet me, and you'd find out bad things about me, and you'd probably walk right out the door.'

'What things could I possibly find out?'

I looked at him. '*You know*. Stuff that sends a nice boy in a hat careening off in the opposite direction.'

'Maybe, maybe not. I'm still stupid when it comes to dark-haired, green-eyed girls.'

On the way back, it began to rain. It was difficult to manoeuvre my cane on the moist and loamy ground. 'Lean into me,' he said. 'I won't let you fall.'

The next day, I went back out to the deck. I had found an old copy of *Sense and Sensibility* on the bookshelf in the office, and I had decided to read it.

'You read a lot these days,' Win said.

'I've taken it up now that I'm a shut-in.'

'Well, I won't interrupt you,' he said.

He lay down on the chair next to mine and picked up his book.

His presence distracted me from my reading. 'How is school?' I said.

'You always ask that. We spoke of it yesterday.'

'I'm interested. I didn't get to go to college.'

'You could still go.' He put his hand over my face to shield it from the sun. 'You should get a sun hat, by the way.'

'It seems too late for that.'

'Which? College or sun hats?'

'Both. I meant college, though I've never been a hat person,' I said.

He took off his own hat and set it on my head. 'I've never known a girl who needed a hat more. Why wouldn't you want an added layer of protection from the sun and everything else? By the way, you're only twenty.'

'Twenty-one next month.'

'People go to college at different times,' Win said. 'You have the money.'

I looked at Win. 'I'm a shadow crime boss. I run nightclubs. I don't see college in my future.'

'As you like, Anya.' He set down his book. '*No*. Do you know what your problem is?'

'I suppose you are going to tell me.'

'You have always been far too fatalistic. I've wanted to say that to you for the longest time.'

'Why didn't you? Get it off your chest. It isn't good to keep your feelings inside, I should know.'

'When I was your boyfriend, I had an interest in avoiding conflict.'

'So you let me think I was right?' I said. 'The whole time we were together?'

'Not the whole time. Sometimes.'

'Until that last time, and then you were out the door.' I tried to make this a joke. 'For a couple of days, I thought you might come back.'

'So did I. But I was so angry with you. Besides, wouldn't you have hated me if I had come back? That's what I told myself. If I relent, she won't love me anyway. So better to have some dignity.'

'High-school relationships aren't meant to last forever,' I said. 'It seems like we're talking about other people. I don't even feel sad anymore when I think of it.'

'Aren't you the most fantastically evolved young adult on this deck?' He picked up his old paperback book.

'What are you reading anyway?' I asked.

He held up the book.

'*The Godfather*,' I read.

'Yes, it's about an organized-crime family. I should have read it years ago.'

'Are you learning about me?'

'Indeed,' he said with mirth in his voice. 'I finally understand you.'

'So?'

'You had to open that club and you had to do everything

you could to make it succeed. All that had been decided long before I ever met you.'

In August, the weather turned miserable. I could not wear my long dresses and sweaters anymore, which meant showing more of my skin than I was comfortable with. Win's mother suggested that we go swimming in the river. She insisted that swimming would be good for my recovery. She was probably right, but I didn't know how to swim. I had been born in New York City in 2066, the summer the pools had been drained to conserve water. 'Win could teach you,' Ms Rothschild said. 'He's an excellent swimmer.'

Win gave his mother a look that was a pretty close approximation to what I was feeling about the idea of him teaching me to swim.

'Jane, I would rather not,' he said.

Ms Rothschild shook her head at her son. 'I don't like it when you call me Jane. I'm not clueless, Win. I know the two of you were romantic once, but what difference does that make? Anya should learn to swim while she is here. It will be good for her.'

'I don't know,' I said. 'I don't even have a swimsuit.' I had never needed one.

'You'll borrow one of mine,' she said.

In my room, I put on her swimsuit, which hung on me. The swimsuit was pretty modest in cut, though I still felt incredibly exposed. I threw on a T-shirt, but you could still see a bit of the scar that was below my collarbone.

If Win noticed it, he did not say.

Not that he would have. The boy had always had manners.

When I got into the water, he didn't say much actually. He told me to get on my stomach. He held me up. He demonstrated how to kick and how to move my arms. It took me no time to catch on. I was good at swimming, which was easy compared to walking.

'It's too bad they didn't have a swim team at Trinity,' I said. 'Maybe I should say it's too bad there weren't any pools in New York City.'

'Maybe your whole life would have been different.'

'I would have been a jock,' I said.

'I can see that. The famous Balanchine aggression would have been useful in athletic competition.'

'Right. I wouldn't have dumped that lasagne on Gable Arsley's head. I would have had productive channels for my anger.'

'But if you hadn't dumped that lasagne on Gable's head, how would I have known where to come and meet you?'

I swam a bit away from the deck. After a minute, he swam after me. 'Not so fast,' he said. 'You're still a beginner.'

He grabbed my arm and pulled me to him so that we were facing each other in the water.

'Sometimes,' he said, 'I think my mother is as manipulative as my father.'

'What do you mean?'

'My mother, with her absurd and transparent notion that I should teach you to swim. And my father . . . I think he has the idea that if he can get us back together, then he'll have redeemed himself for 2082.'

'Ridiculous man,' I said. 'It was really 2082 and 2083.'

'But one must ask the question: Is the only reason that stupid boy ever liked you because his ambitious father objected? Isn't that what you always told me? My point is, maybe Dad's plan is faulty. Because maybe those cute young people need obstacles, you and me. Maybe once the star-crossed become unstar-crossed, Romeo gets bored with Juliet.'

'Well, there are still a few obstacles,' I said. 'I was married, and no matter how you look at it, it was basically a marriage of convenience.'

'You're saying I should consider the fact that you are a person of low morals, ethics, and character to be an impediment.'

'Yes, that is what I'm saying.'

He shrugged. 'I knew that about you a long time ago.'

'And I killed someone. In self-defence, but still. And my body is broken. I'm pretty much like a fifty-year-old woman. I move about as fast as my nana.'

'You look OK,' he said. He tucked a curl behind my ear.

'And the timing is wrong. I want to come to you when I am strong and beautiful and successful.'

'Do you want me to say that you are all those things still, or will you roll your pretty green eyes at me?'

'I *will* roll my eyes at you. I have a mirror, Win, though I try to avoid it.'

'From where I am, the view is not that bad.'

'You haven't seen me naked,' I said.

He cleared his throat. 'I'm not sure how to respond to that.'

'Well, it wasn't an invitation, if that's what you're thinking. It was reportage.'

'I'm' – he cleared his throat again – 'I'm sure it's not so bad.'

'Come closer,' I said. I thought I'd settle the matter. I lowered the scoop neck of my T-shirt to show him the large, bumpy pink scar from my heart surgery and the one from where the sword had gone all the way through.

His eyes grew wide and he inhaled sharply. 'It is a bad scar,' he said in a subdued voice. He put his hand on the scar that ran below my collarbone, which was dangerously close to my breast. 'Did it hurt?'

'Like crazy,' I said. He closed his eyes and looked like he might kiss me. I pulled my T-shirt back up. I swam over to the dock, my heart beating just short of an attack, and I climbed up the ladder as quickly as I could.

XXII

I BID FAREWELL TO SUMMER IN A SERIES OF UNCOMFORTABLY EMOTIONAL VIGNETTES

'I HATE WHEN SUMMER ENDS,' Ms Rothschild said, waving her hand in front of her face. I had found her crying in the farm's library. 'Don't mind me, though. Come sit for a spell.' She patted the place on the couch next to her. I returned *Persuasion* to the shelf – I'd worked my way through all of Jane Austen that summer – and then I sat down. Ms Rothschild put her arm around my shoulders. 'It has been a good summer, hasn't it? You look a tiny bit plumper and rosier, I think.'

'I feel better,' I said.

'I am glad to hear it. I hope you have been happy here. It has been delightful having you and your sister. Please come back anytime. I am thankful to my ex-husband for thinking of it. I always liked you, you know, even when Charlie was so dead set against the match with Win. We argued about it quite a bit back then. He insisted it was just a high-school romance, and I said, no, that girl is special. But these many years later, Mr Delacroix has come to the opinion that I was right, which he always does, by the way, and I know we both have had our fingers crossed that you and Win might find your way back together.'

'It's not to be.'

'May I ask why, Anya?'

'Well . . . I was widowed less than a year ago, and I was so badly hurt. It's hard to imagine a relationship with anyone until I feel more like myself. And, the truth is, romantically, I question a lot of the choices I've made. I've made so many mistakes while thinking I was doing exactly the right thing. I think I need a break from relationships.'

'That is probably sensible,' Ms Rothschild said after a pause.

'Besides, I think what Win truly feels toward me is nostalgia, and he is good to me because of our shared past,' I said. 'You raised the world's most decent boy, so congratulations for that.'

'I had help,' she said. 'Win forgets, but Charlie was a pretty good father most of the time, too.'

'I can believe that,' I said.

'Can you? Most people look at me like I'm insane when I defend that man . . .' She shook her head. 'Do you know what? I am done listing Charles Delacroix's attributes. I've been defending him nearly my whole life. To my friends. To my parents. To our son. I am done.'

'We spoke of you quite often in Japan. He still loves you, you know.'

'Yes, but that isn't enough. I've been disappointed in him for twenty-five years. I am finally done with that, too,' she said.

'I think Mr Delacroix has changed.'

'But then the election will happen and he'll go right back to the way he was before.' She nodded to herself, then she took out her phone. 'Have you ever seen a picture of Win's sister?'

I shook my head and looked at the screen. She had light brown, wavy hair, and blue eyes like Win's. In the photo, she was rolling those eyes. Aside from the expression, I didn't see a resemblance.

'The problem with meeting new people is not that you might not like them, but that you will like them too much. Now that I know you, I'll worry about you in the city, Anya,' Ms Rothschild said. She clasped my hand in hers.

'I've been on my own for years. I'll be fine.'

She looked at me, then she brushed my hair away from my forehead. 'I'm certain you will be.'

When I went back to our room, Natty wasn't there so I went outside to look for her. I found her crying in the gazebo. 'Please, Anya, leave me alone.'

'What is it, Natty? What has happened?'

'I love him,' she said.

'You love who?' I asked.

'Who do you think?' She paused. 'Win. Of course, Win.'

I considered this information. 'I knew you had a crush on him when you were a child, but I had no idea you still did.'

'He is so good, Annie. Look how he has been this summer, trying to make you feel better, even after so much time has passed.' She sighed. 'He still sees me like a kid, though.'

'How do you know? Have you spoken to him?'

'I've more than spoken to him. I tried to kiss him.'

'Natty!'

'We were picking apples for his mother. The first ones are starting to come in. And he looked so handsome, standing there in his blue-checked shirt. I'm sick with loving him,' she said.

'Natty, I had no idea you felt this way.'

'How could you not know? I've loved him since I was twelve. Since the moment we met him in Headmaster's office.'

'What did he do when you tried to kiss him?'

'He pushed me away, and said he didn't think of me like that. And I said I was seventeen, and that was hardly a child. And he said in fact it was. And I said you met Anya when you were sixteen. And he said that was different because he'd been young then, too. And then he said that he loved me like a friend and like a brother and that he would always be there for me. But then I pushed him away. I told him I didn't want to be loved that way. I can't even stand to look at him anymore.'

She sobbed with her entire body – her shoulders, her stomach, her mouth, and all her other parts were aligned in a unified display of misery.

'Oh, Natty, please don't cry.'

'Why shouldn't I? I told him what you said at the beginning of the summer. I told him that you said that you would never get back together with him, but I think maybe he still has hope. Maybe if he knew there wasn't any hope, he could love me instead. We're not so different.'

'My darling Natty, would you honestly want some boy to love you because he thought you were like me?'

'I don't care why. I wouldn't even care! That's how much I love him.'

'I don't think Win thinks that we're getting back together. But do you want me to try to talk to him?' I wanted her happiness more than my own.

'Would you?' Those eyes were wet and hopeful.

'I will make sure he understands,' I said. 'And before summer is over, too.'

After dinner, I asked Win if he would go on a walk with me.

We wandered into the orchard, where the last peaches of summer were dropping from the trees. Win found one still on the branch and picked it. His torso was long and lean as he extended his arm to reach it. He offered me the peach, but I declined.

'I want to talk to you about something,' I said.

'What is it?' He took a bite of the peach.

'My sister,' I said.

'Yes, I thought that subject might come up.'

'She has the idea that if you knew that I didn't think we were ever getting back together that you might be more open to . . . I'm sorry, this is awkward.'

'Perhaps I can help. She thinks that the reason I don't want to start a relationship with her is because I still have feelings for you. And to answer your query, she's wrong. I think she's smart and adorable and everything a girl should be, but even if there were no Anya, Natty would not be for me.

241

Are you sure you don't want a peach? They're very sweet this time of year.'

'Then why have you spent so much time with her? You can understand why she might have gotten the wrong idea.'

'Because you asked me to. Or have you forgotten that you did? Three years ago, you dispatched me to Sacred Heart.'

'Win.'

'I did it because it was something I could do for you. You so rarely, even when we were dating, asked me for help. Even though our relationship had ended badly, I was happy to do something for you.'

'Why are you so good?'

'Because I have nice parents, who loved me as best they could. That's probably why.'

'Even your dad.'

'Yes, even my father. He wants to do big things, like you, and that isn't easy. He did his best. I'm older now, and I see that. He was adamant that I come stay here for the summer, by the way.'

'What do you mean?'

'He said that you had been very injured and that you and your sister would be staying at the house. He said that he had grown very fond of you and wanted you to spend your summer among young people and friends. I, in his estimation, was both.'

'He told me with absolute authority that you wouldn't be here. Do you know that?'

'That's Dad.'

'I almost wish I could love your sister,' Win said. 'She

242

looks like you, except she's taller and her hair is straighter. She's less moody than you, and pretty good company, too. But even if she weren't seventeen years old, I couldn't. She is not you.

'But back to what you should tell Natty,' he said. 'You may tell her that I feel bad if she misunderstood what my feelings were for her. I understand how she may have been misled. Though I never thought of her as anything but a friend, I loved her in her sister's place for three years. I was eager to see her above anyone else because I wanted to hear all her sister's news.

'You may tell her that I was already aware, even before I got on the train to Niskayuna, that there was very little chance of her sister and me getting back together. I know that her sister is too stubborn and probably won't ever forgive me for not supporting her when the club was opening. I know her sister sees impediments that don't exist, like the fact that she has been through some physical traumas. I wish her sister knew how much I admired her, how much I regret not standing by her, how much I could love her still if someday, when she is feeling herself again, she might let me. You may tell her that when it comes to her sister, I have not much in the way of self-preservation instincts or dignity. She could marry ten other men, and it wouldn't matter.'

'You shouldn't wait for me, Win. I can't right now. I wish I could, but I can't. I'm sorry.'

I did not expect him to smile at me, but that is what he did. He smiled at me and he wiped a tear from my cheek. 'I thought you might say that. So here's the deal and it's a very simple

243

one. I will love you forever. And in return, you can decide if you want to do anything with that love at some point down the road. But know there is no other girl for me but you. Not your sister. Or anyone else. My lot is to be the boy who loves Anya Balanchine. I made the wrong choice once upon a time and I think I've paid for it.' He took my chin in his hand. 'And the good thing about my not being your boyfriend or your husband is that you don't get to tell me what to do,' he said. 'So I will wait, because I would rather wait for you than waste my time with someone who isn't you. And I will focus on the long game. As they say in baseball, losing game one and even game two is no reason to give up on the whole series. When you're ready, if you're ever ready, give me the word.'

I looked at the peaches dying on the orchard ground. I watched the sun as it set. I saw the river streaming past. I heard him breathing, softly, and felt my own heart beating, beating. The world became still, and I tried to picture myself in the future. In the future, I was strong and I could run again and I was alone. 'What's the word?' I said softly. 'In case I am ever ready. You know I'm not good with these things. What do I say?'

'I'll make it easy for you, then. All you have to do is tell me to walk you home.'

As the planning for his mayoral campaign had kept him in the city, Mr Delacroix had been around only intermittently that summer. He came back the day before Natty and I were to leave to help Win's mother close up the house. I had gone to pick a bag of apples to bring back to the city, and I was taking them into the house when I saw him crossing the lawn toward me.

'You're looking awfully robust,' he said. 'I am feeling pleased with myself for having sent you here.'

'You are always pleased with yourself,' I said.

We went to sit on the deck. He took out the chess set and arranged it on the table.

'Win is gone, I see,' he said.

'Yes.'

'My plan was a complete failure, then?'

I didn't reply.

'Well, I cannot be blamed. I've never tried to play matchmaker before.'

'What a strange man you are. You break something up only to try to put it back together years later.'

'I love my son,' Mr Delacroix said. 'I suspected he hadn't quite gotten over you, and so I tried to contrive a meeting. I thought your heart might be open to a reunion and that such a reunion might lead to a spot of joy for you. You have had a hard time these years, and it pleased me to imagine that you might be happy for a time. And, as I am not a perfect man, I did not mind the thought of perhaps a little redemption for me.'

I moved my castle. 'I don't know how you ever thought that would work. No one likes being set up by his father. Even if I was gullible enough to believe your lies, Win knew what you were up to from the beginning.'

He positioned his king away from my queen.

I was about to move my queen closer but then I stopped.

'Honestly, *a few days in August*? You might have run the plan by me. If this were business, I'd fire you. I don't like being set up.'

'Point taken. I am good at plotting, but it is easier to deal with pawns and politicians than human hearts, I am afraid. I see right through you. You are stalling for time. Move, Anya.'

I left my queen where she was and used my pawn to block his other bishop.

'It was a nice plan,' I said, 'but I think I am too different from when I was in high school.'

'I don't know about that,' he said.

I decided to change the subject. 'When I get back to the city, I've been thinking about looking into producing a line of Dark Room cacao "candy" bars. A bar that people could take home instead of eating at the club. Cacao for shut-ins like myself. There's still money to be made in chocolate bars, I'd say.'

'It's an interesting notion.' He advanced his queen and then he looked at me. 'Anya, I have something I need to say to you. I imagine you already know what it is. The mayoral campaign means that I will have to step down from the Dark Room. I can help you hire a different lawyer—'

'No, it's fine,' I said coldly. 'I will look for one as soon as I am back in the city.'

'I can make recommendations—'

'I am capable of finding a lawyer, Mr Delacroix. I found you, didn't I? I have known lawyers my whole life. The kind of life I've led has made me an expert in such arrangements.'

'Anya, are you angry at me? You must have known this day would come.'

The truth was, I had grown very attached to him. I would miss him, but it was too hard to say. I had worked steadfastly to never need anyone my whole life.

'We will see each other,' he said. 'I'd even hoped you would be involved in the campaign.'

'Why would you want someone like me involved?' I asked. Yes, I was pouting.

'Listen, stop being foolish, Anya. If there's anything you ever need, I will provide it, assuming it's within my ability to do so. Do you know what I'm saying?'

'Good luck, colleague,' I said. I got up and left. I was not very fast though, and he might have caught up with me if he'd wanted to.

I was almost to my room, which I would soon surrender to summer, to the past. As I set my hand on the knob, I wondered what was wrong with me that I could not say to him, *Thank you and good luck with the campaign.*

I felt a hand on my shoulder. 'Don't go this way,' Mr Delacroix said. 'I know exactly what you are thinking. I know you so well. I know exactly what thoughts turn behind that opaque visage of yours. You have been abandoned so many times. You think if our business relationship ends, that we will not be in each other's lives anymore. But we will. You are my friend. You are as dear to me as my own flesh and blood, and as improbable as this is, I love you like my daughter. So good luck, *colleague*, if that's what it must be,' he said. He hugged me hard. 'And please be well.'

The next day, Natty and I went to the train station.

'I'm still so embarrassed,' she said. I had conveyed Win's message, leaving out the parts where he said he still loved me.

'Don't be,' I said. 'I'm sure he understands.'

'Do you love him?' she asked me after a while. 'I know you said you didn't, but do you?'

'I don't know.'

'Well, I couldn't sleep last night. The more I thought about it, the more I started to realize that what I had thought was his love for me was, in fact, love for you. And my face grew hot and I started to sweat and I was so mortified I wanted to physically leave my body. I started to think of the day I told him how worried I was about you not eating – you are still scrawny – but that it was hard to deal with you because you are stoic, and you won't ask for help or even admit when you are in pain and you are used to being strong and caring for everyone else. And he said he would try to get you to eat something, if I wanted. I told him I'd be grateful to him for trying, but that I doubted he would have much luck. I went back to the room, and I could see the two of you on the deck. I watched him take that crown of leaves off the berry, and I watched him get down on his knees, and I watched him hold out his hand to you, and I watched you. I watched you take that berry from him. And he looked incredibly sweet in that moment. How could I not love him? He was so good to my poor sister, who he had not even been with for three years. And I thought he was doing that for me, but now I know better: it was for you.' She shook her head.

'I'm a smart person, but what a fool I've been,' she said.

'Natty,' I said.

'You say you don't love him anymore, but maybe you are lying to yourself. That boy, our Win, took off the leaves for you. If that's not an act of love, I honestly don't know what is.

'I had a glimpse into my future this morning, Annie. Would you like to know what I saw?'

'I'm not sure.' Natty's visions had often involved my untimely death.

'Maybe it's Thanksgiving,' she said. 'Win is there and you are there and the three of us are having a good laugh over the fact that one summer Natty the genius let herself fall in love with Win even though it was obvious to everyone how much he still loved Anya. *It. Was. So. Obvious*. And I don't even feel embarrassed anymore, because it's the future and I am fantastic.'

'I love you better than anyone in the world,' I told her.

'Don't you think I know that?' she asked.

They announced the train for Boston. 'Have a good semester,' I said.

'Call me every day, Argon,' Natty said.

XXIV

I HAVE THOUGHTS ON THE TRAIN
BACK TO NEW YORK; ON LOVE

IT TAKES NOTHING, save a spot of courage, to kiss a pretty teenager at a high school dance.

It takes nothing to say you love a person when she is perfect and her mistakes can be dealt with in a ten-minute confession.

Love was a boy getting down on one knee, not to ask her to marry him, but to beg a damaged girl to eat a berry: *Please, Annie, have this one.*

Love was the way he had removed the leaves from that berry, the way he had held his palm to me and bowed his head. Love was the humility of those gestures.

Love came three years after he had walked away, and it felt as palpable to me as that strawberry in his hand.

My sister was the romantic; I did not believe in that kind of love.

Sometimes, this good old world does not much care what you believe.

(NB: I knew this, but I was not yet ready to take that walk with him.)

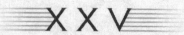

I RETURN TO WORK; AM SURPRISED BY MY BROTHER; BECOME A GODMOTHER AGAIN!

THE BEGINNING OF SEPTEMBER was always a wretched time in New York – summer is over, but the weather hasn't caught on. Still, I was glad to be restored to my life and to be in the city, even if I navigated it at a more deliberate pace than I once had.

At long last, I went to get my hair cut. Bangs seemed like a good idea, and so I got them. Probably a mistake considering the shape of my face and texture of my hair, though no worse a mistake than marrying Yuji Ono in 2086 or taking up with the DA's son back in 2082. In any case, I did not cry. *(NB: This, dear reader, is what is known as perspective.)*

Scarlet and Felix had moved to a place of their own downtown. She'd left her job at the club and she was making a living from acting in the theatre. She was playing Juliet in *Romeo and Juliet*. I made it back to New York in time to see the closing night of the show.

Afterward, I met her in her dressing room, which had a

star on it. That star filled me with something I can only describe as joy. Scarlet burst into tears when she saw me. 'OMG, I'm sorry I couldn't go to Japan or upstate, but between Felix and the play, I haven't been able to leave town.'

'It's fine. I'm sorry I've been such a neglectful godmother. Plus, I wasn't really up for company. You were wonderful, by the way. I didn't like Juliet when we read the play in school, but you made me like her for some reason. You played her so determined and focused.'

Scarlet laughed though I wasn't sure I'd said anything funny. She took off her wig, which was long, black, and curly.

'For a second there, we could have almost been mistaken for sisters,' I said.

'I think that every night. Let's go to dinner,' she said. 'And then you can spend the night at my place and see Felix in the morning.'

'I doubt he'll even remember me. It's been so long.'

'Oh, I don't know. You send presents so that probably will help jog his memory.'

At dinner, we ordered too much food and talked about everything. I hadn't seen her in so long, and I'd missed her more than I even thought was possible.

'It's like we haven't even been apart,' she said.

'I know.'

'Do you know what you said before about me playing Juliet "determined and focused"? I have a secret about that.'

'Oh?'

'The day of the audition, I was thinking of you and wishing

I could go to Japan to see you,' Scarlet said. 'And then I started to remember you in high school. I knew other girls at the audition would be playing Juliet romantic and dreamy, but I thought, wouldn't it be cool to play her like Anya? So I imagined that Juliet hated being star-crossed. I imagined she would have preferred not to have met Romeo, that it was completely inconvenient for her to like someone whose parents her parents didn't get along with. And I imagined that Juliet wished she was into Paris, because he was the boy that wouldn't cause her any problems.'

'I thought I liked your Juliet for some reason,' I said.

'The director thought my take was unique, so I guess you could say my choice to play you worked out well. The reviews have been nice, too. Not that those matter. But it's better than bad ones.'

'Congratulations,' I said. 'I mean it. And I'm flattered for any small part I might have had in it.'

'The only thing I have trouble with is the end, because I know you would never plunge a dagger into your chest, no matter how bleak the plot.'

'Probably not.' Someone else's chest maybe.

'Let's get dessert, OK? I don't want to go home yet. The truth about Romeo and Juliet,' Scarlet said, 'is that they lack perspective. That's what I think. She's so young, and he's not much older. And what they don't know is that sometimes life works itself out, if given a little time. Everyone's parents cool off. And once that happened, that's when they'd know if they were truly in love.'

My cheeks grew warm. I suddenly felt like we weren't

talking about the play anymore. 'To whom have you been speaking?'

'*To whom* do you think? You don't imagine I could play Juliet without asking Romeo a couple of questions first?' Scarlet asked.

'We aren't together yet, Scarlet.'

'But you will be,' she said. 'I know it. I've known it all along.'

The club's expansion had continued without me. There were decisions I might not have approved (locations I did not agree with, hires I might not have made), but I was almost disappointed to note how little an effect my absence had left. Theo said it was testimony to what a good infrastructure I had built that the business had run so smoothly without me. As that sentiment will no doubt indicate, he wasn't angry with me anymore. He had a girlfriend – Lucy, the mixologist. They seemed happy, but what did I know of happiness? I suppose what I mean is that he seemed charmed by that woman and also to have forgotten that he had ever loved me at all.

Mouse had heard very little from the Russians. Perhaps killing Fats had been enough of a statement or perhaps it was out of respect for my incapacitation or perhaps they had other problems with which to deal or perhaps the thought of taking on two crime families at once was too much for them (as Yuji had hoped). We made plans to begin production and distribution of our own line of cacao 'candy' bars.

I flew around the country to check the progress on our other locations. My final stop was in San Francisco to see Leo and Noriko. I had not seen my brother since I'd been hurt, and I had even missed the opening of the San Francisco club last October. In its first eleven months of business, receipts had been strong, and we were considering opening a second San Francisco location. By any standard, Leo, Noriko, and Simon Green had been a good team.

Leo held me to him. 'Noriko can't wait to see you, and I can't wait for you to see the club,' he said.

We rode a ferry to an island off the coast of San Francisco. The ferry reminded me a bit of the trip to Liberty, but I tried to push such associations from my mind and enjoy the breeze on my face. This was the new Zen Anya.

We got off the boat and walked up a set of stairs that led to the rocky island. 'What did this place use to be again?' I asked Leo.

'It was a prison,' he said. 'And then a tourist attraction. And now it's a nightclub. So life is funny, right?'

Inside the club, Noriko and Simon were waiting.

'Anya,' Noriko said, 'we are so glad to see that you are well again.'

I wasn't one hundred per cent. I still had a cane and felt I moved at a glacial pace. But I wasn't in much pain anymore, and it wasn't as if I had to go through life in a bathing suit.

Simon shook my hand. 'Let's give her the tour,' he said.

Alcatraz was truly the strangest place for a nightclub. There were private tables in little rooms that used to be jail cells. Silver curtains had been hung over the bars, and the cells were painted bright white. The main bar and the dance floor were in a former prison cafeteria. They'd hung crystal-and-chrome chandeliers from the ceilings, and everything was so gleaming and sparkling that it was easy to forget you were in a former prison. I was beyond impressed with what they had done. Honestly, my hopes had not been particularly high when I'd sent Leo and Noriko to San Francisco. I'd made the decision not from logic but from love and loyalty. I'd thought that maybe in a year I'd have to hire someone new to run or revamp the club. But my brother and his wife had surprised me. I hugged Leo. 'Leo, this is wonderful! Well done, you.'

He gestured toward Simon and Noriko, who were grinning like crazy. 'You really like it?'

'I do. I thought it was weird when I heard that you wanted to open it in a prison, but I decided to wait and see what happened' – and also I'd been sort of totally incapacitated, but that was neither here nor there – 'and what happened is brilliant. You've turned a prison, a dark place, into something fun and cheerful, and I'm so proud of you all. I know I keep saying it. I can't seem to stop.'

'Simon thought it was a good metaphor for what you had done with the first club. Take something illegal and make it legal,' Noriko said.

'From darkness, light,' Simon said shyly. 'Isn't that what they say?'

Leo and I went to lunch by ourselves at a noodle shop back on the mainland. 'I've been thinking of you a lot this past year,' I said to my brother.

'That's nice,' he said.

'Since I was hurt,' I said, 'I've wanted to say I was sorry.'

'Sorry?' Leo asked. 'For what?'

'When you were recovering from your accident, I don't know that I was always as patient with you as I should have been. I didn't understand what it was to be seriously injured or how long it took to get back to normal.'

'Annie,' Leo said, 'don't apologize to me ever. You are the best sister in the world. You've done *everything* for me.'

'I've tried, but . . .'

'No, you have done *everything*. You protected me from the Family. You got me out of the country. You went to jail for me. You trusted me with this job. And that's not counting the little deeds you did for me every day. Do you see my life, Annie? I run a nightclub where I am important and people listen to me! I have a beautiful and smart wife who is going to have a baby! I have friends and love and everything a person could possibly want. I have two great sisters, who have both achieved so much. I am the luckiest person on the whole planet, Annie. And I have the most amazing little sister that anyone ever had.' He grabbed my head with both his hands and kissed me on the forehead. 'Please don't ever doubt it.'

'Leo,' I asked, 'did you say that Noriko is pregnant?'

He put his hand over his mouth. 'We aren't telling people yet. It's only six weeks.'

'I won't let on I know.'

'Darn it,' Leo said. 'She wanted to tell you herself. Noriko's going to ask you to be the godmother.'

'Me?'

'Who else would be a better godmother than you?'

Simon Green saw me to the airport. 'I know our relationship hasn't always been the best – probably most of that's my fault,' I said before we were to part. 'But I truly appreciate what you've done here. Let me know if there's anything I can do for you.'

'Well, I'll be in New York in October,' Simon said. 'My birthday. Maybe we could get together.'

'I'd like that,' I said. I realized that I meant it.

'I've wondered,' he said, 'what's happening with Mr Delacroix's job?'

'Are you interested in it?'

'I love San Francisco, but New York is my home, Anya. Even with the terrible things that happened to me there, nowhere else will ever be home to me.'

'I feel the same way,' I said. I hadn't decided what I wanted to do with Mr Delacroix's job, but I promised Simon Green that I would keep him in mind.

XXVI

I DISCOVER WHERE THE ADULTS ARE KEPT; DEFEND MY OWN HONOUR ONE MORE TIME BEFORE THE END

By October, the weather had cooled in New York, and Japan had begun to seem like a dream. I did not hear from Win, though I'm not sure I expected to. He had said he would wait for me to contact him, and he was keeping his word. I did not talk much to his father either, though I saw him a great deal. His face was on the sides of buses once again.

From my desk at the Dark Room, I could hear what I thought of as the symphony of my club: the blenders whirring, the shoes dancing, and, occasionally, the glasses breaking or the couples fighting. I was thinking how I loved this music more than any other when a siren began to wail.

I rushed out to the hallway. Through a bullhorn, an official-sounding voice announced, 'This is the New York City Police Department. By order of the Department of Health and the laws of the state of New York, the Dark Room will be shut down until further notice. Please proceed in an orderly fashion to the nearest exit. If you have chocolate on your person, please surrender it to the trash cans by the door. Those displaying signs of chocolate intoxication should be prepared to show their prescriptions on their way out. Thank you for your cooperation.'

To get a better sense of what was happening, I pushed my way to the main room of the club. People were flooding out in every direction, and the flow of the crowd ran opposite to where I wanted to be. Peripherally, I saw one policeman checking a woman's prescription, and another putting a man in handcuffs. A woman tripped on her dress and would have been trampled if Jones hadn't helped her up.

I found Theo by the stockroom. He was gesturing wildly at a police officer who was using a dolly to wheel away a sack of cacao.

'You have no business stealing this,' Theo said. 'This is property of the Dark Room.'

'It's evidence,' the police officer said.

'Evidence of what?' Theo countered.

'Theo!' I yelled. 'Stay cool! Let them have it. We can get more cacao once we sort this out. I can't afford for you to be arrested.'

He nodded. 'Should we call Delacroix?' he asked.

I had yet to hire another lawyer, but I didn't think we should call Mr Delacroix. 'No,' I said. 'He doesn't work with us anymore. We'll be fine. I'm going outside to see if I can get some answers from whoever's in charge.'

Jones stood guard near the front. 'Anya, I don't know why,

but the cops have blocked the door from the outside. It's making people panic. You'll have to go around.' I pushed on the door, but it wouldn't budge. I could hear a rhythmic banging coming from the other side. I had counselled Theo to stay cool but I was starting to feel not very cool myself.

I forced my way through the crowd and out the side doors. I ran – or I should say I did what passed for running for me, more like hopping/limping – back around to the front. Police jammed the steps, and reporters had begun to arrive, too. Barricades had been erected. Several wooden boards were being nailed across the front door.

I pulled myself awkwardly over a barricade. A cop tried to stop me, but I was too quick. When I got close enough, I could see a different cop was posting a sign that read: CLOSED UNTIL FURTHER NOTICE.

'What is going on?' I demanded of the man who was nailing my door shut.

'Who are you?'

'I'm Anya Balanchine. This is my place. Why are you closing it?'

'Orders.' He pointed to the sign. 'I'd stay back if I were you, lady.'

I wasn't thinking; I was feeling. My heart was beating in the jaunty, familiar way that let me know I was about to do something stupid. I lunged toward the cop and tried to grab the hammer from his hand. For the record, it is never a great idea to try to grab someone's hammer. The hammer smacked me in the shoulder. It hurt like hell, but I was grateful it wasn't my head and besides, I had gotten quite good at pain management. I stumbled back a few paces, at which point I was immediately pinned to the ground by several police officers.

'You have the right to remain silent . . .' You know the drill.

Wisely, Theo, who had followed me out, did not try to get between the police officers and me. I could see him pulling out his phone.

'Call Simon Green,' I yelled. I had planned to have dinner with him the next evening, and I knew he was already in town.

When you are a minor and you are arrested, they put you in an isolated cell. But now I was a grown woman of twenty-one, which meant I had graduated to the adults' communal holding cell. I kept to myself and tried to determine whether my shoulder was broken. I concluded it wasn't though actually I wasn't even sure if a shoulder could be broken.

I'd been there about an hour when I was summoned to the visiting area.

'That was foolish.' Mr Delacroix glared at me from across the glass.

'I told Theo to call Simon Green,' I said. 'I told him not to bother you. You do not work for me anymore.'

'Fortunately, Theo didn't have Simon's number so he called me. You're bleeding. Show me your shoulder.'

I did. He shook his head, but did not speak. He took out his phone and snapped a picture.

'They want to leave you in here overnight, and I'm not sure it's a bad idea.'

I didn't answer him.

'But luckily for you, I still know a few people. I've woken a judge, and there'll be a bail hearing later tonight, where they will probably set some exorbitant number. You'll happily pay it and then you'll go home.' He looked at me sternly, and I felt sixteen again. 'You always have to go and make matters worse, don't you? Seemed a grand idea to you to assault a police officer, eh?'

'They were shutting down the club! And I didn't assault anyone. I only tried to grab his hammer. What even happened tonight?'

'Someone tipped off the cops that there were people at the Dark Room without prescriptions. They started checking everyone's prescriptions and some people got upset and when people get upset, they get rowdy. The cops began confiscating the cacao, saying the club was dealing chocolate illegally, which, as we know, isn't true.'

'What's the upshot?' I asked.

'The upshot is that the Dark Room is shut down until the city decides what to do.'

I worried how the shutdown could affect our other locations. 'When's that Department of Health hearing?'

'Tomorrow.'

'Why are they suddenly interested in the Dark Room? Why now? We've been open for over three years.'

'I thought about that,' Mr Delacroix said. 'And the answer can only be politics. It's an election year, as you well know. And I think this is a plan to make me look like I was involved in illegal dealings. My campaign is predicated on the idea that bad legislation needs to go, that we change the laws and bring new business to the city. The Dark Room is an accomplishment for me. Shut it down, and it takes away from that.'

'You're wrong, Mr Delacroix. Your accomplishments extend beyond the Dark Room. Maybe it's best to cut ties with me and the club altogether. Say you were only involved in contracts and such. It isn't far from true.'

'Yes, that could be a way to go,' he said.

'Listen, I'm going to bring on Simon Green tomorrow. He's my half-brother, and I trust him. It was foolish of me to put off hiring your replacement. You can't take this on right now. The election is in less than two months. I won't let you take this on.'

'You won't *let* me?'

'I want you to be mayor. And by the way, I am glad to see you.' I leaned casually on the glass. I don't know why, but it was easier to speak from the heart with a six-inch-thick panel of glass between us. 'I am sorry for the way we parted. I've been trying to tell you that for weeks. I just didn't know how.'

'So you thought you'd attack a police officer? There are easier ways to contact me. Pick up the phone. If you were feeling old-fashioned, a slate message.'

'Several times I apologized to your face on the side of a bus.'

'Yes, I don't always get those messages.'

'And also, I'm thankful to you. You owe me nothing, Mr Delacroix. We are even, and I don't expect you to ruin your campaign to try to help me out.'

Mr Delacroix considered this. 'Fine, Anya. There is no point in arguing. But let me hire a lawyer for you. It isn't that

265

I doubt your ability to do it, but you won't have much time before the hearing tomorrow, and Simon Green is too – forgive the pun – *green* for such a responsibility.'

'Simon's not so bad.'

'In a few years, he'll be perfect. And I am glad you've made peace with him, but he doesn't know the ins and outs of how this city is run. You require someone who does.'

I got very little sleep that night, but in the morning, I received a message from Mr Delacroix that the new lawyer would meet me at the Department of Health, where the hearing was to be held.

When I arrived, Mr Delacroix was waiting for me. 'Where is the new lawyer?' I asked.

'I am the new lawyer,' he said. 'I couldn't find anyone on such short notice.'

'Mr Delacroix, you can't do this.'

'I can. And, really, I have to. Look, I've made mistakes. That is no secret. But you can't run a campaign by trying to separate yourself from your accomplishments. Not a successful one, at least. I am proud of the Dark Room. I am going to defend it even if it costs me the campaign. Yes, that's how strongly I feel about this. But listen, you have to hire me again, or I can't defend you.'

'I won't,' I said. 'I'd rather defend myself.'

'Don't be a martyr. Hire me. I am your friend. I want to help and I have the skills to do so.'

'I don't need anyone to rescue me, if that's what you think you are doing.'

'Hiring someone to assist you is not the same as being rescued. I thought we'd settled that years ago. It's plain good sense. We can only do the jobs we can do in this life. What happens here is important and will determine what happens in San Francisco with Leo, and in Japan, Chicago, Seattle, Philadelphia, and everywhere else. We have to go inside in thirty seconds.'

I didn't like being forced to do anything. And I wasn't sure that he was even right.

'Fifteen seconds. One last reason. I am certain that I am the cause of this situation. Do you want my wife to hate me? My son? What good is being mayor if your family hates you? Can I leave the love of my son's life to defend herself?'

'That isn't true, and I'm not even sure it's rel—'

'Five seconds. What say you?'

The hearing was open to the public, and when I got inside, the crowd that had gathered astounded me. Half the city seemed to have taken an interest in this little proceeding. Every seat was filled in the mezzanine and the balcony, and people were standing by the doors. Mouse and people from the Family had come, as had Theo, Simon, and most of my staff from the Manhattan and Brooklyn clubs. In the very back of the mezzanine, I saw Win and Natty. I hadn't even told them about the hearing, but somehow they had gotten here, and quickly. There was a certain amount of press, but most of the crowd consisted of what appeared to be regular people – that is to say, the kind of people who came to my club.

'This is a hearing to discuss the club on Fifth Avenue at

Forty-Second Street in Manhattan County, New York. Today's hearing is largely discovery, and everyone who would like to speak will have a chance. At the end, we will determine whether the Dark Room should be allowed to remain open. This is not a criminal proceeding though in fact a criminal proceeding may follow depending on what is revealed in this forum.' The head of the board read the complaints against the Dark Room and its president, me: essentially that I was serving chocolate illegally, that some patrons at my club were obtaining chocolate without prescriptions, and that cacao was actually chocolate. 'By calling chocolate "cacao", Ms Balanchine, who is the daughter of a deceased organized-crime boss and still maintains connections to that family and other known international crime families, has introduced what is little more than a term of art to shield her criminal dealings. Though the city has chosen to look the other way for some time, it has become increasingly apparent that the Dark Room is a front for illegal activity.'

A chorus of boos from the gallery.

Mr Delacroix spoke first. He offered our legal justification for the business (chocolate was not served at the club, cacao for health benefits was not illegal) and asserted that we were not in violation of any laws or ordinances of the city. 'On a personal note,' Mr Delacroix said, 'I find the timing of this to be suspicious. Why now, after the club has been open for three years, in the middle of a mayoral election? This whole proceeding is offensive. The Dark Room is a credit to this city. It has created hundreds of jobs and brought in innumerable tourists. The entire section of Midtown around the club is reinvigorated. This young woman, whom I have worked with for the past four years, is a credit to this city, too, and should not be subject to persecution because of who her father was.'

I thought Mr Delacroix was being a bit grandiose, but that was his way.

At that point, the hearing was opened to the public for thoughts and opinions. Theo went up to the microphone first. He spoke about the health benefits of cacao, and the ethical way the cacao was grown. Doctor Param, who still worked at the club, spoke of the precautions he and the other doctors took, and then he went off on a rant about the stupidity of the Rimbaud Act. Mouse spoke of the Balanchines' attempts to turn the Family to legal operations, and how I had spearheaded that. Lucy spoke of the standards we had implemented to keep the recipes as healthful as possible. Natty spoke about how hard it had been for me when we were young and how it had always been my dream to legalize chocolate. Scarlet, who was getting to be known as an actress, spoke of the fact that I was godmother to her son, and the most loyal person she knew. Win spoke of the sacrifices I had made for my family and how important the club was to me. And those were the people I knew! Little old ladies spoke about the transformation of the neighbourhood around the club. High-school kids talked about how they liked having somewhere safe to go. It went on for hours. Amazingly, not a single person spoke against the club or me.

'But the connection to organized crime cannot be denied,' one of the board members said. 'Look at who we are talking about. She is an accused poisoner. As a teenager, she went to

Liberty multiple times. She is her father's daughter. I notice that Ms Balanchine has not spoken a word during these proceedings. Perhaps she is worried that, if she speaks, she might impugn herself.'

Mr Delacroix whispered to me, 'You don't have to let yourself be baited. This is going very well. Everything that needs to be said has already been said.'

I am certain it was good advice.

I stood and went up to the podium. 'Yes, it is true. My father was Leonyd Balanchine. He was a mobster and he was a good man. He went to sleep one day, and when he woke up, the business his family was in had become illegal. He spent his whole life trying to figure out how to run a chocolate business legally, but he never could. He died trying. When I became an adult, I took up the cause. I did not have a choice. Mr Chairman, you say that the difference between cacao and chocolate is little more than a "term of art". And I suppose this is true. The fact is, I would not have gone into cacao if not for who my father was, and so the connection to chocolate is there. As much as I have tried to in my life, I cannot escape it. But what I know – what I know in my soul – is that the club is good for New York. We who work there want nothing but the best for the public. We are not motivated by money or the desire to trick the system. We are citizens who want our city to be healthy and safe, to have sensible laws that protect the people. I am a *mafiya* daughter. I am my father's daughter. I am a daughter of New York.'

I was about to sit, but then I decided I had even more to say. 'You shut down the club because you thought there were people in there without prescriptions. Well, I don't know if this is true, but what I do know is that there shouldn't *have to be* prescriptions. The city or this board should grant any establishment that wants to serve cacao a cacao licence, and that should be the end of that. You want less crime? Make it so there are less criminals.'

And then I really was done.

The board voted to allow the Dark Room to remain open: seven yeas, two nays, and two abstentions. There would not be a criminal case brought against me.

I shook Mr Delacroix's hand.

'You ignored my advice,' he said.

'I ignored some of your advice. But thank you anyway for being there to give it.'

'Well, I won't make the mistake of ignoring yours. If I manage to become mayor, I will look into amending the Rimbaud laws in the city.'

'You'd do that for me?'

'I'd do that because it is the right thing to do. Now go celebrate. Your sister and my son are waiting for you.'

'You won't come with us?'

'I wish I could, but the campaign calls.'

I shook his hand again. And he put both his hands around mine. 'This may sound condescending, but you know that I have come to think of you as my daughter. And it is in this context that I find myself wanting to say how very proud I was of you today.' He stood up straight. 'Go have some fun, will you? I am very much rooting for a happy ending when it comes to that loyal boy of mine and you.'

'How sentimental.'

'I am certainly more invested in the outcome of this little high-school romance than I ever thought I would be. But I care about the characters, and forgive me for wanting everything to turn out for the plucky heroine.' He leaned down and kissed the top of my head.

We went to dinner at a new restaurant near Penn Station. 'I didn't expect to see you two at the hearing,' I said to Natty and Win.

'My father called me,' Win said. 'He told me he was going to be representing you and that you could use support. I asked him what I could do to help you, and he said that I should get on a train to New York and round up as many people as I could find who might have kind words to say about the club and you.'

'That must have been hard.'

'It wasn't. Almost everyone I called was willing to come. Theo helped me. Dad thought the hearing would become a referendum on what people thought of you.'

'My character.'

'Yes, your character. That if the city believed you were good, they would believe the club was good.'

'And you dropped everything to do this?'

'I did. You probably think less of me.'

'Win, I am older now. I take help when it is given, and what's more, I say thank you.' Hadn't I learned that lesson six hours ago?

I leaned across the table, and since I was feeling in high spirits, I kissed him on the cheek. How long had it been since I had kissed that boy?

I should say, *that man*.

Just on the cheek, friendly-like, but still.

Natty began to chatter about a project involving the extraction of water from garbage. She'd been working on this for years. It was probably going to save all of us, but I wasn't paying any attention.

Win smiled at me, a bit ruefully.

I smiled at him – *Don't read into this.*

He cocked his head at me and I felt like I could read his mind – *Are we going to do this?*

I shook my head and shrugged my shoulders a little – *I still don't know.*

He put his hands on the table, palms up – *Hurt me. Go ahead and try, my girl. I've got the thickest and the thinnest skin imaginable when it comes to you. I'm half rhinoceros, half baby bird.*

I folded my hands in my lap – *I'm old, Win. I'm a widow. I'm beaten up. I'm a little scared to try this again. The last time was disastrous. Don't you like being friends? Don't you like sitting here civilly, smiling at each other and having dinner? Are you so eager to sign up for another round of pain? Being with me has never made a single person happy. Not for very long at least. I think I'm good alone. And why do people need to be in couples anyway?*

He shrugged his shoulders – *I wish there was someone else for me. I honestly wish there was. But you get to hurt me, because you, I love. I love you. So I'll be sitting here. Maybe forever. Looking like an idiot. And it's OK. I've made peace with it. Love me or don't. I love you either way. Cos I am the one boy who can't get over the girl I met in high school. I'm that dumb, hopeful boy. I've tried, my girl. Have I tried. Don't you think I'd rather be in my dorm right now reading* Gray's Anatomy? *But I have to be here with you, the best, worst girl in the world. The only girl in the world as far as I'm concerned.*

A second rueful smile from Win.

But maybe this exchange was only in my head.

No one was speaking and so I turned to Natty. 'And you! You should be in school.'

'I had to tell them what a good sister you are.'

I turned to Win. 'You called her?'

'Annie, I am allowed to call who I like.'

'Still – you should both be in school.'

'We're going back tonight,' Win said.

I walked them over to the train station, which was a manageable distance for me. 'Hey Win,' I said when Natty was buying gum. 'Might I do a favour for you sometime?'

'Like what?'

'I mean, you've helped me a million times over. It seems one-sided. I'd like to do a good turn for you.'

'Listen, Annie, I've been lucky in my life. As unlucky as you've been, I've been lucky. Life works out for me.'

'Probably I'm the unluckiest thing that ever happened to you.'

'Probably so.' He took off his hat. He leaned down and whispered in my ear, 'I'll see you when I see you, OK?'

274

'Win,' I said, 'there are other girls, you know. Ones with fewer issues than me.'

'As far as I'm concerned, you're the only girl in the world, Annie, and I think you already know that.'

XXVI

A FINAL EXPERIMENT IN ANCIENT TECHNOLOGY; I LEARN WHAT AN EMOTICON IS AND I DON'T LIKE IT

anyaschka66: *Hey Win, people don't end up with the boys they meet in high school.*

win-win: *Yes, I got home safely. Thanks for asking. The train wasn't too crowded.*

win-win: *Some people do, Annie. Otherwise it wouldn't be such an enduring cliché.*

anyaschka66: *I'm not a happy-ending person.*

win-win: *Sure you are.*

win-win: ☺

anyaschka66: *What's that?*

win-win: *Didn't your nana teach you about emoticons?*

anyaschka66: *It's creepy. I feel like it's looking at me.*

win-win: ☺

anyaschka66: *Ugh, what's it doing now?*

win-win: *It's winking.* ☺

anyaschka66: *Gross. I wish it wouldn't.*

win-win: ☺

anyaschka66: *When someone looks at me the wrong way, I start reaching for my machete. I'm very damaged, Win.*

win-win: *I know, but you're sturdy, too.*

anyaschka66: *Goodnight, Win. See you at Thanksgiving.*

win-win: ☺

XXVII

I SPOT A TULIP IN JANUARY;
WALK DOWN THE AISLE;
HAVE MY CAKE

Because life is curious, long if you're lucky, and filled with twists, I found myself at City Hall on a bitterly cold afternoon in January, having a lunch meeting with the newly inaugurated mayor of New York City. When I arrived, I had been told by his assistant that my former enemy had no more than a half-hour for lunch. 'The mayor is a very busy man,' she said, as if I did not know that already.

At lunch, the mayor and I spoke of my business for a while, and of his plans to introduce legislation to amend the Rimbaud laws. We spoke of his son briefly, though I would not have minded a more detailed report as far as that was concerned. About five minutes before lunch was over, my old colleague looked at me with a very solemn expression.

'Anya,' Mr – now mayor, though always Mr Delacroix to me – Delacroix said, 'I did not summon you to lunch purely for chatter. I have a request.'

I braced myself. I had known some unpleasant requests from this man in my life. What might he demand from me now that he was so much more powerful than he had been?

He looked at me steadily; I did not blink. 'I am getting married, and I would like you to be my best woman.'

'Congratulations!' I reached across the table to shake his hand. 'But who is she?' Mr Delacroix had always been secretive about his personal life, and I had not even known he was dating anyone.

'She is Ms Rothschild. The former Mrs Delacroix.'

'You are remarrying Win's mother?'

'I am. What do you think?'

'I think . . . Frankly, I can think of nothing more shocking! What has caused this turnabout?'

'Last summer, during my failed attempt at matchmaking for you and Win, I succeeded in matchmaking for Jane and me. Had I not sent you to that farm, which necessitated my going there myself, I doubt very much that I would be telling you this tale. Jane finds me to be less fearsome and selfish than I once was. She thinks it might have been your influence, which I have informed her is absurd. And for my part, I love her. I never stopped loving her. I have loved that woman my whole life, since I was fifteen years old.'

'And even though she knows what you are like, she still wants to marry you again?'

'I am not sure if I should be insulted by that question. But yes, she does. As strange as that may seem. She forgives me and she loves me. Despite the fact that I am awful. Perhaps she thinks that life is better with company. Anya, you are crying.'

'I'm not.'

'You are.' He reached across the table and wiped my eyes with the sleeve of his dress shirt.

'I'm so happy for you,' I said. And how could one not be happy when presented with evidence that love could bloom from ground once considered barren? I threw my arms around Mr Delacroix and kissed him on both his cheeks. He smiled boyishly, and it reminded me of Win.

'What does Win say?' I asked.

'He rolled his eyes quite a lot. He said that we – and particularly his mother – were crazy. He will, of course, walk Jane down the aisle. The wedding is in March. It will only be a little affair, but you still have not said if you will stand up for me.'

'Of course I will. I am honoured to be asked. Am I truly the best friend you have?'

'Yes, just about. It's been a lonely life. And Jane and I are grateful to you. In a strange way, she thinks you belong to us, though I told her that Anya Balanchine belongs to no one except herself. In any case, we could think of no other we wanted standing beside us more, except our own daughter, had she lived.' He held me to him, and I tried not to cry again. (*Aside: How much of this book – nay, my life – have I spent 'trying not to cry'? When I think of the wasted effort!*)

His assistant came into the office. The half-hour was up. He shook my hand, and I went back out to the street. The January air was cold and bright, and it seemed as if the colours of the city were more vivid than before.

In the gutter, a yellow tulip improbably pushed its way

through the mud and the trash and the ice. Apologies for the cliché, but I must tell it like I see it. The tulip *was there* – it is not my place to speculate why or how such miracles occur.

The wedding was in March though the day felt more like May. Win's parents were not young people and they had already done this before, so it was not a grand wedding – only a justice of the peace at the Dark Room, Manhattan. Aside from Win and myself, the only other people there were a few of their colleagues, including Theo, who had brought Lucy. Rumour had it that Theo and the mixologist were engaged, but Theo and I didn't discuss these matters. Natty had wanted to come, but she couldn't get away from school.

I wore a pink dress that Ms Rothschild had selected for me. Though I didn't agree, she thought pink was my colour, that it complemented my black hair. Win wore his usual grey suit, which I had seen several times – I hadn't yet tired of it.

I wore heels, low ones, for the first time since I'd been hurt. I still had a pronounced limp, but I felt girlish, strong, and even a little sexy. Last year, I had never thought I'd feel pretty again.

Win's parents said their vows. I snuck a glance at Win, who was standing beside me and who I had not seen since Christmas. He grinned at me, then leaned over and whispered in my ear, 'You look awfully sweet, Annie.'

The wedding was over by three. As a present, Theo had provided the cake for the occasion – chocolate. Mr Delacroix had recently pushed through legislation that amended the Rimbaud laws within New York City to allow for cacao to be served with a licence, and so it made sense that chocolate cake would be featured at his wedding. There were no more prescriptions needed at the New York clubs either. Instead, we had a certificate on the wall that said the city permitted cacao-based products of all kinds to be served on the premises.

It was so warm out that I wanted to walk home, even though it was kind of a long walk for me. So I had Theo cut me two pieces of cake to go, and then I asked Win if he would walk me home. 'If you don't have anything else to do, that is. I'll probably take forever.'

He looked at me a long time. 'You're sure you're good to walk home,' he asked. 'It's a long way.'

'I'm sure,' I said. 'I'm stronger than I was in the fall, Win. I think I'm finally ready.' I slipped my arm through his. 'Is this OK?'

'It is,' he said after a pause.

'Let's head west,' I said. 'I'd like to go past Trinity.'

'That's a bit out of the way,' he said.

'I'm feeling sentimental, I guess.'

'All right, Annie,' he said. 'Let me carry the cake.' He took the box from me, and we made our way uptown.

'Any spring plans?' he asked as we crossed into Central Park.

'I'm going to Russia with Mouse. We've approached the Balanchiadze about manufacturing a line of cacao bars.'

'Aren't you worried about working with them?' Win asked.

'No,' I said. 'Not anymore. They're in my business whether I want them there or not. I think the best option is to try to convert them to the good side.'

'That seems optimistic for you.'

'I'm optimistic now, Win. Why shouldn't I be? I'm twenty-one years old, and I may have had a hard time and made a few pretty shady decisions, but I've stayed alive and mainly everything has worked out for me, hasn't it? Look at your dad. Look at your parents. Who would ever have thought that they would get married again? I can't help but feel hopeful today.'

'I think my mother is crazy,' Win said. 'I don't remember if I mentioned that.'

'I know they're your parents. But don't you find it romantic, even a little? They were high-school sweethearts.'

He looked at me steadily. 'Where has Anya Balanchine gone? Isn't she the girl who told me no one ever ends up with anyone they dated in high school?'

'Your parents have proven me wrong. I am humbled yet again.'

'I don't even know who I'm walking with right now.' He was smiling at me, and there were wrinkles around his eyes. I liked his face when it got squinty that way.

'How can you not feel happy when it is almost springtime and the air smells like flowers and you can walk across the park without getting mugged?'

He put his hand on my forehead. 'Spring fever,' he said. 'Clearly.' He laughed at me. 'I should get you home.'

'No, let's not go home. Let's stay out the whole day. We'll find a park bench and we'll eat our cake out here, too. You don't have somewhere you have to be, do you?'

'I do not,' he said. 'Going back to what we were talking about before, it'll be kind of dangerous for you in Russia, no?'

283

'Maybe,' I said. 'Though I don't think anyone wants me dead at the moment.'

'Well, that's a relief.' He rolled his eyes. 'I rather prefer you alive. Maybe that comes off as too forward for you.'

'Scandalous. That pretty boy must really like me if he doesn't want me dead! Actually, I'm excited to go to Russia,' I said. 'I'm reasonably sure I'll survive, and what's more, I've never been. People think of me as Russian, but I honestly don't know a thing about it.' Suddenly, I stopped. 'Win, look at that!' We were halfway through Central Park. 'There's water in the lake!'

'What do you know.' Win said.

'Is your dad behind that, do you think?' One of Mr Delacroix's stump speeches had been about how people in a city needed more than essentials. The reason he thought that the Dark Room had improved Midtown so much was because it had reminded citizens that life could be more than survival. And so Mr Delacroix had promised to plant flowers in the medians and reopen museums and, yes, fill the man-made lakes with water. He said that even if the cost seemed exorbitant, it was worth it – a city with hope is a city with less crime, and policy decisions made on cost alone were often shortsighted. It was a very good speech. But politicians – my dear colleague included – had been known to make lofty statements when they were campaigning. I hadn't known if Mr Delacroix would get around to filling the lakes when he was elected. But today, miracle of miracles, I was looking at a lake! Five years ago, I remembered running past a dirt hole while Natty had almost gotten herself mugged.

'Could be,' Win said. 'Annie, what would you think if I went to Russia with you?'

'You wouldn't be trying to protect me, would you? Because I'm hardy, you know.'

'Nah, I know that. I've always wanted to visit Russia. Maybe you weren't aware of it, but I'm kind of into Russian girls.'

I thought about kissing him, but I didn't. I was not afraid. No, not anymore. I knew with absolute confidence that I would kiss him again. I knew I might even be kissing him for the rest of my life, though one would rather not tempt fate with such outlandish proclamations. But at that moment, the promise of that first kiss hung in the air like the promise of springtime on a balmy March day. What I didn't know when I was sixteen was the exquisite pleasures that can be found in the waiting, the anticipation. How lovely it was to look at fallow ground and know that any day a flower might poke her head out. How lovely it was to be outside, to be young, and to know that, oh yes, there would be a kiss. How lovely to know with authority that this future kiss would be a good one, because I had kissed him before. I knew what that mouth felt like, those lips, that tongue. That future kiss was like a delightful secret that we both already knew. The day had been so filled with happiness. Why not save a portion of joy for tomorrow?

'Do you want to have the cake now?' he asked. We'd been walking for an hour at least, and I was hungry. We sat down on a bench near the lake. It was nearing sunset, and the sky was pregnant with evening. Win took the cake out of the box, and he handed me my piece.

I took a bite. Perhaps the irony of my life was that I had never truly loved the taste of chocolate. Yes, I'd built a business out of it, and I could recognize good quality chocolate like Balanchine Special Dark. I could even enjoy a cacao drink if it was mixed just so or a dish of chicken *mole* at Granja. But chocolate had never been my favourite flavour – I much preferred citrus or cinnamon. When I tasted chocolate, the bitter tones were what I tended to fixate on, to the exclusion of every other taste, and I never felt like I was experiencing what others seemed to describe when they ate it. But on that almost-springtime night, as the chocolate rapidly dissolved on my tongue and that good, good man sat beside me, I began to see the appeal. Once I surrendered to it, all I tasted was the sweetness.

ACKNOWLEDGEMENTS

As a reader, I don't particularly like acknowledgements. As a writer, I must acknowledge their necessity. Thank you to Ash Nukui for advice about all things Japan, and to Cari Barsher Hernandez, Stephanie Feldman Gutt, and Marie-Ann Geißler for their assistance with the German and Spanish translations. Of course, mistakes and liberties should be considered mine.

This is a book about friendship as much as it is about love or chocolate, and for this, I must thank my longtime editor, Janine O'Malley. Ms O'Malley rescued Scarlet from an uncertain fate and saved Anya multiple times from herself and from the clutches of a disreputable gentleman who shall remain nameless. As readers have noted, the book's original title was *In the Days of Death and Chocolate* – the transformation of 'death' into 'love' may be attributed, in part, to Ms O'Malley. Such alchemy could not have been accomplished without the additional support of my ardent copy editor, Chandra Wohleber; Doug Stewart, who is as fine an agent as there has ever been; Hans Canosa, who had to endure many speeches from me about feminism and the limitations of the

287

Bechdel test; and, of course, the patience and goodwill of my publisher.

Thanks especially to Jean Feiwel, Simon Boughton, Joy Peskin, Elizabeth Fithian, Jon Yaged, Lauren Burniac, Katie Fee, Alicia Hudnett, Véronique Sweet, Alison Verost, Kate Lied, Lucy del Priore, and Polly Nolan. For a variety of reasons, I am also grateful to Madeleine Clark, Stuart Gelwarg, Rich Green, Carolyn MacKler, Jenn Northington, Shirley Stewart, and Richard and AeRan Zevin.

Finally, I am thankful to the readers who have taken my prickly, pious, ambitious, guarded, old-fashioned heroine into their hearts. Because I am often asked this question, I want to mention that I never saw the series as a dystopia. Aside from a noun or two, Anya's world is pretty much like our own, and her battle is not against the forces of a terrifying and dehumanizing fictional society, but within herself. How do you get over your past and your mistakes? How do you find light when so much in the world seems dark, and sweetness when so much seems bitter? I ask these questions myself. I don't have answers, but here is an observation: whether you are fictional or real, the world is as dark as you choose to see it.

ABOUT THE AUTHOR

Gabrielle Zevin is the bestselling author of *Elsewhere*. She writes novels for adults and for young adults and these have been translated into more than eighteen languages. She is also a successful and critically acclaimed screenwriter.

Gabrielle lives in New York and is a graduate of Harvard University.

In the Age of Love and Chocolate is the third part of her original and compelling Birthright trilogy.

ALL
THESE
THINGS
I'VE
DONE

GABRIELLE ZEVIN

FOR ANYA, LOVE WILL BECOME A LIFE-OR-DEATH CHOICE . . .

New York 2082. When Anya is arrested for attempted murder, the District Attorney offers her a choice: stay away from his son or watch helplessly as he destroys her family. It should be a straightforward decision. Except that the DA's son is the boy Anya loves, and her family is at the dark heart of the city's criminal underworld.

Anya must choose between love and loyalty, knowing that whatever she decides will have shattering consequences: heartbreak or a gangland war that will tear the city apart.